CH00663331

THE NAKED FISHERMAN

BOOK ONE

JEWEL E. ANN

This book is a work of fiction. Any resemblances to actual persons, living or dead, events, or locales are purely coincidental.

Copyright © 2021 by Jewel E. Ann

ISBN 978-1-955520-03-4

Print Edition

All rights reserved.

Cover Designer: Estella Vukovic

Formatting: Jenn Beach

The Naked Fisherman

JEWEL E. ANN

PLAYLIST

James TW — "Butterflies"
Holly Humberstone — "Livewire"
Holly Humberstone — "Please Don't Leave Just Yet"
Natalie Taylor — "Wrecked"
Drew Holcomb & The Neighbors — "Live Forever"
Judah & The Lion — "Only To Be With You"
(Unplugged)
Matt Maeson — "Put It on Me"
Matt Maeson — "Tribulation"
Matt Maeson — "Hallucinogenics"
John Legend — "Wild"
Josie Dunne — "Good Boys"
James Bay — "Wild Love"
ZAYN — "It's You"
HRVY — "Me Because of You"
The Driver Era — "Natural"

For Jenn, if only Fisher were Scottish ... this would be perfection.

CHAPTER ONE

THE DAY I met the naked fisherman, I was a whole-some eighteen-year-old girl, fresh out of high school with lots of opinions and zero big ideas. The perfect target. I had only heard about men like him through sermons and Bible studies on temptation.

However, as I spent the morning packing, I was unaware of his existence. I should have embraced the final few hours of my innocence instead of fretting over the thought of seeing my mom for the first time in over five years. It made me want to throw up my scrambled eggs and at least one piece of buttered toast. Six months earlier, she'd been released from a women's correctional facility in Nebraska. Apparently, she had a few too many marijuana plants growing in the storage room of her hair salon. My dad said he knew nothing about it, and the judge believed him.

My grandma snatched everything I tossed into my

suitcase and refolded it. "You're an adult now, Therese. You don't have to live with her ... or us. You don't have to live with anyone. Are you sure you don't want to get an apartment with some friends? There are mission trips that can take you all around the world."

Three years earlier, my dad's heart had stopped working. A congenital defect he didn't know he had. No high blood pressure. No high cholesterol. Not a single sign before he just ... keeled over while sitting at his drawing board. We'd had pasta that night. I still couldn't look at pasta without tearing up.

He was a brilliant architect. My grandparents (his parents) got custody of me since my mom was in prison and her parents lived in a dinky but expensive apartment in Boston. They were Catholic liberals with a special detest for my father's parents—conservatives who took advantage of my mom's incarceration and my dad's death by enrolling me in a private Christian academy in Houston, Texas.

"She's my mom. I haven't seen her in five years. And it's only temporary until I decide what I want to do with my life." I gave my grandma a reassuring smile, but her frown told me she wasn't feeling the least bit reassured.

"You didn't invite her to your graduation. Why are you so curious now?"

Coughing before laughing, I shook my head. "Pa talked me out of inviting her, just like Dad would have done. And she's my *mom*, not a zoo animal I'm 'curious'

2

about. If she's not what I remember, if she feels like a complete stranger and I feel no connection to her, then I'll come home."

"Therese, I worry that by not going to college right away, you'll never go. And your father would have wanted you to get a degree."

I tossed a pair of sandals and flip-flops on top of the clothes she'd just refolded. "Statistically, people who take a gap year do better when they do go to college." A true statistic I played on repeat.

Lack of direction wasn't fun. At my graduation party, everyone asked where I was going to school ... what I planned on doing. I cringed and threw out my brilliant Gap Year Plan. It felt like code for "smart kid who happened to be an underachiever with little to no direction." Nobody actually said that to me, but I saw it on their faces. Then they listed all of the things I could do, as if I simply needed a good idea.

Grandma pressed her hands to my cheeks for a second before stroking my hair down my shoulders. My straight, dark brown hair and blue eyes were all my mom, but my grandma always said I looked like my dad. He had blond hair and hazel eyes. The only things I got from him were my full lips and obsession with crossword puzzles.

"I also worry your mom won't be the best influence." Grandma frowned as she continued to stroke my hair. There it was—her real fear.

"If she's on drugs or if she has taken up smoking

three packs a day, I'll come home. Besides, I've already found a church to attend, and I'm sure I'll find good Christian friends who will keep me from falling under my mom's spell." I winked at Grandma. I was only half serious. There wasn't a rule book for reuniting with your mother after years of separation due to incarceration. Would she expect me to call her "Mom?" Would it feel natural to call her that? It felt natural at thirteen, the day I last saw her and cried fat tears while they removed her from the courtroom in handcuffs. Her tears matched mine as she mouthed, "I love you."

Dad hugged me and promised I'd see her soon.

Soon ...

That didn't happen.

"You can come back. Anytime. You know this, right?"

I nodded while zipping my suitcase. "Yep. That's why I've told you a million times that I'll come home if it doesn't work out. Besides, half of my stuff is still here. Of course I'm coming back. I just want to see what she's like now and see if I like Colorado."

Grandma's eyes glossed over with emotion. "Therese, I'm going to miss you so much. It's like I'm losing your dad all over again."

"God will watch over me."

"I know, honey." She kissed my forehead. "Let's have Pa load up your suitcase and drive you to the airport so you don't feel rushed getting to the gate. I still can't believe we're letting you fly by yourself."

I laughed a little. "I'm an adult now. I've got this." I

wasn't sure eighteen felt like adulthood, but I put on a brave face because my friends were going on summer trips and preparing to head off to college. They were leaving the nest. I was moving to a different nest. The least I could do was fly by myself and pretend that I was a real adult for a few hours.

CHAPTER TWO

I WOULD HAVE BEEN LYING HAD I said I wasn't scared to death. My hands and my voice shook, fumbling my bags and ID while going through airport security. Everything freaked me out. Strange men looking at me. Women corralling their young kids while eyeing me like they wondered if they should report me to airport security—a young woman possibly being smuggled to some faraway place (like Colorado) to be sold as a sex slave. For five hours, I feigned confidence. When I exited the secured area of the Denver airport, it took me only a few seconds to spot my mom: brown almost black short hair, not quite touching her chin with bangs cut a little too short (just my opinion), and skinny as a rail. She sent me pictures after we made contact shortly after my eighteenth birthday, but she looked even thinner in person.

The mom I remembered from the courtroom had curves. She wasn't overweight, but she looked healthy and well nourished. Post-prison Mom looked like she ate to live and not one bite more. Her bones protruded from her cheeks, shoulders, and hips. Sunken blue eyes the color of a stormy sky at sunset eyed me with anticipation. And not as much as a single speck of makeup could be found on her face. The owner of a salon, she used to have long hair, nearly to her butt, always curled in princess-like ringlets.

Where did the hairdresser go? Makeup? Nail polish? Perfectly styled hair? I wondered if she remembered that person or if that person died over the five years I hadn't seen her. Over the five years she didn't get to see me.

"Reese!" She hooked her crossbody handbag over her shoulder and ran toward me.

Reese ... I hadn't been called that in years. I was Therese to my dad and my grandparents. I was Therese at the Christian academy and to my new Christian friends.

My body stiffened, panicked by the stranger ready to get up close and personal with me. Would she smell the same? Would her embrace feel the same?

"Hi," I croaked as she knocked the wind out of me and nearly tackled me to the ground.

"Oh my baby ..." She cried. Literally cried.

I had thought I would cry too, but there were no tears in sight. Nerves and sheer awkwardness gobbled them up before my eyes had a prayer of shedding even a single one.

Everything felt different.

Her embrace was not as comforting, probably too many bones and not enough fat.

She smelled woodsy, not the floral scent of her perfume I remembered.

I thanked God for reuniting us. My mind should have stopped there. That was all that mattered, but I couldn't stop thinking about all the ways she was a little *less* than I remembered. Did my thirteen-year-old self have her on a pedestal? Or was the eighteen-year-old version of me being unfairly judgmental?

Thou shalt not judge ...

That was always a hard one to obey.

"You've grown into the most beautiful young lady." She grabbed my shoulders and held me at arm's length, getting a good look at me.

"Thanks." I smiled.

"Well, let's get your luggage and head home. We have so much catching up to do before I leave town." She looped her arm around mine and led me toward the baggage claim.

"What? You're leaving?"

"It's just for a month. Six weeks tops. My new employer is sending me to L.A. to work at his salon there and get refreshed on my skills. I'll be working with people who do hair and makeup for celebrities. How awesome is that?"

"Um ... really awesome, I guess. So, I'll be living alone, in your house?"

"Yes and no." We stopped and waited for my luggage at the carousel. "And it's my landlord's house.

Not mine. I just rent the basement. It has its own entrance at the back. He's the nicest guy. And adorable. We've become good friends. I've told him all about you. And he's also willing to give you a temporary job this summer while you figure out what you want to do."

"What kind of job?" I watched for my suitcase, sparing a quick side-glance for my mom.

"He owns a construction company. I'm not sure what you'd be doing, but I'm sure you couldn't ask for a better boss."

"Construction? Building houses? I'm not that great with a hammer." With a nervous laugh, I considered the bigger picture. My hammer abilities were the least of my concerns. My mom was leaving me with an *adorable* man. Adorable as in old and quirky?

She laughed. "I'm sure there's office stuff you can do."

I nodded several times, trying hard to formulate an image of adorable in my head. Kittens were adorable. "Okay. Yes, I can do office work. Thanks for asking him." *Mr. Adorable.*

She glanced over at me and smiled. "Of course. I want to do everything I can for you. Lots of lost time to make up for."

CHAPTER THREE

It took us forty-five minutes to get to her place. I'd never been to Colorado. Never seen the Rockies. I couldn't stop gawking at them in the distance. How had we lived in Nebraska for nearly fifteen years and never headed west? We'd made a million trips straight south to Texas and a few trips out east to visit my mom's parents. But never west.

"Home sweet home. I know it's not as nice as your grandparents' home in Houston, but I want you to feel like it's yours. We can decorate your room. Paint. Whatever you want. Fisher said as long as we don't tear down walls, the sky's the limit."

"Fisher?" I asked while climbing out of her Subaru Outback.

"Fisher Mann. My landlord."

"Interesting name." I chuckled while my mom retrieved my suitcase from the back of her car.

"It is." She grinned, nodding toward a cobblestone

path that wound around to the side of the sprawling ranch home with an unobstructed view of the mountains.

"There's a door to the house through the screened-in porch, but I usually go in through here because there's a locker area to put coats, shoes, purses, etcetera."

She unlocked the door, and I followed her into the basement. It was nice—way nicer than I expected, not basement feeling at all. A wall of west-facing windows gave it depth, not that it needed any illusion. The vast family room held a mammoth sectional, big screen TV, and a pool table.

"You've bought a lot of stuff."

"Pfft ..." She shook her head. "No. The family room came furnished. I purchased beds for the two bedrooms and bedding. Towels. Kitchen stuff. And by me, I mean my parents loaned me the money."

"I see." My other grandparents. I saw them three times while my mom was incarcerated. My father wasn't exactly accommodating.

"Let's see if Fisher is upstairs. I want you to meet him; then we can grab food and spend the rest of the evening catching up."

Catching up ... I found that odd. The catching up would be very one-sided. There was no way she had that much to catch me up on in regard to her life.

I followed her up the split staircase. She knocked on the door and waited a full two seconds before unlocking it and opening it. It was odd that there weren't locks on both sides like connected hotel rooms. As I followed her into a spacious kitchen with high ceilings, I glanced back and noticed there was a lock on his side. He just hadn't locked it.

"Fisher?" she called and waited a few seconds. "I'll check the garage. Sometimes he's working on a project or spit-shining his motorcycle."

I nodded, feeling nerves tighten in my stomach. Why? I wasn't sure, but two seconds later I quickly figured it out.

"Hey."

I turned toward the deep, male voice.

"Oh my gosh!" I made another quick turn, completing a full three-sixty in total. "I'm sorry."

"Why? Did you break in? Or are you Rory's daughter?"

I cleared my throat. "That ... um ... yeah ... Rory's daughter."

"Ah, Reese Capshaw. It's nice to finally meet you. Rory talks about you nonstop."

I nodded a half dozen times, refusing to turn back toward him and his nearly naked body. My initial glance caught lots of chest and water dripping down said chest and a loosely tied navy-blue towel hanging low on his waist. Oh ... yeah ... his hair was messy, wet, and light brown or maybe dark blond.

"Where's your mom?" He brushed past me. Like ... physically brushed past me. His wet arm bumped mine. And he didn't say "excuse me." Instead, he turned a few degrees just before reaching for the garage door handle. He eyed me from head to toe, a smirk reshaping his mouth into something I didn't trust. "You look just like your mom. Lucky girl."

In that moment, I knew Fisher Mann was bad news.

"There you are!" Mom started to open the door at the same moment Fisher turned the handle and pulled inward.

Was it the right time to tell my mom she couldn't go to Los Angeles because her landlord looked at me like his next meal? But more than that ... I couldn't believe she had no response to his nearly naked body on full display in front of her daughter.

"Sorry. I was in the shower," Fisher said while he gave his towel a slight adjustment *in the wrong direction!* He lowered it an inch.

Heat gathered in my cheeks. I had only seen men like him on television or with my friends when no one's parents were home. It felt forbidden then, and it didn't feel any less forbidden with my mom standing between us.

"So you met Reese. Isn't she beautiful? Even more stunning than her pictures. Don't you think?"

Dear God, please make this stop. Make HIM stop.

Stop being so ... everything.

My mom, too busy giving me her most adoring expression, looked on the verge of crying again, while Sin—with his disheveled hair, overexposed flesh, and hard muscles—wet his lips and nodded. "She's perfect, Rory. Almost angelic."

What was that supposed to mean? I contemplated his wording. Did he know I went to a Christian academy? Was he making a jab at my religion? My faith? My youth? My level of experience? Maybe it wasn't a biblical reference to an actual angel. What if he thought I was truly beautiful?

I quickly shook my head to derail that train of thought. Of course, I didn't want Fisher to find me attractive to any degree. He was older than me by more than a few years. He didn't look like a man of faith. Yes, I realized that was another judgment, but my mind did its own thing. Was he with my mom ... as in *with* her in the biblical sense?

"I told Reese you might have a job for her." She glanced back at the naked fisherman.

Ugh! Why did that have to go through my head? I would forever imagine him naked with a fishing pole in his hand ... maybe naked except for a pair of those fly-fishing boots reaching his mid-thigh region.

Stop!

"Sure. I can keep her busy with lots of odds and ends. Some days you could work in the office with my secretary, Hailey. Other days you might come with me to job sites. Drop off lunches. Grab supplies."

There was a long silence.

"Reese?" my mom said.

"Huh?" I hummed, slightly incoherently.

Fisher bent to the side like he was lowering his body to fit into the view of a camera lens. But there was no camera, just my gaze affixed to his abs and the teasing of dark hair peeking out from the top of his towel. The coveted happy trail. No not coveted. At least, not by me. Nope.

"Hello?" Fisher said, and that was when I realized he'd caught me gawking at him, just inches from his ... uh ... lower pelvic area.

I needed the fire department to extinguish the embarrassment from my face. "S-sorry ..." I jerked my gaze away from him and folded my arms over my chest, staring down at my feet as I rocked back and forth on the balls of them several times. "A job. Yes. That would be great. Thanks."

"Everything okay?" my mom asked.

"Yeah. It's just been a long day of traveling. That's all." I shifted my focus to things around the kitchen. He kept it rather clean, unsure of what I expected from a guy who worked in construction. And he liked bananas and apples. He must have had two dozen bananas and an equal number of apples in a glass bowl by his toaster. Apples ... the fruit of temptation. How appropriate.

"We'll let you get dressed before your towel falls off, and you show Reese more than she wants to see. I haven't had the sex talk with her yet."

Let. Me. Die!

She really said that. To *him!* Prison had done things to my mom. I couldn't remember her being so forward, so blunt, so embarrassing.

"Oh my gosh ..." I covered my face with my hands.

"Thanks for embarrassing me. I'm an adult now, ya know?"

I was an adult covering her flushed face. I was an adult who hadn't had sex because I wasn't married. I was an adult who fit in with my grandparents, my church family, and my friends from the Christian academy. Apparently, I wasn't an adult in my mom's eyes, and something told me I wasn't an adult in Fisher's eyes. Or maybe I was. *That* was the most terrifying thought at that moment.

CHAPTER FOUR

"I'm sorry. I didn't mean to embarrass you." My mom laughed as we headed back downstairs. "I've been stressing out over how to treat you." She opened the fridge and plucked two sodas from the bottom shelf, handing one to me.

Orange soda. She used to give me that as a special treat. I wondered if she had those graham crackers shaped like bears as well since that used to be my favorite snack—when I was five years younger.

"I mean ... the last time I saw you, you weren't even old enough to drive a car. You hadn't gotten your period yet. And now you're a grown woman. I know it in my head, but my heart still remembers the little girl. I guess I want to get back time, but I can't."

"Thanks." I took the soda and sat on the U-shaped leather sectional. "I know. It's weird for me too. I guess we'll just have to pray about it, and God will help us through this."

Pausing the bottle at her lips, she shook her head. "Boy ... they did a fine job of indoctrinating you. Didn't they?"

"What do you mean?"

"I mean the 'we'll just have to pray about it.' That's not what the average eighteen-year-old girl says. I've been a little isolated for a few years, but I know that much hasn't changed. You talk like a girl who's been reading the Bible more than romance novels. A girl who spends more time praying than watching Netflix."

"I have a love for Christ. Is that so wrong? We went to church before you went to prison."

She chuckled and took a sip of her orange soda. "We were Catholic."

"So? What's that matter?"

Again, she laughed. "Oh, it matters. But I don't want to talk religion with you. Your faith is between you and God. I want to know all the big moments you've experienced over the past five years. Your first boyfriend. Your first kiss. Your first heartbreak. I want you to tell me all about your friends. Did you keep in touch with your old friends? Or did you make new ones at your Christian school? Did your dad ever find another woman? Or did he die a lonely man?"

She had a lot of questions. I had only anticipated one or two of them. Maybe the boyfriend question and the one about my old friends from public school. Everything else left me a little speechless, especially the questions about Dad finding someone new after divorcing her.

"I've had a boyfriend. Two, actually."

"And ..." Her grin grew into something weird. A grin like my friends used to give me after I'd gone out on a date.

It was hard to separate Rory from Mom. In fact, I hadn't used either name yet to her face because I wasn't sure what I should call her.

"It didn't last long either time."

"That's it?" She gave me a raised eyebrow. "That's the best you can do? What about your first kiss?"

I shrugged. "It was okay."

"You seem hesitant. Is it because I'm your mom? We used to talk about stuff all the time. You'd come home from school and tell me about your day." She sighed with a contented smile, like her five years in prison never happened. Like we should've been able to pick up where we left off.

I remembered watching a show about this plane that disappeared and then returned years later. Families assumed the plane went down, and there were no survivors. So when the plane returned home, things were different. Kids were older. Spouses remarried. But the people on the plane couldn't understand that because, for them, nothing had changed. My mom's time in prison was like her being on that plane.

"I wanted to visit you in prison." I changed the subject to what I had imagined we'd talk about.

Why Dad convinced me it was in my best interest to *not* visit her.

Why I didn't push harder to see her after he died.

How I felt the three times I did get to see her parents.

What it felt like being in prison.

How it changed her.

Literally anything but my dating life and details of my first kiss.

"I know." She frowned and dropped her chin. "I mean ... I didn't *know*, but I believed it in my heart. I knew someone had probably filled your head with reasons it was best to not visit me. And honestly, there were times that I was glad you didn't see me in that place. But..." she glanced up and forced a smile "...that was all then. This is now. If you don't want to relive any of that, if you don't want to share your 'firsts' with me, then we don't have to do that. We can start fresh. Well ..." Her eyes rolled dramatically, like I had done to my dad a million times. "We can start fresh when I get back from L.A. I leave in two days."

Two days.

I had two days before my mom, who was in many ways a stranger to me, left me with the naked fisherman.

THAT SOUND ... that echoing siren. I didn't have to think twice. I knew it was a tornado siren. Just my luck. My first night in Denver, first night with my mom in over five years, and the sirens went off.

"Reese, sweetie, come into the back room with us."

Rory poked her head into my room and shined a flashlight on me.

I sat up in bed and rubbed my eyes. Taking two steps, I froze. "Oh!" My hands covered my boobs. They weren't out and about or anything crazy like that. I had on a thin white tank top, no bra. "Jeez, you ..."

The naked fisherman (okay, he had shorts on) eyed me and wore a smirk that wasn't all that comforting. "Yes, me. The basement is the safest place. Utility room. Let's go." He held up an actual flashlight, one of those long metal ones.

I guarded my eyes with one hand and snatched the blanket from the bed with my other hand.

"I can't remember the last time I heard the sirens go off, aside from testing it," Fisher said, shutting the door to the unfinished utility area.

"We should pray. I can do it."

My mom and Fisher stared blankly at me while we huddled in a small circle, sitting atop large plastic storage containers like the ones she used to store my old clothes and sentimental things from my childhood. I wondered what happened to those.

"Sure." Mom smiled. "Can't hurt. Do you want us to join hands?"

Eyeing the naked fisherman, I shook my head slowly. "We don't have to."

"What the heck. If we're asking God to spare our lives, holding hands might be the best way to show sincerity." He grabbed my mom's hand and then mine.

It felt small in his strong, calloused hand. Warm.

Unfamiliar. And it jumbled my thoughts. It sent my mind into rewind, replaying him smirking at me, wearing nothing but a low hanging towel.

Abs.

Veiny arms.

Rivulets of water dotting his broad chest muscles.

"Is this a silent prayer?" Fisher asked, once again startling me back to reality. He squinted one eye at me like he'd just had both closed for the prayer. "Will you at least say the Amen part out loud?"

"Dear Lord ..." I jumped into prayer instead of acknowledging the awkward pause. "We pray that you watch over us and keep us safe from the storm. Amen."

"Amen," my mom and Fisher echoed.

"So we're good?" Fisher winked at me while releasing my hand. "Protected?"

I narrowed my eyes. "Are you being sarcastic?"

"It's the middle of the night, Reese. He's just tired, and it's probably coming across like he's a little punchy." My mom stuck up for him. That had to have meant they were together—a thing.

How did I feel about my mom being with a younger man? Well, that was a hard question to answer at the time because it had been so long since I'd not only seen my mom, but also since I'd seen my parents together.

"I'm not being punchy, Rory. I'm being a smart-ass. You can only take fifty percent of the things I say seriously, Reese. If you're going to work for me, you'll need to keep that in mind."

I twisted my lips and nodded slowly. "That's a bit vague. Kinda feels like you're setting me up to fail. Or did my grandparents call and ask you to ensure I fail so that I'll go crawling off to college?"

"Is ... everything okay, sweetie?"

Sweetie.

I'd wondered if my mom would call me that again. It used to be the only thing she called me. It made me feel loved and special. At eighteen, sitting next to the naked fisherman in his basement, it felt a little conde-scending—like everyone needed to remember that I was the youngest, least experienced one in the room. That sealed the deal. I wasn't going to call her "Mom."

"I'm good, Rory."

Her eyebrows slid toward the bridge of her nose as if I'd offended her in some way.

"Reese ... I don't think you are good. And I leave in less than forty-eight hours. I don't want to go if you're not okay here. I can do something else. I can tell my boss it's not good timing."

"Christ, Rory. She'll be fine. Stop coddling her." Fisher yawned and stretched his arms over his head. It made me feel like a twelve-year-old someone snuck into an R-rated movie. Was I old enough to see so much male skin in person? And why couldn't I stop thinking about what it would be like to have sex with him? That was the truth. And I wasn't happy that God could read my mind, but I also wasn't happy that my mind kept going there without my permission.

That Christian academy made it easy to keep my

virginity, but nearly impossible to keep my sanity. A focused mind. A *clean* mind.

Dear Lord, please forgive me for my thoughts. Please fill my mind and spirit with your love and all things that bring you glory.

"Do you feel coddled, Reese?" Rory asked.

Confused?

Sinful?

Anxious?

Yes.

"No. I don't feel coddled."

She eyed Fisher with a frown. "See?"

"You've been reunited for all of ten seconds. Reese wouldn't tell you if she did feel coddled."

The sirens stopped.

"Thank god! I have to pee." My mom ran out of the back room.

Fisher stood and held out his hand. "We're alive. Looks like your prayer was answered."

I didn't take his hand or give any more attention to his statement because I felt certain that it fell into the fifty percent category that I needed to ignore.

He waited at the door for me to exit the back room. As I squeezed past him, I shot him a quick glance and inhaled deeply, proving that God didn't answer all my prayers.

"So ..." he rubbed his lips together.

I gulped a mouthful of saliva, unable to tear my gaze away from him.

"When do you want to do it?" His voice deepened.

My heart pounded to the point of feeling it in my throat. What if my mom had heard him? I wasn't having sex with him. And I lost all ability to speak those words because it was the boldest thing a man had ever said to me.

"Start working for me. When do you want to start working for me?" His voice was no longer low. And he slowed his words as if he were talking to a child or someone who didn't speak English well.

Embarrassed wasn't the right word to describe how I felt in that moment. More like ... mortified. And when Fisher smiled, as if he'd been reading my mind the whole time, I wanted to do physical harm to him. Never had I felt so angry toward another human in my whole life. The most frustrating part? I wasn't sure why I was so angry with him. For not wearing a shirt? For having a sinful body? For winking and smiling? Maybe talking in a slightly deeper voice, which tripped my imagination, sending it tumbling into a dark, forbidden place.

"We can do it ... I mean ..." I pinched the bridge of my nose. "I can start working for you. Well ... your business ... whenever." *Gah!* I might as well of had "parochial-schooled virgin" tattooed on my forehead.

CHAPTER FIVE

THE NEXT DAY, my mom took me to lunch and gave me a quick tour of Denver, promising me we'd go to a Rockies game when she returned from Los Angeles. That night, I sat on her bed next to her suitcase while she packed.

"Is it weird?" I finally got the nerve to broach the subject. "Being with someone so much younger than you?" It wasn't the question I needed to ask her, but I hadn't worked up the nerve to ask her why she was growing pot in the storage room of her salon.

She folded a pair of black pants and added them to the growing pile in the suitcase. "You're my daughter." A hearty laugh followed her answer. "Or are you meaning that the women I was around in the correctional facility were all my age? Because they weren't. Crime comes in all ages, sizes, colors, and social statuses."

"No. I mean Fisher."

She shrugged. "He's my landlord. I think he's twelve years younger than me. So ... twenty-eight. I suppose I'm a little envious that he's been so successful this early in his life. But it doesn't bother me to have a landlord younger than me."

My nose wrinkled. "Again, that's not what I'm talking about."

Her eyes narrowed, lips still curved into a grin. We had the same smile. My dad used to say it before she went to prison. Then he stopped comparing me to her at all. But she had tiny dimples like mine, and her smile was a little crooked like mine. Hair. Eyes. I was her mini me.

"Then what are you talking about?"

"Fisher is ... your boyfriend. Right? I mean ... I know he's your landlord too, but you seem to be close to him, more so than a landlord-tenant relationship."

Her lips parted, eyes unblinking for several seconds. "N-no ..." She coughed a laugh. "We're just friends. I can promise you that."

"Really?"

Another laugh. "Really."

"Does he have a girlfriend?" That question came out so quickly I didn't have a single second to stop it.

Adding more clothes to her suitcase, her eyebrows lifted a fraction. "No. Why? Are you into older men? Please say no."

"Of course not. I mean ... I'm not saying there's anything wrong with a year or two older, but not ten years older. I only asked because I noticed he didn't lock his side of the door at the top of the stairs. And I think if he had someone living with him or even visiting, he wouldn't want you going into his space unannounced. I'm not *at all* interested in him." I rolled my eyes.

My mom bit her lips and nodded slowly. "I see. Well, I knocked, so that was my announcement, and he started it, so I know he's okay with me going upstairs."

"What do you mean he started it?"

"We're friends. *Just* friends. Sometimes we watch TV together down here. Sometimes we hang out and have a beer or two. I don't even know when it happened really, but he'd knock twice to come down here, and I'd have to go up the stairs to unlock the door. So eventually, I stopped locking it on my side, and he stopped locking it on his side. But, by all means, if it makes you more comfortable, you can lock it while I'm gone."

I traced my fingernail along the zipper to her suitcase. "It's no big deal. I might lock it if I remember." Oh ... I was locking it. That was a guarantee. However, there was no need for my mom to know just how little I trusted the naked fisherman.

"Well, I trust him. I wouldn't leave you in the same house with someone unless I trusted them with my life and yours. I'm a good judge of character. Fisher is one of the good ones. I mean..." she smirked "...don't get me wrong, I told him I'd remove his testicles if he for one minute looked at you inappropriately." She laughed.

I wasn't sure what she was laughing about because

I felt certain he had already given me that look more than once.

So I wasn't so sure about his "good one" status, but I knew I was about to find out.

"Do you have a boyfriend?"

Keeping her gaze on the shirt in her hands, she smiled. A sad smile. "I don't have a boyfriend. I'm pretty sure I'm done with men."

"But you have so much life left to live. I've prayed for you. I've prayed that you would find happiness again. I've prayed that you would be able to stay clean too."

"Clean?" She glanced up.

"The marijuana."

After a few seconds of intense contemplation, she found her sad smile again. "Thanks for praying for me. I'm not sure God's ready to give me His grace yet, but I do appreciate you thinking I deserve it."

I let her finish packing without asking anymore questions, but I had a lot. There was so much Dad didn't tell me. Maybe he thought he was protecting me, but I didn't feel protected when he died, leaving me with so many unanswered questions.

"Fisher's taking me to the airport in the morning. We're leaving early ... four-thirty. You can come if you want to, but I understand if you want to sleep in." She zipped her suitcase and set it by her bedroom door next to her carry-on bag.

"I'll come."

That seemed to make her smile, a real one that

showed both of her dimples. "Great. I've written down things for you. My number and the number for the salon where I'll be. Wi-Fi password. I wrote down Fisher's number too, in case he forgets to give it to you. You have your grandparents' contact information, and I'm leaving you the keys to my car and some money for gas and food."

"No." I shook my head. "You don't have to leave me money. I have money from Dad's ..." My nose wrinkled.

She blinked a few times before recognition ghosted along her face. "His life insurance."

"Yeah," I whispered.

We didn't talk anymore about my dad or the money that I had, the money that would be given to me in increments as I got older, including money assigned to my college fund that I wasn't sure I'd use.

We ate dinner. Watched TV. And turned in early for bed.

Four-thirty came too soon. I pulled my hair back into a ponytail and stretched on yoga pants and an oversized tee.

"Coffee?" Rory asked.

I shook my head and yawned. "I might go back to sleep when I get back here."

"Good idea. Let's go then. Fisher has already carried my suitcase up to his truck, and he's waiting on us."

"K" was all I managed on a second yawn as I followed her out the door and around to the front of the house, where a white truck with Mann Construction, Inc. on the side of it waited for us.

"Morning, ladies." Fisher smiled as I climbed into the back seat and my mom hopped into the front seat.

"Morning. I think Reese might be regretting her decision to ride with us to the airport." My mom laughed.

"I'm good," I said on yet another yawn.

Fisher and my mom chatted on the way to the airport while I grabbed a quick nap. When he pulled to a stop in the drop-off lane, I climbed out and stretched while he retrieved the suitcase from the bed of the truck.

"Take care of yourself, and take care of my baby girl," Mom said while giving Fisher a big hug. "And remember ... she's my *baby* girl. Nothing more."

What did that mean? Fisher winked at me over her shoulder. Really? What the heck was that all about?

I looked at him differently, knowing he wasn't my mom's boyfriend. I shouldn't have, but it made him even sexier. My gaze ate up everything about him— that strong jaw with a permanent five o'clock shadow that showed his maturity, not like the young men in caps and gowns at my graduation ceremony with molestaches.

Blue eyes with thick lashes.

Messy, dirty blond hair peeking out from under his baseball cap.

Defined arms.

Just six-plus solid feet of *strong man*.

Who ... wasn't my mom's boyfriend.

"Bye, sweetie. Call me. FaceTime. Text. Just ... let me know how you're doing or if you need anything." She hugged me.

Fisher glanced around while slipping his hands into the front pockets of his jeans as if he was giving us a little bubble of privacy.

All too quickly, she released me, slung her carry-on over her shoulder, and wheeled her suitcase toward the entrance with nothing but a quick glance back and a big smile.

"Breakfast?" Fisher asked while climbing into the truck.

I hopped into the passenger's seat and fastened my seat belt with shaky hands. It was officially just me and the naked fisherman. "It's five. Who eats breakfast at five?"

"Well, if you're working for me this summer, then *we* do." Pulling away from the curb, he chuckled and shook his head.

I couldn't stop staring at him. The veins in his arms that continued to his large hands loosely gripping the steering wheel. His scent—all man, but like I imagined the mountains would smell. I was well in over my head with a river of inappropriate thoughts pulling me under.

"THOUGHT YOU SAID we were going to breakfast?" I asked Fisher as he pulled his truck into the driveway.

"We are." He hopped out and walked into the garage.

Maybe he forgot something.

His wallet.

His phone.

I jumped as my door opened.

"This isn't a date. But good for you for insisting a guy open the door for you. I'll do it this one time, but my other employees can't see me doing this for you. So pull this lever toward you then push out on the door next time." Fisher smirked, really proud of himself for making me feel stupid.

I assumed we were leaving again. And I knew how to open a door.

Jerk.

"Thanks." I scowled at him while sliding out of his truck. "I thought we were going to breakfast."

"Jeez, we are. You must be starving since you can't stop asking me about it."

I followed him into his kitchen. "I'm not really that hungry. I'm just confused."

"Well, this is bread." He held up a loaf of bread. "And I put it in this little appliance that cooks it nice and brown to create something called toast." He dropped four slices into the toaster. "After that, the sky's the limit, baby. We can put almost anything we want on top of it. Think of it as the perfect vehicle to anywhere. I personally like going to peanut butter town with banana slices, but you can do butter, jelly, avocado, hummus, marshmallow cream ... really, the options are endless." After he set two white plates on the counter, he turned toward me and grinned.

"Why do you treat me like I'm eight instead of eighteen?" I crossed my arms over my chest and flipped out my hip.

"Because you wear this permanent deer-in-the-headlights look. I don't know if you're scared of me or just really confused. But since I don't think I'm a scary person, I have to assume you're confused. I don't know how they do things in Texas, so I'm just walking you through my routine."

"We have toasters in Texas. And for the record, I spent most of my life in Nebraska. It's a neighboring state to Colorado, in case you don't have good geography skills."

My reaction pleased him, or at least that was the look he chose to give me. Complete amusement.

I wasn't trying to amuse or please him.

"I'm not sure yoga pants are the best choice for work apparel. I suggest jeans for sure. Leather work boots for visiting job sites. And whatever shirt you want as long as you don't care if it gets dirty."

"I didn't know I was starting work today. And I don't have work boots. I have tennis shoes."

"Those will work." He grabbed the toast when it popped up and deposited two pieces onto each plate. "We'll get you work boots later. Maybe over our lunch break."

"Sounds ..." I started to say "sexy." Why? I didn't know. But I quickly replaced it with something less provocative. "Fashionable."

"Fashionable?" He glanced over his shoulder while spreading the peanut butter. "This isn't a job where you have to worry about being fashionable. Practical and safe for the win."

"I don't like peanut butter." I eyed his hand spreading it onto my toast too.

"Jesus, woman ... are you even human?" He scraped the peanut butter off the bread and returned it to the jar. "There's the fridge. Have at it. Put whatever you want on your toast."

It would still smell like peanut butter, but I opted to keep my mouth shut and just gut it down. He added his sliced bananas and took a seat on one of the painted metal barstools while I found a stick of butter and smeared lots of it over the residual peanut butter.

"I threw up a bunch of puppy chow ... you know, the corn or rice cereal with peanut butter, melted chocolate, and powdered sugar? And since then, I haven't been able to eat peanut butter."

"Thanks for sharing your peanut butter vomit story while I'm eating peanut butter."

I glanced over my shoulder while returning the butter to the fridge. "Oops. Sorry. Cinnamon?"

He nodded to the spice rack by the stove.

"Sugar?" I grabbed the cinnamon.

"Pantry."

"Where is your pantry?"

"The door to your right." He took a big bite of his toast and nodded to the cabinet door.

"Here?" I opened the door and a light turned on to a hidden pantry and walked inside. "This is cool."

"Second shelf on the right, clear to the back."

I plucked the bag of cane sugar from the shelf and exited the hidden pantry. "Did you build this house?"

"I did."

"Seriously?"

He chuckled. "If you didn't think I could *seriously* build this house, then why did you ask?"

I shrugged. "Just making conversation." I did my best to play it cool. When, in actuality, I was on a high.

Eighteen.

In a new state.

Mom out of town.

Living with a twenty-eight-year-old man who rented a large portion of space in my head. Dominating my thoughts—corrupting my thoughts. He even interrupted my prayer time. I quickly discovered that my on-and-off anger toward him was because he made me think and feel things that felt sinful. I wondered if I could have an innocent crush on him? He wasn't married. And if I didn't act on it, could it be a big deal? An actual sin?

"I built it three years ago. My dad is an electrician. My uncle is a plumber and a welder. I started working for a construction company when I was fourteen, over the summer. And I loved it. I knew I wanted to build houses. So my dad and uncle helped me get up and going. And things took off. I have more business than my crew and I can handle most days."

"So you have a crew?" I took a seat at the counter, leaving two chairs between us, and he smirked when he noticed that I was avoiding close proximity to him. "Does that mean you don't build the houses anymore?"

"I don't build as much, but I still do a lot of the trim carpentry in the custom homes we build."

I wasn't sure what that meant, but I didn't want to be the deer-in-the-headlights girl with him, so I nodded like I totally understood.

"You ever been married?" Why? Why did it happen again? Why couldn't I control my curiosity?

"No. You?"

I smiled over my bite of toast while wiping cinnamon and sugar from my lips. "Duh."

"Boyfriend?"

I did it. I started it. And he jumped on board, making me regret saying anything.

"No."

"Girlfriend?" he asked.

I whipped my head to the side, stopping mid-chew. "Um ... no."

He sipped his coffee and shrugged. "Don't look so offended. You're eighteen. You're supposed to be woke enough to not be offended by the question like there's something wrong with being a lesbian."

"I ... I ..." Swallowing, I shook my head. "I didn't say there's anything wrong with being a lesbian. It's not their fault."

"Fault?" His jaw dropped. "Oh man, I'm embarrassed for you."

"What does that mean?" I set my toast down, no longer feeling hungry. Not that I was anyway because it was too dang early in the morning to eat.

"I'm pretty sure implying being a lesbian is a 'fault' would not score you points with a lot of people."

I felt so backed into a corner. I didn't know what to say. I knew all the things my grandparents had told me and all the things I was taught at the Christian academy. "You know what I mean," I said softly.

After a few seconds of eyeing me until I felt two inches tall, he nodded. "I do. I know what you mean. But not everyone would."

"You're gay," I said as it hit me. Everything so clear. Of course my mom wasn't with him. He was gay. That explained his reaction to what I said.

Without a shred of offense, he shook his head. "No. I'm not gay."

I frowned. "It's wrong." Rubbing my lips together, I shrugged. "I was taught that it's wrong."

He stared at the last bite of his toast for a few moments before popping it into his mouth and lifting a shoulder in a half shrug. "Well, good thing you're out of that place they called a school. Now you can fucking think for yourself."

Cringing at his use of the F-word, I felt insecure and completely exposed. I had no idea Fisher Mann would teach me *so* much during our time alone.

CHAPTER SIX

"What?" I looked down at my jeans, gray tee, and white tennis shoes as Fisher leaned against the back of his truck with one foot propped up behind him on the bumper, eyes taking way too much liberty with inspecting me.

"Approximately seventy percent of my young male crew will try to get into your pants. I'll do my best to keep them from humping your legs and licking your face, but I just want you to remember that they went to public school and lost their virginity before they could legally drive a car."

I hugged my arms to my waist. "And that makes it okay to act like animals?"

"No." He laughed, pushing off the truck. "They're not animals. Just guys being assholes because they haven't had a good woman to keep their dicks in check. Give them a day or two to get used to you before you go filing any sexual harassment complaints because they looked at you the wrong way or whistled a little too loudly. They're good workers. I need them more than I need you."

I should have been offended that he was suggesting I turn a forty-eight-hour blind eye to his crew's bad behavior—but I wasn't because I was too preoccupied with how he didn't need me. "If I'm nothing more than a burden, I don't have to work for you. I'm sure there are plenty of other people who would love to have me."

Fisher's crew? *Ha!*

He looked at me the wrong way, rarely keeping his gaze on mine. My boobs? Those he could have picked out in a lineup.

"Oh..." he forced his wandering gaze back to my face "...I'm sure there are lots of people who would love to have you. But for now, you're mine. So get in the truck."

Did I want to be his? *Pfft ... No.*

If God was keeping count of my lies, that one got a tally mark.

As soon as we pulled out of the driveway, he played music from a playlist on his phone. I hadn't heard the song. It was loud. Hard rock. Littered with swear words. And all about sex.

Conflict muddled my thoughts. I was an adult. I could hear bad words, even if I wasn't comfortable saying them. Technically, I could get married and have sex. So explicit music should not have felt so wrong. After all, it wasn't *my* playlist. But I felt uncomfortable because, like all sin, it tempted me. It tempted my mind. It made me think inappropriate things about my new boss.

"Too loud?" he asked, after the song ended.

I shook my head, a tight shake.

"Why are you so stiff?"

Blowing out a slow breath, I tried to relax my body and my mind. "Just ... just nervous about my first day." I pulled a pad of paper and pencil out of my backpack and opened it.

"Is that a crossword puzzle?" He turned down the music.

I nodded, adding boxes for my next word.

"Are you ... solving one or making your own?"

"I'm constructing my own."

"Why?" He laughed, but it was an odd laugh, a little forced.

"Because I enjoy doing it. My dad was an architect, and he also enjoyed crossword puzzles. Then he started making them just for fun. Eventually, he was submitting them to different places for publication." I wrote out the next clue.

Seven down: Clownish

Then I filled in the four letters: ZANY

"Doing it makes me feel like he's ... not as dead."

Fisher glanced over at me for a beat. "Not as dead. I like that. So ... what do you do with your puzzles?"

"Not a lot at the moment. However, when I was in school, I got extra credit from my English teachers for making them. The school had an online newsletter, and it included my puzzles. I don't know what I'll do with them now. Maybe I'll look for an online publication for them like my dad did. Maybe..." I grinned without taking my gaze off my paper "...they'll make it in *The New York Times*. That would get me some blogger buzz."

"People blog about crossword puzzles?"

Chuckling, I nodded several times. "Um ... there are bloggers for everything. There are plenty of programs to generate puzzles now, but this is authentic. I hope big publications always favor the diehard cruciverbalist."

"The diehard what?" He held his hand to his ear.

"Cruciverbalist. A person who is skilled at constructing or solving crossword puzzles."

"Damn. You're a nerd, Reese."

"No. I just do slightly unusual things to keep the memories of my parents alive."

"Parents? Your mom is still alive. You know this, right?"

"Yes. But I felt like I lost her five years ago."

"Did you do something that made you think of her like your dad and the crosswords?"

On a nervous laugh, I glanced up from my pad of paper and watched the traffic for a few seconds. "I ... do. Uh ..." More nervous laughter filled the air.

"What?"

"Just ... I collect stuff that she used to collect. Now that she's out of pris—" It occurred to me that Fisher might not know her past. Maybe he didn't do background checks on his tenants. I wasn't sure if Rory freely offered that information to people.

"I know she was in prison."

On a breath of relief, I nodded several times. "Okay. I mean, I figured she probably mentioned it. Background check. References. Surely she had to be accountable for the previous five years."

"I didn't ask. No background checks. She told me."

"Oh, okay."

After a few seconds, where I hoped he would forget what we were discussing, he cut his eyes to me for a few seconds. "So ... what did she and then you collect?"

As a young girl, my mom's hobby was cool. And I benefited from it. As an eighteen-year-old young woman with a slight crush on a guy ten years older than me, my mom's hobby that I took over no longer felt cool. In fact, embarrassed was the only word to describe it.

"She collected..." I needed to remind him that it wasn't really my hobby "...toys from Happy Meals."

"McDonald's Happy Meals?"

"Yeah. She felt certain that, eventually, they'd be worth a lot of money. So she bought Happy Meals. *Lots* of Happy Meals. Sometimes the same toy would be offered for a week or two, maybe even longer if it was really popular. When that happened, I scored a trip to McDonald's for a Happy Meal. She'd get two so I didn't feel cheated out of the toy. But when there were multiple interrelated items available at the same time, like collector cards or something like that, she'd buy *so* many Happy Meals just to get all of them. And since she was likely to get a lot of repeats before getting one of each ... whatever it was ... she'd buy more than we would ever consume, even taking a minivan full of my friends. So she'd take Happy Meals, minus the toys, and give them to homeless people. Well, I take that back. When the toys were repeats, she'd give them the toy too."

Fisher said nothing for a minute or two. The longest minute or two of my life. What must he have been thinking of Rory? Of me?

"And now *you* get Happy Meals for the toys?"

He was right. I had a nerd gene I didn't like to admit. But when he made that statement, even I couldn't deny I was a little zany.

"I don't, really. Not now, of course, because she's out of prison. There's no need for me to do it now. If she wants to continue, she can do it on her own."

The grin on his face swelled, and I wanted to crawl in a corner and die. "Did she ask you to do this while she was in prison?"

"Not exactly."

"Have you told her you did it?"

"Not yet. I really haven't had the chance to talk to her. I no sooner showed up and she left for California. I'll mention it when she comes home."

"But you're done? You won't be getting anymore Happy Meals. I mean ... isn't there an age limit for that?"

I rolled my eyes. "What are they going to do? Ask for the birth certificate of the child for whom you're buying the Happy Meal?"

Fisher shrugged. "They probably should. Wouldn't that be an interesting twist. Your mom going to prison for something that's now legal in most states, and you going to prison for Happy Meal fraud."

Covering my mouth, I giggled. He was being so ridiculous.

"Good thing you're done now."

I wasn't exactly done. There were Pokémon cards that month, and I still had three to get. Then I would be done. It felt weird ending with something as incomplete as Pokémon cards. "Yup." I popped my lips. "Good thing."

"I collected rocks."

Glancing at him as his attention remained affixed to the road, I ate up that grin of his—a mix between boyish and mischievous. "Like geodes and crystals? Precious stones?"

Pursing his lips upward a bit, he inched his head side to side. "No. Just rocks. Yard rocks. Playground rocks. Pebbles stuck in the soles of my shoes."

Biting back my smile, I nodded. "Sounds awesome. Do you still have your collection? Or do you still collect? I bet you find a lot of rocks in your line of work."

"I think my mom still has my shoeboxes full of rocks at home. I'll have to ask her. Why? Do you want to see it? I can show you my rocks, and you can show me your Happy Meal toys."

Again, he made me want to laugh, but I didn't trust myself to not be too transparent with my tiny crush on him. So I cleared my throat and swallowed back my amusement. "I didn't bring the collection with me. It's uh ..."

"A lot of shit? It has to be. I mean ... five years of collecting toys, you must have boxes and boxes of them? Or are they in a safe? Maybe safe deposit boxes for when they become collector items and you or your mom decide it's time to retire early?"

If he only knew ...

A few Christmas-tree sized Rubbermaid containers in my grandparents' basement.

"I don't know. You'll have to ask her. I just tried to continue her hobby while she was incarcerated. It's not like I got all of them. I was in school. I had other things going on. No time to keep militant track of Happy Meal toys."

I didn't miss a single one. If I were honest with him, I would have confessed just how much of my hard-earned money I spent *not* missing a single toy. And I even continued her tradition of giving out the Happy Meals to homeless people during times that required lots of purchases in a short amount of time. So really, I was a Good Samaritan. Feeding the homeless. WWJD? He would have handed out Happy Meals to everyone.

"I think that's cool. I mean, that you did that to feel

connected to your mom. Just like the crosswords and your dad. Rory's a good person, even if she took the leap of faith and trusted me to keep an eye on you."

"Wait ..." My head jerked backward. "What do you mean by that? You make it sound like it was foolish of her. Which it might have been. I was a little surprised she trusted you. And for the record, I don't need anyone's eyes on me."

"You don't trust me?"

"No." I shifted my attention to the side window to hide my truth. Did I trust him? Not really. Did that give me a slight thrill? Unfortunately.

A hint of amusement lingered at his lips as he focused on the road. "That's fair. But I'm your boss during the day, so save your distrust for nights."

Oh my gosh ...

"That's ... a little creepy."

"Oh, Reese ... we're going to have so much fun." He turned up the music again. I glanced at his phone.

Matt Maeson, "Put It on Me."

The base vibrated my bones, and the lyrics rushed through my veins like ice water. A seductive and chilling song. It did nothing to make me trust the naked fisherman.

Rory must have felt desperate to find a friend—any friend—which made her susceptible to blind trust.

CHAPTER SEVEN

"Morning, Bossman." A wavy-haired blonde glanced up from a tiny desk nestled between a water cooler and a coffee machine.

"Morning. Hailey, this is Reese, Rory's daughter. If you have stuff for her to do here in the office, she'll hang with you today. Otherwise, I'll take her with me."

"Hi." I gave Hailey my best smile, silently begging for her to have some office work for me.

"Hey, Reese. Nice to meet you. I don't really have much today. But Monday you can help me enter bids in the computer and send them off."

Fisher grabbed a cup of coffee and sat at a desk opposite Hailey's. It was the smallest office I had ever seen.

"Or we could do it today," I suggested with a little too much enthusiasm.

"Sorry. I'm cutting out early for a doctor's appointment." She refocused on her computer.

I stood in the middle of the dinky room with my hands folded behind my back.

"Guess you're with me," Fisher said with a half grin, shooting me a quick glance before returning his attention to blueprints taking up his whole desk—sans a small corner where he set his coffee. "We need to get you some boots anyway."

"Yay …" I said with zero enthusiasm.

"Atta girl, way to bring so much energy on a Friday."

Hailey snorted. "You're one to talk. I was surprised I got a full good morning from you today. Weren't you up extra early to take Rory to the airport?"

"Mmm … yes, I was." He studied the plans, and I quickly learned I liked looking at him with or without clothes. He'd turned his baseball cap backward as if the bill somehow blocked his view or disrupted his thinking process.

"Fisher is not a morning person or a Monday person. He doesn't like his coffee cold or his water warm. He growls when he's mad at someone else and grumbles when he's mad at you."

"Hailey is full of shit. None of that is in the employee handbook."

"Because we don't have an employee handbook." She rolled her eyes.

"Not true. You just never took the time to read it." He reached in his pocket for his phone. "Fisher," he answered.

I made mental notes.

Growl = mad at someone else.

Grumble = mad at me.

"You're young." Hailey eyed me. "Sixteen? Seventeen?"

She wasn't exactly old either.

"Eighteen." I tipped my chin up and pushed out my chest. I was five-nine with a solid B-cup. "How old are you?"

"Twenty-eight, like Bossman."

I wouldn't have guessed that. Maybe twenty-three or twenty-four.

"I'll make sure the guys don't razz you too much. Except Jeremiah. He's twenty-one, really cute, and single," she said.

"Well, I'm not sure how long I'll be staying. My plans are just for the summer at this point."

With a conspiratorial grin, she winked. "Nothing wrong with hooking up just for the summer."

I wasn't hooking up. That would have required getting married, and I wasn't rushing into marriage just to have sex.

"Ready to head out to the first job site?" Fisher slipped his phone back into his pocket.

"The one they're roofing today?" Hailey asked.

"Yeah, that's one stop." Fisher turned his hat the right way again while nodding at me to head toward the door.

"Jeremiah is there. Make sure you introduce him to Reese. I said he'd be a good summer hookup."

"Reese isn't hooking up with Jeremiah this summer."

"Why?" Hailey asked as if I wasn't standing in the middle of their conversation about me and my sex life.

"Because Rory left me in charge of her." He disappeared out the door, and I shot out after him.

"Hey, you're not in charge of me. Maybe you're my boss when I'm working, but Rory didn't leave you in charge of me. I'm an adult."

"You're eighteen." He hopped into the truck.

"Yeah ..." I fastened my seat belt. "Eighteen is a legal adult."

"Legal yes. But not in the practical sense."

I scowled at him, but he ignored me. When we got to the first site, I started to climb out of the truck.

"Stay put." He opened his door.

"Why?"

"Because it's a work site, and you don't have a hard hat yet."

I peered out the window at the crew roofing the house. "They're not wearing hard hats."

"They're on the roof. Nothing's going to fall onto them." He started to shut the door.

"Where's your hat?"

"I'm hardheaded. I'll be fine." The door shut before I had a chance for a rebuttal.

For three job inspections in a row, I waited in the truck and basically got paid to work on my crossword puzzles. Then we pulled into a supply and apparel store parking lot.

"Let's get you some boots and a hard hat." He jumped out of the truck and strode a good twenty feet before he turned around. After holding out his hands, he let them flop to his sides, returning to the truck and opening my door. "Did you already forget how to operate the little lever called the door handle?"

"No. I just wasn't sure if I was allowed to exit the truck yet." I hopped out of the truck, and he shut and locked the door.

"I said we're getting you boots and a hard hat."

"Yes, Boss."

He glanced over at me, one eyebrow peaked. "Boss, huh?"

"That's what Hailey calls you. Bossman."

"I'm not sure she means it with any sort of respect."

"I'm not sure I'm saying it with any respect either."

He laughed and shook his head. "You're a spitfire, like your mom." Opening the door to the store, he waited for me to go inside.

I nodded for him to go first. "It's not a date."

"You're right. My mistake." He stepped inside and let go of the door.

It quickly started to close, and I grabbed the handle. My shoulder jerked in the direction of the door. It was a lot heavier than I anticipated. After I lugged it open and squeezed inside the store, I jogged to catch up to Fisher who was already halfway toward the back of the store.

"What's your shoe size?" he asked.

"Nine."

"Really?" He glanced back at me. "Big feet."

My nose wrinkled. "Nine isn't that big."

"For a woman it is."

"Pfft ..." I shook my head.

"Sit." He nodded toward a bench.

"I'm not a dog." I held my own to prove ... well ... that I wasn't a dog.

"You're right. A dog would be better behaved."

"Jerk." I plopped onto the bench while Fisher tracked down an employee.

A few minutes later, he returned with three boxes. "Take off your shoes."

I slipped out of my tennis shoes.

"Reese ..." He stared at my feet. "Where are your socks?"

"My shoes have wool inserts. They don't require socks."

He grumbled. That meant he was mad at me.

"Well, they don't." I shrugged.

Dropping the three boxes onto the bench next to me, he stomped his work boots in the direction of a rack of socks. After quickly picking a pair, he ripped the tag off them and handed them to me. "Put these socks on." His no-nonsense attitude prevented me from saying or doing anything but exactly what he asked me to do.

"Here." He retrieved a boot from the first box and loosened the laces before handing it to me.

I shoved my foot into it, but before I could tie it, Fisher hunched in front of me and tied the laces with fast and furious hands. "Walk."

Standing on command like a good dog, I walked, really hobbled because I only had on one boot. Stopping at a floor mirror, I inspected it.

"Well?" he said.

"They're ugly."

Another grumble. At least, I thought it was a grumble. Maybe it was a growl. "You know what else is ugly? Toes with nails poked through them or toes crushed by heavy objects. Let me reframe my question. How do they fit?"

"They? You mean it? Trying on one boot tells me nothing except that it's ugly ... and hard to walk in one boot."

"Great. Glad you like them. Here. Put on the other boot, and let's get you a hard hat."

I slipped on the other boot and tied it much slower than Fisher did. Then I followed him to another part of the store as he carried the boot box holding my tennis shoes and the tag to my socks.

"Let's see how this fits." He put a hard hat on my head.

"It's loose."

He removed it and tightened the inside strap.

"How about now?"

I nodded. "Better."

"Let's go."

"Did I do something wrong?" I asked, scurrying to catch up to him.

"Nope. We just have a busy afternoon."

"And I didn't wear socks."

"And you didn't wear socks," he echoed me, setting the box and the hard hat on the register counter.

"Are you going to fire me?"

The employee on the other side of the counter eyed us cautiously.

"Not until we get to the truck." He tapped his credit card to the machine and slipped it back in his wallet.

The employee's eyes widened, focusing mainly on me.

"Do I have to reimburse you for the boots and hat if you fire me?"

"Yes." He grabbed the box before she could put it in a bag, then shoved the hat on my head, a little crooked. "Let's go."

"That ... all of that back there ... it was part of the fifty percent that I should ignore. Right?"

"You're on the clock. Never ignore me when you're on the clock."

"So I can ignore you when I clock out?"

"You can do whatever you want to me when you clock out."

Gah!

There it was again. His words were so suggestive, leaving me with no choice but to let my mind think the most inappropriate things.

"What if I want to ..." I stopped. I had no clue where I was going with that. At least, not consciously.

He opened my door despite his rules about not opening it for me. "What if you want to what?"

"Nothing." I climbed into the seat and grabbed the box from him.

"I worry about you. What lies beneath the surface ..." He shook his head slowly.

Before I could act offended or actually be offended, he slammed my door shut.

MY FIRST NIGHT ALONE, truly alone, was weird. I locked the door at the top of the stairs to keep the naked fisherman out of the basement. Yet, every time I heard a strange noise, all I wanted to do was run up the stairs and ask him to figure out where the noise came from. It didn't take long to understand what Fisher meant when he said I was only an adult in age. Hiding beneath my blankets, I felt like a ten-year-old hiding from the boogie man.

I didn't see Fisher at all on Saturday—then again, I never left the basement. On Sunday, I made my first big solo outing to a nearby church. They dressed a little more casual than what I was used to at my grandparents' church in Texas, but everyone was nice. I left with at least a dozen new contacts in my phone from members offering to help me get acclimated to the area in any way possible.

"What's the occasion?"

Getting out of my mom's Outback, I turned toward Fisher's voice. Seriously, did he ever wear a shirt at home? He was, in my mom's words, spit-shining his motorcycle in the driveway next to his truck.

Shorts that hung too low in front.

No shoes or socks.

Tan from head to toe. He was a mix of Theo James and Liam Hemsworth. Definitely Theo's smile when he wasn't grumbling.

"What do you mean?" I moseyed in his direction, sliding my purse strap onto my shoulder.

"The dress. Hair. Makeup." He shot me a quick glance before returning his attention to the motorcycle, working the chrome by the tires.

"Well, in all fairness, you've seen me after a long flight. With bedhead in the middle of the night. And thrown together early in the morning to take my mom to the airport."

"Let me rephrase. Where have you been?"

I stood next to his truck, keeping a good six feet between us. "Not that it's any of your business, because it's Sunday and I don't work for you today, but I went to church."

"Oh yeah? How'd that go?"

"Fine. I made a lot of friends."

"I can see that about you."

"Making friends?"

"Making friends at church."

"Ha. Ha. I can make friends outside of church too. But my boss won't let me out of his truck for more than two seconds, so I never get the chance to ..."

"To what?" He gave me another quick glance while wiping his arm along his forehead.

"To meet people like Jeremiah." I lifted a shoulder, casually hinting at my interest in Jeremiah whom I hadn't met yet.

"Like him? Or him?"

"Either."

"I don't think he attends church."

"Doesn't matter." Oh, it mattered a lot, but I hated the way Fisher made me feel like a prim and proper church girl.

"He swears," Fisher said.

"So?"

"So, I notice you cringe when I say fuck, shit, damn, crap, even dick. And dick's not a swear word, right? It's more of a body part or synonym for asshole, which you don't like either."

"What's your point?"

"My point is, would you really enjoy being around Jeremiah if he used that language in all of his sentences?"

"It's not me saying it, so whatever."

"Really?" He stopped his polishing again to inspect me, to read me. "What if he wants to do more than hang out with you? Is that something you're down for?"

"I don't think the things I'm *down for* are any of your business."

"Maybe you should stick to your new church friends. I'd feel better about it and so would Rory."

"Well, I'm—"

"Yeah, yeah ... you're an adult. I've heard you mention it a time or two."

"Well, it's true. So that means I don't need your permission or Rory's permission to hang out with whomever I want to hang out with."

"How rebellious of you. Are you throwing your V-card to the wind and having a hot girl summer?"

"What makes you so sure I have my V-card?" I knew I was marching, with zero regard for self-preservation, straight into a snake pit.

He stood tall and draped the towel over his shoulder while scratching his jaw with his other hand, lips corkscrewed. "Just a wild guess."

"Because I went to a Christian school?"

"No." He chuckled. "That might actually make a better case for you not having your V-card. Repression and all that shit."

"Then what?"

"Just little things like the way you're so quick to get defensive, like now. Or the way you fidget when I make you uncomfortable with a topic like this. But really, it was the way you looked at me the day we met. Like you hadn't seen a guy without his shirt on. The way you're looking at me right now."

My gaze snapped from his chest to his face and embarrassment flamed up my neck to my cheeks. "You're a little too full of yourself. I've seen plenty of shirtless men."

"But have you seen any naked men?"

Dang it!

I walked right into that. Why did I stop and engage in conversation with him? I should have kept walking toward the basement. "I mean ..."

He grinned like he'd caught me. And my lack of ability to answer right away only added to his proof. "You wouldn't have had to technically see the guy's entire naked body to have sex with him, but I'd hope you would have insisted on it. The visual is half the fun."

The sun was no match for the heat in my face and really, everywhere along my body. Nobody had ever talked to me like Fisher talked to me. On one hand, he liked to treat me like a child, on the other hand, he spoke to me in a way that felt crude and borderline inappropriate.

But inappropriate for whom? His employee? Yes. The daughter of his tenant? Probably. An eighteen-year-old girl ... woman? Well, the *woman* in me wanted to say no, but the girl who did in fact still have her V-card cringed everywhere. That girl felt like a ten-year-old who just had a perv expose himself to her on the playground.

"I've seen a naked man."

Man. Yes, as in man oh man ... why couldn't I shut my stupid mouth and go bury my head beneath a pillow for the rest of the day? Or the rest of my life?

"Oh yeah?" He squinted against the sun. "That's good to know. It takes the pressure off me. I'm a clothing optional kind of guy. Rory has seen more than she bargained for. Of course, she was cool about it. Like mother like daughter, huh?"

Was I cool with seeing the naked fisherman? No. Could he not see my face? I was the complete opposite of cool. No 'like mother like daughter.' My mom had seen a naked man before. Maybe more than one. I never asked my parents about their relationships before they met each other. I never got the chance.

"I'm going to change my clothes and maybe head into the mountains. I've never been."

"Wait. What? You grew up in Nebraska and you've never been to the mountains?" he asked with the right amount of shock because it was shocking. A crime, really.

"No. Not the Rockies."

"That's insane. And you thinking your first trip into the mountains should be by yourself is just as insane. Let me change my clothes. I'll take you."

"I don't need a chaperone. Really. I have navigation on my phone. It's not snowing up there, is it?"

"Unlikely. But you'll encounter some steep grades. And people drive crazy fast on some of those winding roads because they're used to them. You're not used to them. Rory would kill me if I let you go alone."

"I'll let her know it was my decision."

"Your decision to get eaten by a bear or bitten by a rattlesnake. Great. Just what I need."

"What do you mean bears and rattlesnakes?"

"I mean the mammal that's brown or black and has

sharp teeth and even sharper claws. And snakes are reptiles—"

"Fisher! I get it. I know what bears and snakes are. I just wasn't aware that they were a concern for a day trip to the mountains."

"Chill." He held up his hands in surrender. "I was only looking out for you. The problem with new adults, such as yourself, is that you abandon all common sense in the name of independence. You've been *all grown up* for two seconds. You've been here for less than two seconds. It's okay to ask for help or allow someone to go places with you when there's a chance you could get into a bad situation."

Widening my stance, I crossed my arms over my chest. "Are you going to spend the day lecturing me? Are you going to complain if I don't wear the right shoes or go without socks? Are you going to—"

"Fuck it, woman. No." He shook his head and sauntered into the garage. "I'm not going with you. It's my day off, and I shouldn't have to subject myself to your attitude. I regret mentioning any of it. Go conquer the world. I'm out of fucks to give."

I flinched with every "fuck," thankful he didn't see me because it would have confirmed his earlier accusations. Without another word, I escaped to the basement. He'd planted the seed, making me doubt my ability or even my sanity for going into the mountains alone. If I didn't go, it would've looked like I'd succumbed to his fear tactics. If I did go and anything bad happened, he would have to tell Rory, making me look like the stubborn, immature, fake adult he pegged me for.

"Gah! Stupid naked fisherman!" I ripped off my dress and pulled on a pair of shorts and a fitted red T-shirt. Then I found a pair of socks to wear with my tennis shoes.

Sunscreen.

Bug spray.

Water bottle.

Energy bar.

Cell phone.

What more could a girl need? I wasn't staying for a week, roughing it in the wilderness.

As I slung my backpack over my shoulder, my phone rang.

Rory.

"Hey." I headed out the door and closed and locked it behind me.

"Hey, sweetie. I just called Fisher to check in. He mentioned you taking a trip into the mountains today. It's not a good idea to go by yourself, given the fact you've never driven in the mountains."

"Thanks for your concern, but I'll be fine." I gazed out at the mountains. They didn't look so tough from where I stood.

"I'd feel better if Fisher went with you."

"Well, that makes one of us."

"Do you have a problem with Fisher?"

I closed my eyes and blew out a breath. "No. No problems with Fisher. It's just that he's my boss now, and maybe I don't want to be under his watchful eye on the weekend too. And really, do you think he wants to deal with me on his day off? No. I don't think so."

"He said he'd love to take you today."

Liar.

"He did, did he? Well, that's not what he said to me."

"Oh? What did he say to you?"

I couldn't tell her. It involved using the F-word twice, and I wasn't comfortable with saying it outside of my head.

"He basically said he didn't want to go because it's his day off. His day off from me."

"Wait until I get home. We'll go together."

"You want me to wait half the summer to go up into the mountains? That's not fair."

"Reese ..."

"I've got this. Really."

"I'm going to call Fisher back."

"No! I mean ... just let it go. Stop treating me like a child who needs a chaperone. I don't need someone watching me anymore. I didn't come here to have you or your *friend* watch me. I came here to be with you. Now you're gone, so I'm on my own. And that's fine. I get it. But don't think that Fisher is your replacement."

After a long pause, she cleared her throat. "Okay. You're right. Just ... be careful and text me when you get home, so I know you made it back safely."

"Fine." I huffed while ending the call.

College was starting to sound better and better,

even if I had no clue what I would study if I got there. At least my life would have felt like mine. Mine to succeed. Mine to fail.

I marched past Fisher's driveway to Rory's Outback parked on the street. Without giving him a single glance, I tossed my backpack in the back seat and slipped into the driver's seat. Turning the key, nothing happened. I tried again. And again, nothing happened. Not a single sound.

"Are you kidding me? Dear Lord, please let this car start." I tried one more time.

Silence. Not one peep like the engine was making a single effort to turn on. I'd *just* driven it to church and back. God wasn't answering my prayer that day.

After reaching around and snatching my backpack from the back seat, I made the walk of shame past the driveway.

"Battery's dead. I've been telling Rory for weeks she needs a new one. I'll drop a new battery in it tomorrow after work."

I glanced over at Fisher using a squeegee to remove the water from his clean garage floor. "I can call someone."

"Or..." he shook his head and grinned "...you can call someone on your own."

I sulked toward the side of the house.

"I'm going for a ride on my motorcycle. Want to come along?"

"I'm sure my mom would think riding on the back of your motorcycle is a terrible idea."

"Probably." He hooked the squeegee on the wall and grabbed a towel to dry his hands. "That's why we won't tell her."

"Like you didn't tell her I was going into the mountains?"

He shrugged. "I didn't know it was a secret."

"I'm going to work on my crossword puzzles." I ducked my head and kept walking.

"I'm going to shower. I'll be leaving in fifteen minutes. If you're going, change into jeans."

"Have fun," I called back with virtually no sincerity.

CHAPTER EIGHT

AFTER DEPOSITING my bag onto my bed, I made myself a sandwich. Ten minutes later, with half of my sandwich gone, I eyed the time on my phone.

Fisher was leaving in less than five minutes. On his motorcycle. I'd never been on a motorcycle. They were dangerous and would have required me to hold on to his waist. It was a terrible idea. I had things to do. Puzzles to construct. Bible passages to study before Wednesday night, if I planned on attending the singles' group. That was where I would find a nice guy who didn't swear or make suggestive comments.

A guy who wore a shirt.

A guy closer to my age.

A guy who didn't care if I wore socks or not.

A guy who didn't ride a motorcycle.

After letting those sensible thoughts settle in my mind, I tossed the rest of my sandwich in the trash, changed into jeans, grabbed my backpack, and sprinted around the house just as Fisher started to pull out of the driveway.

"Wait!"

He stopped and slid up the visor to his helmet. I had no idea if one could truly have an orgasm just by looking at a guy. It seemed unlikely. A myth. But ... Fisher in jeans, black leather boots and jacket, and black gloves made me feel a little dizzy as something between my tummy and my chest tickled me in the most unfamiliar way. I imagined it was what it felt like to have a glass of wine or maybe get a little high. Not that I would ever find that out. I had a firm no drug policy for many reasons, but mainly because of my mom.

He said nothing, like I was supposed to read his mind, but really, I was asking him to read mine. That would have been embarrassing beyond my imagination.

"I'd like to go with you."

He made me squirm with his silence for a few seconds before killing the engine and removing his helmet. "Follow me."

In a matter of days, I'd become irritatingly infatuated with a man ten years older than me. I followed Fisher Mann into his garage, but I would have followed him off the edge of the mountain. That was the effect Devil in a Tool Belt had on me. I really hoped the whole once-saved-always-saved thing was true because there was a good chance I'd need that unconditional salvation.

"It's a woman's size." He tugged a helmet onto my head and fastened it under my chin.

"For all your women?" I tried to play coy, but my face felt too heated to make anyone believe I could pull off coy or subtle at that point.

"Yes, for my harem." Turning toward a cabinet, he retrieved a riding jacket like his. "You have long arms, so this might be a little small on you. Something is better than nothing."

"Long arms? I don't have long arms." I threaded my arms through the jacket while he held it up for me. As he zipped the jacket, I tugged on the cuffs of the sleeves.

Fisher smirked. Yes, the sleeves were a little short.

"It's okay. Your legs are long too. And guys will overlook your octopus arms because you have legs for days."

"I'm not a giraffe."

"I didn't say that." He strutted to his bike, and I followed him ... to his bike ... off the side of the mountain.

He climbed onto his bike, and that feeling that stretched from the pit of my stomach to the center of my chest returned, only stronger as he helped me climb on behind him. When he reached around and grabbed my ass, pulling me closer to him, I almost died. It was the most forbidden feeling I had ever experienced. I realized how crazy that would seem to anyone else, but I was, in fact, the girl who spent the last three years of high school living with grandparents, attending a Christian academy.

"Rory can never know," I said.

"Hold on," Fisher replied.

I snaked my arms around his waist, trying not to actually press my hands to his stomach or my chest to his back.

"Hold on like your life depends on it ... because it does."

I tightened my grip, a lot. And two seconds later, he kicked the bike into gear, and we shot off down the street. It was unreal.

Me on the back of a motorcycle holding on to the sexiest man I had ever seen.

My heart in my throat.

The seeds of possibilities sprouting in my head.

It felt like an alternate universe where my mom hadn't gone to prison. My dad hadn't died. And I never left Nebraska and the public school with all my friends. I was daring, and flirting with mischief was my only purpose. Church was a ritual, an afterthought. And the God I worshipped wasn't anyone to fear. I was ... normal.

Wild oats were mine to sow.

And my reality was whatever dream I dared to chase.

Fisher took me through town. I anticipated him heading back home, but he didn't. He drove me up the winding roads into the mountains—the steep inclines and the rollercoaster trips down hills at insane speeds.

We passed cars, weaving from one lane to the next. Rory would have died had she seen her only child on the back of Fisher's motorcycle, flying through the increasingly steep terrain of the mountain highway.

"WOO HOO!" I let my lungs loose as we drove through the Eisenhower Tunnel.

Fisher's hand left the handlebar for a few seconds to press against my leg, giving it a soft squeeze. My arms tightened around him. We rode and rode. My butt went numb. Eventually, he pulled off at a scenic stop. My legs were numb too as I hobbled off the bike and unfastened my helmet.

"If you're enjoying the tour..." he took my helmet from me "...don't forget to leave a Yelp review."

I giggled. "Is this a side gig? And here I felt kind of special." I inched closer to the guardrail and a canyon filled with trees for miles. The view ... there were no words. "I bet this means nothing to you."

"The view?" he asked.

Of course the view. What did he think I meant? Tossing him a quick sideways glance, I nodded. "Yeah, the view."

"I think there are some things that are meant to provide a lifetime of awe. The mountains. The oceans. Rainbows. Shooting stars. First kisses."

Ten years. There were ten years between us. And he admitted that fifty percent of everything that left his mouth was not to be trusted. First kisses ... he was baiting me. I was surprised he didn't say unicorns.

"I have jaded memories," I said. "Not like my

friends who vacationed every summer. Trips to Disney. Key West. The Grand Canyon. My big moments involved my parents fighting. My mom leaving our house in handcuffs. The day she was convicted. My dad didn't want me there, but I begged him. I told him I would never forgive him if he didn't let me go with him. She mouthed 'I love you,' as they took her away. I remember my dad telling me to let her go. He said she lost the privilege of being my mom because she chose the wrong path. He said she should have loved me more. And sometimes ... I believed him. Then he died. Another memory taking up so much space in my head. So this..." I nodded to the view "...it's a great picture to pin on top of the other pictures that don't take my breath away."

For several minutes, Fisher didn't reply. I'm sure it all sounded crazy to him. It sounded crazy to me, yet I couldn't roll my eyes and let it be someone else's pathetic life.

"You deserve to have your breath taken away ... every day."

Those. Those ten words. They wrapped around my heart like sticky peanut butter and jelly fingers.

Pure.

Innocent.

Unforgettable.

Perfect.

"Well..." I kept my gaze on the feathery green canvas "...mission accomplished."

"Want me to take a picture of you?" he asked, retrieving his phone from his pocket.

"Okay." I bit my lower lip to hide my true level of giddiness.

"Say, 'Sorry Rory.'"

I laughed. "Sorry Rory."

He studied the screen of his phone. "Perfect. I'll airdrop them to you when we get home."

"Want me to take your picture?"

He chuckled. "I'm good. I have at least a million already."

I tilted my head and wrinkled my nose. "Yeah, but not with me."

Something quite like a genuine smile bent his lips. "True." He stood next to me, one arm around my waist, pulling me close while he stretched out his other arm with the phone and took a selfie with me.

That was the one I wanted him to send me. It wasn't just the mountains; it was him, the motorcycle, the feeling (although foolish) that I was a woman enjoying the perfect Sunday afternoon with a man. The naked fisherman.

On our way back home, we stopped in Idaho Springs, an old mining town, for pizza at Beau Jo's. Not just any pizza. Nope. Thick wheat crust with loads of toppings. And we dipped our crust ends in honey. It blew my mind.

He blew my mind.

Fisher told me about his family. Two older sisters and a younger brother. His love for building things that started at an early age. And his all-star jock status in high school. All State everything. His coaches thought he would go on to college to do something—basketball, baseball, track. But he didn't love any of it as much as he loved his tool belt and the smell of fresh-cut lumber.

"Are you awake?" he asked, killing the engine inside his garage.

"Sort of," I mumbled as I almost fell on my butt getting off the back of his bike.

He grabbed my arm to steady me. "I got Rory's daughter back in one piece. Phew." He removed my helmet and unzipped my jacket.

"But she'll never know because we aren't telling her."

"She won't hear anything from me." He winked, removing his jacket.

"Thanks. I realize you probably weren't planning on a tagalong today."

"You can tag along anytime."

"Well ..." I nodded toward the garage door. "I'd better get to bed. My boss isn't a morning person or a Monday person, so I have to bring enough awesomeness for the both of us."

He smirked. "I'm sure your boss's reputation is unfair and exaggerated."

I shrugged. "Maybe. But just in case ... I'm off to bed. Goodnight." I headed toward the open garage door.

"Reese, you can go through the house. It's dark. No need to walk around the side of the house."

"You sure?"

Fisher held open the door to his house for me. "I'm sure. Just don't steal anything on your way through my kitchen."

With an eye roll, I stepped into his house and removed my shoes, carrying them through his kitchen. "Are you going to lock your basement door behind me?"

"Why? *Are* you going to rob me?"

"No." I giggled, opening the basement door.

"Are you going to sneak up in the middle of the night and do weird shit to me while I sleep?"

"What?" I coughed. "Um ... no. I just think if I rented out my basement, I'd lock my door."

"Noted. You have no self-control, and therefore I need to lock my door."

"I'm locking my side."

"I don't doubt that." He shoved his hands into his back pockets and rested his shoulder against the threshold into the kitchen from the garage entrance.

Fisher and his overabundance of sexiness continued to give me all the feels. "Am I driving to the office in the morning or going with you?"

"The Outback's battery is dead."

I frowned. "That's right."

"We'll leave at six."

"Six." I gave him an unavoidable smile before shutting the door ... and locking it. As I tiptoed down the stairs, I listened for him to lock it on his side.

He never did.

CHAPTER NINE

MONDAY, I spent the day with Hailey sending out bids. Fisher put a new battery in the Outback then disappeared for the rest of the evening on his motorcycle. I didn't get an invite to join him.

Tuesday, I went with Hailey to pick up flooring for a kitchen. She drove a company pickup, and for some reason, I found that kind of cool. After that, we picked up lunch for the crew. Apparently, it was a perk Fisher offered his guys, not the norm in construction. I found that rather cool too.

Wednesday, I was back with Fisher and that thrilled me.

"Yesterday, Hailey introduced me to some of your crew. So you don't have to worry about introductions now. Except your dad and uncle. When will I meet them?"

"My dad is out of town until next week. My uncle just had knee surgery, so he's out for a while." Fisher lifted a brow and gave me a quick sidelong glance while we waited in the drive-thru to pick up our coffees on the way to the first job. "And it's a relief that I don't have to introduce you to anyone because that was high on my list of priorities today."

"Is that sarcasm?"

He pulled forward and grabbed our coffees. "Nope." He handed me both drinks and rolled up his window.

"Have you talked to Rory since Sunday?" I handed him his coffee.

"Nope." He sipped his drink and wrinkled his nose. "This one is not mine. It's sweet and disgusting." After depositing it in my cup holder, he reached over and snagged my coffee—his coffee—from me.

I frowned at the one in the drink holder. "Now you've tasted it."

"So? I'm not sick."

"Yeah, but you drank out of it."

He chuckled. "Have you never swapped a little saliva with anyone? I didn't spit anything back into the cup. It's the equivalent of a peck on the lips. I'm sure you've had a few tongues down your throat. What's the big deal?"

Sliding the drink from the holder, I brought it to my mouth and took a cautious sip.

Fisher shook his head at my hesitation. "Do I gross you out that much?"

Just the opposite. It felt intimate sharing a cup of coffee with him. I took another sip, trying to not think too hard about how I liked the idea of my mouth touching the same spot his lips had touched.

"It's fine." I stared out my window while sipping the coffee, brushing my lips over the lid a little too much.

"Reese?"

"Hmm?"

"You have kissed a guy before. Right?"

I scoffed. "Yes."

"An open-mouthed kiss? Tongue? Saliva swapping?" He was so crude. I loved it and hated it in equal parts.

"Duh."

"Duh is not an answer."

"Hailey invited me to her house for a party on Friday. Well, not this Friday ... next Friday." My attention remained steadfast out my window.

"You dodged my question."

"I think I'll go. It's a chance to make new friends if I don't have much luck tonight."

"What's tonight?"

"Singles' Bible study at the church."

"Sounds ... titillating."

"You could come with me."

Fisher laughed, a little too hard. "As tempting as the offer is, I have a date. Sorry."

A date.

Fisher had a date. That was okay. Of course he dated since he wasn't married, and he wasn't dating Rory. I bet he had sex too. That didn't feel quite as okay to me for utterly ridiculous reasons. It wasn't like Fisher Mann was mine no matter how incredibly sexy I found him, no matter how many thoughts he owned in my head. It wasn't like he was going to wait for me to figure my life out, marry me, and take my virginity on our wedding night.

Nope.

None of that was happening, so it was just great, awesome really, that Fisher had a date.

"A new date? Someone you've gone out with before?"

"Blind date. A friend of a friend."

I nodded slowly. "Where are you going?"

"Concert downtown."

"Sounds fun."

"I suppose."

"How old is she?"

He grinned before sipping his coffee. "I'm not sure. Why?"

"No reason."

"Well, if you decide to bring someone home from Bible study, I won't tell your mom. And the house is insulated really well, so don't ever worry about me hearing anything."

Oh my gosh ...

I bit my tongue so hard. What he implied was offensive and yes ... crude. As if I was going to pick up some guy at Bible study and bring him back to have sex. Clearly, Fisher had never attended church, which meant he probably wasn't saved. And I needed to remember that. I needed to remember all the reasons I shouldn't have obsessed over the naked fisherman.

"So I won't hear you either." I felt incredibly brave saying that to him. For a breath, I tried to feel like an equal. An adult who dated and had loud sex. But inside it really ... really bothered me to think of him having sex with someone else.

Or me, of course.

But mostly someone else.

"I'm not really a screamer. I may drop a few profanities if it's worthy of it."

Stop! Make him stop!

He enjoyed playing with me. I could tell from the smirk he wore like a favorite T-shirt. He ate my reactions up like a shark finding a wounded otter. Fisher knew I was way out of my comfort zone. And his favorite game seemed to be pushing me a few more inches with every remark. I refused to give him the verbal satisfaction, even if my feelings were on full display in the color of my face or the uncontrolled fidgeting of my hands.

"It won't matter. I'll probably be late anyway. Someone mentioned getting ice cream afterward." It sounded ridiculous the second I said it.

Biting his lips to mask more of his amusement, he nodded several times. "I can see that. Well, you have my number if things get too crazy and you need a ride home. Gut ache. Sugar jitters. Brain freeze. Whatever."

"Jerk." I couldn't help it. He brought out the worst in me, the crazy in me.

Fisher sniggered as he pulled to a stop at the first job site. The framers were already busy constructing the interior walls in the basement.

"Am I allowed out?" I asked.

Fisher grabbed my hard hat out of the back seat and plopped it on my head. "If you can stay out of trouble and not distract my crew with stories about wild ice cream socials."

Had I used swear words, I would have told him to fuck off, and it would have felt so liberating. But I remained silent because I knew those other words would feel foreign leaving my lips.

"Cat got your tongue?" Fisher grinned as I fumed.

I climbed out and mumbled to myself, "No. Jesus does."

WWJD?

Fisher walked around the perimeter looking at things. What? I had no clue. I assumed he knew what he was doing. I followed a few feet behind him.

"Plumber been here?" he asked one of the guys carrying a stack of two-by-fours on his shoulder and depositing it in the middle of the basement.

"Not yet," the guy said just as he adjusted his jeans and stood erect again.

Whoa ...

He was built like an ox. "Hi. I'm Jason."

"I'm—"

"What about Kevin? Has he been by yet?" Fisher totally cut me off. Rude.

"Not yet." Jason shook his head, scratching the back of his thick, tattooed neck.

I didn't think I was a big fan of tattoos, but Jason changed my mind.

"Christ ... are they fuckin' sleeping in this morning? I don't have time to wait around." Fisher pulled his phone from his pocket and walked a few feet away from me, answering it with a sharp "Fisher."

"Are you the sidekick this summer?" Jason asked, glancing up as he measured and marked a board.

"I guess. I think he offered me the job as a favor to my mom. I feel like a shadow that's in his way. I think I prefer working with Hailey."

"Amen. She's awesome."

"Yeah." I slipped the tips of my fingers into my front pockets, glancing over my shoulder to see if Fisher was still on his phone. "Is he always in such a delightful mood?"

"Just in the mornings. He's not much of a morning person."

I laughed. "That's what Hailey said." I thought of our ride to the job site. He seemed fine with me.

"Let's go, Reese. It's going to be a long day." He made what I felt pretty sure was a growling sound which meant he was mad, but not at me or anyone in our proximity.

I cringed at Jason and he laughed, shaking his head.

"Well, it was nice meeting you."

"See ya around. Good luck with Mr. Sunshine."

"Thanks." I rolled my eyes and smiled. That smile quickly faded when I turned toward Fisher who was not smiling.

"Are you done rolling your eyes and talking about your boss?" Fisher asked me.

I had nothing to lose. I kinda knew he wasn't going to fire Rory's daughter. "For now." I shot him an extra toothy grin.

"No lunch for you," he murmured as he trekked toward his truck with me right behind him.

"I have a Cliff Bar in my bag. I came prepared for your less than stellar attitude. And AHHH!" I tripped. Stupid big boots. I hissed a sharp breath, sitting back on my knees as I brought my hand close to my chest with a dirty nail partially impaled into my palm. "Ouch! Oh my gosh! I'm fine." I hissed again. "I'm not fine. It hurts." Tears stung my eyes, but I refused to set them free in front of Fisher and his all-male framing crew.

"What did you do?" Fisher hunched down and reached for my arm.

"I tripped," I said with a bit of irritation lacing my words. What did he think happened?

"Let me see."

I shook my head and turned my torso, hiding my hand and the nail away from his line of sight. I didn't want him or anyone to touch it because it hurt too much.

"Don't. Touch. It." I felt my control slipping. I needed someone. A female. My grandma. I needed her to fix this. She was good at fixing and mending things.

"I just need to look at it. I won't touch it." Fisher grabbed my forearm and forced me to show him my hand. He frowned. "Well, looks like we'll be adding another stop to our morning."

That did it. That made my tears escape. "I'm sorry," I said with a trembling lower lip.

"Why? It was an accident. Shit happens. We'll get you fixed up. Okay?"

Sniffling. I nodded.

"Can you walk?" he asked. "Or do I need to carry you?"

He didn't want to open my door in front of anyone. I felt certain that carrying me was way out of the question as long as my legs weren't broken.

"I'm fine." I started to stand on the uneven pile of dirt and, just as quickly, my foot turned to the side, and I felt myself going down again, but not before Fisher grabbed my torso.

"I guess I'm carrying you." He lifted me up, cradling me in his arms like a needy two-year-old and carrying me to the truck. After he helped me into my seat, he grabbed my forearm again.

"Don't. Touch. It!"

He laughed. Laughed! "Just chill a sec. I'm going to get my first aid kit from the back and get some antibacterial wipes to clean the dirt off around it."

"Don't pull the nail out." I slowly released my bent arm so he could see my hand.

"I'm not going to pull the nail out. God ... you're a basket case." He disappeared to the back of the truck and returned with the wipes.

"Shouldn't you wear gloves so you don't get my blood on your hands?"

"You have my saliva inside of you. It's only fitting I get a little of your blood. Might as well let everything mingle today. Do you have an STD I need to know about?" Fisher squinted at me as his hands gently cleaned around the wound.

I frowned.

"It's a joke."

"Terrible timing." I jumped when his finger accidentally bumped the nail.

"Sorry." He cringed, giving me a sincere apologetic look. "Here, sit back. I'll get you fastened in." After he fastened the seat belt, he drove me to urgent care where we were ushered back surprisingly quick. They removed the nail. Cleaned the wound. Bandaged it. And gave me a tetanus shot because I couldn't remember the last time I'd had one.

"Do you need to go home?" Fisher asked when we got back into the truck.

"No." I felt stupid. I cried in front of him. How did I expect for him to think of me as a grown woman when I cried over a little puncture wound? I bet his date that night wasn't a crybaby like me.

"Sure?"

I nodded.

We finished off the day with me doing very little

aside from waiting in the truck and holding sacks of food for the roofing crew at the final job where they were working late to finish before the rain.

After a quick stop at the office, we headed home around six.

"What time is your Bible study?" Fisher asked as we pulled into the driveway.

"Seven."

"Are you still going?" He opened his door and paused, eyeing me warily like for the first time he felt bad about my accident.

"Yes," I managed to say like all was good. But I was not going to Bible study. "After a nice soak in the tub, I'll be fine." I shut the door.

"Um ... have you not noticed that there's only a shower downstairs? A nice shower. A huge tiled shower with lots of shower heads, but still a shower."

I'd forgotten. "Shower." I gave him a forced smile. "That's what I meant." I took three more steps before he said my name.

"Reese, you're more than welcome to use my tub. It's a big soaker tub, and I rarely ever use it. I'll shower in my other bathroom."

"No. A shower is great. A shower is what I meant."

"Well, if you change your mind, the offer stands."

"Thanks," I called without looking back as I headed around to the side of the house. "I'm good. Have fun on your date."

CHAPTER TEN

I SHOWERED when I really wanted a bath.

I skipped Bible study because I just needed to sulk.

I stayed up way too late, making a gazillion trips to the top of the stairs to press my ear to the door, listening for any sign of Fisher.

By one in the morning, I gave up and went to bed, a little irritated that he either wasn't coming home at all or was out so late ... on a work night. People who were not morning people needed to get to bed earlier. My grandparents went to bed at eight every night, and they were always a bucket full of smiles in the morning.

Thursday morning, I woke to a text from Fisher.

You're working in the office with Hailey today. Hopefully you can drive yourself. If not, call me.

What did that mean? Did he not come home the

previous night? Was he out too late? Hung over? At *her* place? Naked in her bed?

NO!

I really needed to get control of my thoughts. I should have gone to Bible study instead of going out of my mind eavesdropping on Fisher when he wasn't home.

"Good morning. How's the hand?" Hailey asked as I set my backpack next to her desk. "You can sit at Bossman's desk. I have a bunch of invoices for you to sort through today. Just set his shit in a pile on the floor."

"My hand is fine. Thanks." I gathered the papers and blueprints on his desk and set them on the floor in the corner. "Have you seen him this morning?" I asked.

"Not yet. I assumed you two would be riding together."

"He had a date last night." I poured myself a cup of coffee. "I don't think he came home."

"Oh ..." She lifted her eyebrows and grinned. "Go, Fisher, go."

No. Why did she say that? Maybe because she had sexual fantasies about other men, not her boss. I envied her. It's not like I wanted to pine for Fisher like a pathetic teenager.

Teenager.

Oh my gosh ... it wasn't until the word popped into my brain that I realized I had let the whole "adult" thing go to my head. Sure. Eighteen was legally adulthood, but I was eighteen which meant I was a still a teenager.

That seemed so wrong, to be a teenaged adult. Like an oxymoron.

Fisher got laid by a real woman. A non-teenaged adult woman. What was I thinking? And why couldn't I stop?

"Yay, Fisher," I said, lacking all enthusiasm just like the fake smile I tossed in Hailey's direction as I carried my coffee to Fisher's desk.

"I wonder if it was the orthodontist? Meghan or ... Keegan? I can't remember, but if it's Jason's friend from high school, then it's the orthodontist."

An orthodontist. How was I supposed to compete with that? Highly educated, self-sufficient, real adult orthodontist. Or ... teenaged adult who cried because she scraped her knees and got a little nail prick?

"Think you can hold things down for thirty minutes while I run a quick errand?"

My head snapped up at Hailey, and I nodded quickly. "Um ... sure."

"Cool. So here are the invoices. Just sort them by distributer then alphabetize them. They've all been scanned and saved on the computer, but Fisher likes hardcopy backups to everything."

"Got it."

"Can I get you anything while I'm out? A bagel? Better coffee?"

"I'm good. Thanks."

Twenty minutes into sorting invoices, the office

door opened and *Bossman* sauntered inside carrying a to-go cup of coffee. "That's my desk."

"How was your date?" I kept sorting, refusing to look at him.

No need to see his messy hair, unfairly sexy body in dark jeans, boots, and a black tee with his construction logo on the back. I didn't care about his square jaw and sinful smile.

Nope.

I had stuff to sort.

"Fine. Where's Hailey? Where's my stuff?"

"On the floor." My hands kept sorting papers, but I stopped focusing on any sort of alphabetical order.

"Hailey or my stuff?"

I didn't want to grin, but I did. "Your stuff."

"And Hailey?" He squeezed behind me, pushing his desk chair (and me) forward an inch or so.

"Errands."

"What errands?" He hunched down and thumbed through the stack of papers I'd set on the floor.

"I didn't ask. How was the concert?" I was pretty proud of myself for slipping that in like it was no big deal.

"I said fine."

"No. You said your date was fine. I asked about the concert."

"It was fine too."

"You're such a guy." I rolled my eyes and sneaked a quick peek at him over my shoulder.

"Well, yes, last I checked, I was a guy." Pulling out a manila folder, he stood.

"Hailey thought your date was an orthodontist."

"She thought right."

I felt six inches tall sitting in his desk chair while discussing his date ... that date who had him *all* night.

"How was Bible study? Did you go out for ice cream?"

"It was fine." I covered my face with one hand and sighed. "It was ... well, I didn't go."

Fisher chuckled and rested his butt on the edge of his desk, opening the folder. "Did you just try to lie? Are you incapable of lying?"

"No. Trust me. I can lie just fine. I just don't like to do it."

"Then why lie about last night. Why *try* to lie about it?"

"Because I don't want you to think that I didn't go because of my hand. I just didn't feel like it. That's all."

"Hey, you don't owe me an explanation."

I continued alphabetizing invoices while he remained leaning against the desk, close to me. So close I could smell his woodsy soap mixing with the coffee he set on the desk next to him. "So ... you must have been up early this morning. Since you uh ... texted me to drive myself. Were you meeting with the plumber?"

"No."

No? NO?

That was it. One word. No additional details. No

explanation as to why he asked me to drive myself to work.

"You never sent me the photos from our trip into the mountains."

"Oh. Sorry." Without taking his attention away from the contents of the folder, he slipped his phone out of his pocket and unlocked it before handing it to me. "Go for it."

I had Fisher's phone. It felt oddly personal like I had his whole world in the palm of my hand.

Contacts.

Text messages.

Photos.

Apps—which could tell me a lot about a person.

I behaved despite my mind whirling with a million possibilities. Opening his photos app, I quickly found the ones he took of me and us because they were the most recent. My gaze flitted from his phone screen to him several times to see if he was paying any attention to me.

He wasn't.

I airdropped the photos to my phone, then I may have accidentally swiped up a few times to get a quick glimpse of other photos he'd taken. Most were from job sites.

"Did you get them?"

I jumped and fumbled his phone, trying to hand it back to him. "Yeah, thanks."

"Sure." He stood and tossed the folder back onto

the pile on the floor. "Well, I'm out of here. I'll catch you later."

It killed me, as in physical pain clawing at my chest, to not say more to him.

Where was he?

Did he sleep with her?

If so, why?

Was it his MO to sleep with women on first dates?

Was he planning on seeing her—having sex with her—again?

So many crazy, irrational, and completely inappropriate questions chased each other in my head. But all I could do was smile like a sane person, like the adult teenager I was, even if a streak of insanity buzzed just beneath the surface.

OVER THE NEXT WEEK, Fisher tortured me by mowing the lawn without a shirt, eyeing me way too long in all the wrong places, and dropping slightly crude remarks at every chance. Then he'd buy me coffee and treat me like an equal for two seconds before the torture started all over again. I looked forward to every morning, even if all we did was banter and sling questionably appropriate comments at each other. (He was such a bad influence). And I liked the evenings when I'd take a walk only to return to him washing something in the driveway or watering plants—sans a shirt.

The wandering eyes.

The cocky smiles.

The slow wetting and rubbing of his lips together.

It felt like a game of cat and mouse, but I wasn't always sure who was the cat and who was the mouse.

The evenings I didn't like were the ones when he was gone ... the nights I assumed he was with the orthodontist. Every cell in my eighteen-year-old brain hyper-focused on my new crush in bed with another woman. Despite its extreme irrationality, it sucked.

And it sucked the most at my first party. Well, my first adult party at Hailey's house on Friday night. There must have been fifty people there, and she called it a small gathering. A lot of the guys from work showed up, some with wives, girlfriends, and even a few with boyfriends. That made me a little uneasy, and I hated that it made me uneasy. Fisher's words replayed in my head. *Now you can fucking think for yourself.*

That was hard for me. All my beliefs seemed to be interwoven with scripture, parental lectures, or sermons.

"Hey, you came." Jason playfully elbowed me before taking a swig of beer as we stood on the deck overlooking the backyard cluttered with people, yard games, kegs, and loud music.

"Hey, yeah. Good to see you again."

He wore cleaner jeans and a crisp white tee hugging his monstrous chest and arms covered in tattoos. "How's the hand?"

I laughed a little, holding up my hand with the tiny Band-aid. "Fine. Clumsy me."

"Drink?" He held his beer bottle toward me.

More shared germs? Did I want to swap saliva with Jason?

"Bossman!" Hailey hollered from the backyard.

I glanced over the railing to Fisher ... and his date. Hailey handed both of them red plastic cups of beer. Dr. Smile was a petite blonde with normal sized arms and legs—and of course perfect teeth. Mine were fairly perfect, but a few lower teeth had shifted after I stopped wearing my retainer. And she was at least a solid C-cup.

"Where did you get the bottled beer?" I asked Jason, feeling out of sorts with my emotions. I shouldn't have hopped on the back of Fisher's bike. That trip to the mountains messed with me.

"I brought my own beer. Don't care much for keg piss."

Staring at the amber bottle in his hand, I battled wrong and right in my head. Then I gave Fisher and his date another quick glance. She slid her hand around his waist.

"Maybe just a sip." I took the bottle from Jason's hand and brought it to my lips taking a whiff. It smelled like beer. I had no idea if beers had different aromas like wine. Taking a hesitant sip, I let the slow mingling of carbonation and alcohol coat my mouth. It didn't burn like I'd imagined. Maybe that was just hard liquor. It didn't exactly taste great either.

"Let's head down," Jason said as he nodded toward the stairs.

I held the bottle out to him.

"Keep it. I'll get another from my cooler."

"I don't need it."

He chuckled, descending the stairs. "Nobody does, but it's a party, Reese."

My grip on the bottleneck tightened as I followed him down the stairs. Most of the other women were wearing nicer sun dresses or sexy shorts and cute sandals. I wore shorts that nearly hit my knees and a T-shirt that I was pretty sure was a unisex shirt with a big smiley face on it.

Minimal makeup.

No nail polish.

And my hair looked like I'd done nothing more than comb it and let it air dry after a shower ... because that's what I did.

Straight brown hair doing nothing special. No body. No highlights. No funky pink streaks. Could I have been more basic?

"Yo, Bossman," Jason said.

Fisher and his date turned around. He smiled at Jason, but his smile faded a fraction when he saw me standing a few feet back, clutching a beer bottle to my chest. "Having..." he eyed the bottle for a little too long before lifting his gaze to mine "...a good time?" That look, it was too parental.

Too challenging.

Too condescending.

Long-armed, tiny-boobed, fake-adult Reese.

Lifting the bottle to my lips, I nodded. "I believe I am."

Fisher shifted his focus from me to Jason. "Did you give her the beer?"

Jason shrugged. "Maybe."

Fisher nodded slowly. "She's eighteen, which means she's officially your responsibility."

No he didn't. He didn't just call me out like a child.

Jason turned and gave me a sad smile. "Sorry. I'm not in the mood to babysit tonight." He plucked the bottle of beer from my hand.

I was so embarrassed; I wanted to kill Fisher. Then I wanted to cry because it sucked being an adult, only not really a full adult. Jason disappeared, leaving me with an empty hand in front of Satan's awful son and his girlfriend.

"Reese, this is Teagan. Teagan, this is Reese. She and her mom rent out my basement."

I didn't rent squat. But it was *so* generous of him to make me look grown up in front of her after calling out my age and apparent need for a babysitter.

"Nice to meet you." She smiled instead of offering to shake my hand, probably because one of her hands held a beer and the other was still around Fisher's waist.

The ugly jealousy felt terrible. How did I get such an extreme crush on a guy ten years older than me in a matter of weeks? It just added to all the other reasons I wasn't a mature adult yet. I felt certain Teagan didn't get stupid crushes on guys who were out of her league. Then again, she was a beautiful doctor with a great job, great hair, and great boobs. No guy was out of her league.

"Nice to meet you too."

Fisher took a swig of his beer, and I wanted to knock it out of his hand.

"Well, have fun. I'm going to grab something to eat." I wasn't hungry. It was code for "I'm leaving."

"You too," Teagan said. She sounded nice. She worked with a lot of kids, giving them great smiles. Of course she was nice. He deserved her.

I sulked my way through the crowd in the house, but not rushing anything to avoid looking like I was leaving. A few people were just outside the front door vaping—and probably smoking pot too—but they ignored me when I held my phone up to my ear, pretending to talk to someone.

When I got home, I opened a bag of cheese curls and ate half the bag. Then I downloaded some new music to my phone.

Matt Maeson.

After listening to several songs, I settled on "Tribulation." It was fitting in some ways. Tortured love.

Twenty minutes later, I knew every word.

Thirty minutes later, I ascended the stairs. And not surprisingly, he didn't lock his side of the door. I opened it slowly, even though I knew he wasn't home. I stole a banana and ate it. Then I opened the fridge door and frowned at all the peanut butter he had in the door. At least four jars. He must have been scared of a shortage. On the bottom shelf, there was beer. Lots of beer.

Biting my lips together for a few seconds while tapping my nails on the door, I contemplated borrowing ... *taking* just one beer.

One beer led to two beers, and I was buzzed. And it was good. I bobbed around his house holding my phone with music blaring while looking at photos of people I imagined were his family. Then I stumbled upon his bedroom.

"Oh, Fisher ..." I giggled, swaying a bit while I sauntered into his bedroom. "You make your bed like a good boy." I laughed some more and plopped onto my tummy, burying my nose in his pillow. "You smell sooo good." When I was convinced I'd sucked all of his scent from his pillow, I rolled to the side and right onto the floor. "Ouch ..."

More laughter.

More swaying as I lumbered to my feet and continued my self-guided tour, which led me to his bathroom. "There you are ... you big, beautiful tub."

I sighed. His bathroom was ginormous. And he had a wall of switches, at least twenty switches for all kinds of lighting around the sink, the shower, his wall of wardrobe cabinets, by my feet, even under the toilet.

"Too much." I pushed all the bottom buttons which turned off all the lights, leaving only natural moonlight coming from the big window by the tub and the two skylights. "That's better." I stripped, stepped into the soaker tub, and started the water, easing onto my butt with no grace. When the water reached an inch below my neck, I shut it off. "Where's my music?" I realized I'd left my phone on the bed or maybe on the floor, but the music had stopped anyway.

Closing my eyes, I enjoyed the silence ... and my buzz. The silence was interrupted with voices. I had enough sense to kind of care, but not enough sense to get out of the tub or say anything. Instead, I held still, really still ... and listened.

"It's beautiful, Fisher. You're incredibly talented. How long did it take you to build it?"

Teagan.

"About a year. I didn't rush anything, and I had some other jobs I was working on too." His voice got closer.

My senses ... my fight or flight? Yeah, they had the night off.

The lights turned on. All of them. There must have been a master switch. It was a little blinding at the moment. I squinted.

"Jesus ... what are you ..." Fisher turned his head like a real gentleman. No wonder Teagan liked him.

I liked him too.

"Oh! Reese!" Teagan jumped and turned as well. "Why is she in your tub?" she asked Fisher in a tone that made me think she wasn't too pleased.

"You said anytime ... I could use your tub anytime." I chuckled, cupping my hands together at the surface of the water and squirting it in different directions.

"You didn't say I could drink your beer, so ... oops. I'll pay ya back." Another giggle.

"Fisher ..." Teagan's voice wasn't friendly like her smile, like she worked with kids all day. It was really grumpy. Did he offer his tub to her too?

"I'll get out in a minute. When my head stops spinning."

The door shut, and I no longer saw them, but I heard the murmuring of their voices, and it wasn't good. A few moments later, the door opened again. It was Fisher, but he wasn't being as much of a gentleman. No hiding his eyes.

"Reese ..." he said in a slow and steady tone like I was that deer in the headlights he talked about.

"Fish-er ... I like that name. At first ... it was weird, like what were your parents thinking? But I like it now. A little too much. Ya know?"

"I *don't* know." He made his way to the tub, plucking my clothes from the floor one piece at a time. He sat on the edge of the tub with his back to me, holding my clothes in his hands as he drew in a deep breath and let it out slowly in a sound. My fuzzy head had trouble deciphering it. A grumble or a growl?

"Are you mad at me?"

Shaking his head, he pinched the bridge of his nose. "I don't know what I am."

"Is it the beer?"

He didn't respond.

"The bathtub? Were you just kidding about me using it whenever I wanted to?"

No response.

"I think I need a towel."

He nodded toward a tall stack of drawers by the sink on the opposite side of the bathroom. "Bottom drawer."

It might have been his proximity or the shock of him and Teagan showing up so early, but my buzz was quickly wearing off. "Aren't you going to get it for me?"

His lips twisted and he glanced over his shoulder at me. My hands moved to my breasts, and I crossed my legs as a big fat dose of reality began to register. The naked fisherman had seen *me* naked. Not briefly. He took his time, picking up my clothes while inching his way to the tub and my fully exposed body.

No bubbles.

No effort to cover myself.

Nothing.

"I'm not," he said.

"Why not?" My voice shook a bit. Sobriety stole the moment.

"Because I think you need to get it yourself."

"Are you going to leave now?"

"Nope." His gaze slid down my body.

My hands gripped my breasts harder as I squeezed my legs together tighter.

It was so wrong. *He* was so wrong.

Drawing my knees to my chest, I rocked forward and stood, lifting one leg out of the tub followed by the other, inches from Fisher. On a suffocating swallow, I closed my eyes and took a deep breath. He had an unobstructed view of my naked backside. I didn't have enough hands to cover everything.

"I thought you were a gentleman," I mumbled, making the walk of shame to the stack of drawers and hunching down instead of bending over to retrieve a towel.

"Why did you think that?"

Wrapping the towel around my body, I turned toward him. "Because you looked away when you first came into the bathroom."

"That was for Teagan. A gentleman doesn't stare at a naked woman in front of his date."

"So you're a gentleman for her, but not for me?"

He narrowed his eyes a second before returning a slow nod. "That's accurate."

Stupid fu—fudger.

"Because of my age?"

"Maybe."

"You're a real butt. Did you know that?"

"I know."

"So what's the point of all this?" I marched toward him and snatched my clothes from his hand.

"I need you to know that when you make poor decisions, men will take advantage of you."

"You said I could use your bathtub."

"Not drunk."

Hugging my clothes to my chest while keeping a firm grip on the towel, I frowned. "Well, if you're done teaching me ridiculous lessons, then I'm going to bed." Pivoting, I shuffled my feet to the bathroom door.

"I'm not done teaching."

I stopped, but I didn't look back at him.

"What now?"

"You need to bring your own towel. That one's mine. Leave it right where you're standing."

"You're a perv. How do you think Rory will react when she finds out you were being so perverted with her daughter?"

"I don't know, but make sure you start the story with the part where you stole beer from my fridge."

Fucker!

It felt so good to scream it in my head; I just wished my body would have cooperated and screamed it to his face. He knew I'd never tell Rory about the night's events. So he took every opportunity to embarrass me.

"I'm filing a sexual harassment complaint against my boss on Monday."

"You do that." He was a steel beam, an immovable boulder. Always one step ahead of me.

CHAPTER ELEVEN

I SPENT Saturday in shameful regret, not venturing out once.

Sunday morning I bolted to the Outback to go to church and pray ... lots of prayers. And when I returned, God had answered at least one of my prayers: Fisher wasn't outside.

Monday morning, around five-thirty, my luck ran out.

Fisher: You're with me today. We'll leave in twenty minutes.

Someone might as well have said, "You've been found guilty. We're executing you in twenty minutes."

I wore my hair down to hide my face as much as possible. With not a second to spare, I dragged my feet up to the driveway and climbed into the truck, keeping my backpack between my legs on the floor instead of tossing it in the back where I might have accidentally made eye contact with Satan's son.

"Morning." I could feel his gloating expression. His amusement.

"Morning," I mumbled, keeping my head down.

"Listen, there's no need to drag your weekend to work with you on Monday. What happened, happened. No big deal. We move on."

My head snapped up, jaw open. "No big deal? You molested me with your eyes! I wouldn't call that no big deal."

Fisher's molesting eyes flared, a new kind of shock I hadn't seen on him before. I may have spent the whole weekend letting my emotions build into something a little ... explosive.

"You know what your problem is?"

My chin tipped up as my eyes narrowed. Yeah, I knew what my problem was ... *him*.

"You need to get laid. And so help me, if you even think of telling Rory I said that, I will tell her everything."

"I ..." My jaw flapped a few times. I couldn't believe he said it. If I would have had a hundred guesses as to what I imagined he thought my problem was, lack of sex would not have been on that list. "That ... you ..." My head wouldn't stop shaking side to side. "I do not need to get laid. You need to stop being so crude. Some people take sex seriously, not like a game to play with anyone willing to have it with them. It's supposed to be something beautiful between two people who love each other."

"You've clearly never had an orgasm."

"I have too." Once, by accident. And it irked me that he had a way of keeping me on the defensive. I wasn't proud of my accidental orgasm, but I felt the need to own it with him accusing me of needing one.

"Liar." He smirked.

"You can't call me a liar about this when you've known me for a few weeks. You don't know anything about me and my past."

"Did you give it to yourself or did someone else give it to you?"

"This ... this is a stupid topic and really inappropriate. You're my boss, driving me to work."

"I'll be your boss when we get there."

"Then let's go." I faced forward and folded my arms over my chest.

At the first job, he inspected the previous day's work and talked to a few of the workers. The second stop was a meeting with potential clients at an empty lot. I waited in the truck. We grabbed a fast-food lunch (unfortunately not Mickey D's) and headed to the final stop of the afternoon. It was a staircase he'd been working on for a client, but they weren't home.

"Did you buy these?" I asked, running my finger over the intricate details of a spindle.

"Nope. I made them." He slipped on his tool belt.

Although I kinda hated him from our morning

conversation, I couldn't not appreciate how sexy he looked in a tool belt.

The scruff on his face a little longer.

His shirt nice and snug in the chest but loose over his tight abs.

"Are you serious?"

He glanced up, gathering the spindles in his arms to haul them inside the house from the garage. "Why are you constantly doubting my skills?"

Because he was the most amazing man I had ever met, but I couldn't tell him that. I couldn't hand him the last drop of my dignity because I didn't trust him with it.

"I'm just used to seeing you walk around staring at other people's work or barking orders. I have yet to see you in action."

"Well, grab the rest of those spindles, and I'll show you some action."

I carried the spindles into the house.

I handed him tools.

I ran and grabbed stuff from his truck.

I got him ice water.

I answered his phone when people called for him.

I watched Fisher Mann feed my obsession with him to the point where I knew no other man would compare, which meant I'd die a single and barren virgin. Occasionally, he'd lift the front of his T-shirt to wipe the sweat from his face. And on more than one of those occasions, he caught me gawking at his abs while wetting my lips.

"I'm going to start deducting pay from your check if you keep stealing free peeks at my body."

I cleared my throat and glanced at his phone. "Hailey just texted you. She said Brad's crew is done. She wants to know if you're coming by the office before you go home."

"No."

I risked a glance up at him. "You want me to just say no?"

Sliding a pencil behind his ear, he lifted his gaze to me from three steps down. "To Hailey, yes, I want you to say no."

"Who else would I say no to?"

He shrugged. "I'm hoping that's your last no of the day."

What did he mean by that?

I replied with a "no." Then I watched Fisher finish the railing. At some point I started nibbling at my fingernails; I wasn't a nail chewer.

"Grab the vac and clean the dust that didn't stay on the drop cloths."

"Um ... okay." I jumped to attention and did what he asked me to do while he loaded his tools in the trailer parked in their driveway.

"Are you done?" I handed him the vac.

"Almost. I'll finish up tomorrow afternoon." He closed the trailer and locked it.

"Think you can teach me something?" I asked with my hands in my pockets.

Fisher closed his tailgate and walked to my side of

the truck, standing uncomfortably close to me. "Oh, Reese ... I think I can teach you a lot."

Choking on my words for several seconds, I coughed and shook my head. "A-about construction. Can you teach me how to cut and nail things?"

The grin that climbed up his face made me melt like M&Ms on a hundred-degree day. "We might wait on the cutting, but I think I can show you how I nail things."

Another gulp clogged my throat. "I'd ... um ... I'd like that."

"Oh..." his grin did the impossible and grew even bigger "...I have no doubt you'd like it."

Oh my gosh ...

I didn't think he was talking about construction. And I wondered if he understood that I *was* talking about it.

"Well..." I lifted my shoulders and shoved my hands even farther into my pockets "...time to call it a day?"

He eyed me with his signature predatory, ready-to-pounce-on-its-prey look for several seconds. "Definitely."

When we pulled into the driveway after a ride home with no conversation, only music—his sexually explicit music—I jumped out before he got the truck into *Park*.

"Goodnight. See you tomorrow." I ran—sprinted—to the back of the house and fumbled the key with shaky hands. Rocks crushed under big boots—Fisher following me.

"Open!" I begged the key and my hands to work together.

Just as he turned the corner, it opened.

"Are you running from me?"

"Nope." I slid inside and shut the door behind me, locked it too. On a sigh of relief, I turned and made a straight line to my bedroom.

Click.

The door unlocked and opened. Of course he had a key. It was his house. The door clicked again when he shut it behind him.

"Whatcha need?" I asked with the last little bit of breath left in my lungs. His proximity made breathing so hard. It made my heart work even harder. It made my thoughts cross lines that should not have been crossed.

"Why are you running from me?" He was right at my back.

I forced myself to turn toward him, and it took superhero strength. He stepped toward me.

I stepped back.

We did this dance until a wall stopped my retreat.

He pressed his hands to the wall above my head, and my heart rate spiked a thousand percent. The air exchange in my lungs sounded like that of someone finishing a marathon.

Was I reading him wrong?

It wouldn't have been the first time I got it wrong and felt like a fool. But that moment felt different.

The look in his eyes wasn't the same.

The part of his lips.

The increased intensity of his own chest rising and falling.

"You can't have my virginity," I whispered.

It took him a few more breaths to respond. And when he did, it blew my mind.

"What can I have?" he whispered back.

In that most unexpected moment, my foolish, adult teenaged heart cracked open and made room for Fisher Mann. And I immediately wondered how long it took to fall in love.

Years?

Weeks?

Seconds?

Did common sense and timelines rule emotions?

"What do you want?" My words were weak when I wanted—more than anything—to sound brave.

Something so very tiny shifted along his face, like he was smiling without actually smiling. His right hand slid off the wall and cupped my jaw, his thumb teasing my bottom lip that trembled like the rest of me.

"A-are you g-going to kiss me?"

His lips pulled into a hint of amusement. "I was thinking about it." Fisher's patience killed me, completely slayed me. It was as if he had to solve the world's problems in his head before he kissed me.

But I didn't want to be a problem of the world. I wanted to be the girl—the woman—he kissed on a Monday night for no good reason. Not everything in life needed an explanation. Couldn't we steal a few seconds, a kiss, without accountability?

"Will you be done thinking about it anytime soo—"

Fisher kissed me.

It wasn't hard or rushed. It didn't make me feel inexperienced. And it didn't feel wrong.

After a few seconds, he pulled back an inch, maybe two. I sucked in a quick breath, and he kissed me again. It was just like the first kiss.

Perfect.

And just like the first one, he pulled back, but this time he smiled. My own smile came to life too, big and embarrassing.

Every imaginable "what-if" dominated my thoughts. What were we doing? Did those two kisses mean the world to me and nothing to him?

Seventy-two hours earlier, he'd been upstairs showing Teagan the house he built. And she loved it. She didn't question his abilities with a "seriously" because she was too mature for that.

What was he doing kissing *me*?

"I'm going to shower and grab dinner. I'll see you in the morning. Five-forty-five?"

I nodded, still wearing that impossibly huge smile.

He disappeared from my bedroom, his footsteps fading as he climbed the stairs.

CHAPTER TWELVE

I DIDN'T SLEEP that night. I tried, but I couldn't sleep after that kiss. Well, those two kisses. It took too long to figure out why he did it. And I never came up with a good explanation.

My trek around the house to the garage was the longest walk of my life. I couldn't breathe. It was eerily similar to how I felt the previous night. Would he be different with me? Regretful? Act like it never happened? Kiss me again?

I crossed my fingers for the third kiss. Which was why I brushed twice, flossed, and rinsed with mouthwash for a full minute. Just as I rounded the corner to an empty driveway, my phone chimed.

Fisher: You're with Hailey today. Had to go out of town to pick up some things.

Not even a "good morning." No XO. And not a

single emoji. Did he not know how to use emojis? It was the most emotionless, lackluster text ever. It wasn't the text you sent someone you'd kissed.

I typed my reply a dozen times and erased all of them. My drafts contained words like "good morning" and emojis. Hearts and kisses. Maybe it was a dream. Maybe it was another cruel lesson.

Reese: OK

As heartbroken as I was to be just as emotionless, I felt a sense of pride and maybe even a sense of maturity for keeping it professional. When I got to the office with my burning tongue (a minute of swishing mouthwash was *a lot*), Hailey greeted me with her usual bubbly smile and a stack of things to sort through. I got the feeling nothing had been sorted until Fisher hired me.

"Is it the weekend yet? Why did Monday feel like the longest day ever? It should be Thursday not Tuesday."

"Mondays aren't always bad." I shrugged, depositing my backpack on the floor and grabbing coffee.

"Are you ..." She tilted her head. "Blushing?"

"No." I dipped my chin and dove into the messy piles of papers.

"You are. Did you have a hot date last night? A *Monday* date?"

"No." I laughed like it was ridiculous. "No date."

"Okay then. I noticed you left the party early. But so did Bossman and his new girlfriend. She was all over him. I imagine he had quite the Friday night. Was he in a good mood yesterday morning?"

"Um ..." I tried to sound as aloof as possible. "Yeah, he seemed fine."

"Did he mention her? Is it serious? This time of year, I only get to see him for a few seconds a day, at the most. He's always on the go and constantly running thirty minutes behind."

"He didn't mention her. I don't think it's serious, but I'm not really sure."

"Why do you think it's not serious? Did he say something?"

"No. Just a feeling. I'm not sure. Maybe guys don't say much even if they do have serious feelings about someone. Like ... they probably don't send gushing texts or use a bunch of emojis."

"Ha! Not my ex. He sent me the dirtiest texts all the time with a string of eggplant and peach emojis. I bet Bossman sends her dirty texts. I can see him having a dirty side."

Hailey wasn't helping my emotional situation one bit. *Was* he sending Teagan texts? Were they still together? Did he play me? The more I thought about it, I felt so played by him. He and Teagan were having a good laugh over my foolishness.

I spent the better part of my day silently fuming while sorting and alphabetizing invoices and receipts.

Even the lunch Hailey brought me was left half-uneaten because I couldn't stomach it *and* the very real possibility that I was a pawn.

"I'm taking off," I said after placing the last sorted pile into the file box.

"Okay. Have a good night. Will I see you tomorrow?"

"Who knows. I never seem to know myself until the last possible minute."

"Sounds about right." Hailey laughed as I pushed through the door.

On the way home, I stopped at the grocery store and grabbed a few essentials. Then I made the short drive home, parking across the street just as Fisher pulled into the driveway on his motorcycle with a woman on the back.

Unbelievable.

My heart deflated as a cynical voice in my head laughed at me. I grabbed my two bags of groceries from the back and marched past the driveway to the path leading down the hill, not giving a single glance in the direction of Fisher and the dark blonde as they removed their helmets.

"Reese?" he called.

I walked faster.

"Reese?" His voice and the rest of his terrible self followed me.

I unlocked the door and picked up the bags, continuing into the basement like I didn't hear him or see him. Then I told myself not to cry. I even prayed for my tears to stay in check. Crying after one kiss (well, two) was something an eighteen-year-old virgin would do. And even if that was me, I wasn't offering that version to Fisher. Not anymore. He couldn't be trusted with my heart. I wouldn't have trusted him to hold my kite string on a breezy day.

"Why do you make me chase you?"

I hoisted the bags onto the counter and released a slow breath while plastering on a fake smile as I turned toward him. "The question is ... why are you always chasing me? I'm just the *girl* living in your basement. The employee you see several times a week. Seems silly that you're even giving me the time of day right now when you have some blonde waiting for you to ... I don't know ..." Shrugging, I tapped my chin. "Kiss her. Or do more than that."

Resting one hand on his hip and his other hand rubbing the back of his neck, he eyed me with no regret. "Are you done?"

My frown deepened. "Yes."

"I'm not going to kiss the blonde because she's my sister, so that would be weird. Occasionally, she likes to ride with me. That's her red Honda you parked next to."

After processing his explanation, I shrugged. "What about Teagan?"

"What about her?" He unzipped his jacket.

"Are you still with her?"

A slow grin made its way up his face as he shook his head. "I'm not sure I was ever 'with' her, but she's not okay being 'with' me since you were in my bathtub."

Was I a consolation prize? Since the beautiful doctor didn't want to be with him, he got the naked girl in his bathtub? Was I even that? I felt certain he'd had sex with her, yet he didn't think they were together? What could a simple kiss possibly have meant to him?

"Sorry. I shouldn't have taken a bath in your tub." Pivoting, I unloaded my groceries.

"I disagree. I gave you permission. I'm still giving you permission. Do you want to take a bath? Right now?"

Couldn't he let me be mad for a few seconds? No.

Releasing an unavoidable laugh, I shook my head while closing the fridge. "I don't want or need a bath right now. And where's your sister?"

"She had to leave." He slipped off his jacket and tossed it on the sectional.

I folded the paper bags, eyeing his moves as he made his way to me. A wall of shields lifted around my heart as an inner voice chanted, *No. No. No.*

"Did you get a lot of work done today?" He gripped my waist, and my hands flew to his shoulders because I wasn't sure what he was doing. Then he lifted me onto the counter and stepped into the space between my spread legs.

Just like the previous night, everything in my body

kicked into overdrive. "I ..." Swallowing hard, I gave him a nervous smile. "I sorted and filed today."

"That's good." He brushed my hair away from my shoulders and dipped his face into my neck.

I stiffened feeling the warmth of his breath spread along my skin. My hands slid from his shoulders to his hair, searching for control. If I didn't want him to kiss my neck, I could have yanked him away.

But I did.

I wanted to be kissed where I'd never been kissed before. Boys had kissed me, but I'd never *made out* with anyone. No kisses on my neck. No hickeys.

Two things happened at the exact same time, and I didn't know where to give my attention because they both set me ablaze and out of my mind. Fisher's hands shifted from my hips to my legs, his thumbs pressing on my inner thighs *really* close to my crotch as his lips pressed to my neck for only a second before he licked ... *he licked* a path to my ear.

A sharp, audible gasp left my parted lips just as he sucked my earlobe into his mouth and released it a second later by dragging his teeth along it. *All* the weird things happened at once.

Heat in my cheeks worked its way down to *everywhere.*

Pressure built between my legs.

I swear it felt like I'd peed a little, but I knew better.

Heaviness in my breasts.

Even my nipples felt different—sensitive as they pressed against the fabric of my bra.

Copious amounts of saliva required constant swallowing to keep from drooling. I was afraid to be touched anymore yet *needed* to be touched. It was so foreign and impossible to articulate even to myself.

My grip on his hair tightened which made him chuckle, kissing along my jaw. I didn't find anything funny. I was crawling out of my skin in the most wicked way.

"F-Fisher ..." I closed my eyes because everything he did made the room spin.

When his mouth covered mine, he didn't kiss me slowly like the first time. He kissed me like I'd always imagined a *man* kissing a *woman*.

This time he teased my lips with his tongue, tasting me like he'd tasted my neck and my ear. Then he kissed me hard again, and the foreign invasion of his tongue sliding deep into my mouth ... well ... I liked it.

So much.

Too much.

It felt sinful, but I didn't want him to stop.

For a few seconds, I wasn't sure what I was supposed to do with my tongue, but he showed me. Teased it. Teased me. And of all the lessons Fisher had tried to teach me up until that point, kissing was my favorite.

I was a good student. An eager student.

Then my phone rang, and I jumped, tearing myself

away from him. I fished it out of my purse, a few inches away from where I sat on the counter. "Rory," I said on a labored breath while I stared at the screen.

As I swiped the screen and brought it to my ear, Fisher stepped back, rubbing his well-kissed lips together while ...

Oh my gosh!

He adjusted himself, and it gave me a moment's pause, a little shock. I wasn't experienced, but I also wasn't stupid. I knew he was adjusting his *erection*, but for some reason I still felt a little shocked that kissing *me* did that to him.

Seeing my shock, he rolled his eyes and murmured, "Don't look so surprised."

I swallowed and cleared my throat, a tiny smile (a little triumphant) stole my lips as I found my voice. "Hey!"

"Hi. You sound happy. A good day?" Rory asked.

"Yeah, it was ... fine."

Fisher grabbed his jacket from the sectional and walked up the stairs. No look back. No kisses blown in my direction. I realized it was his way of giving me some privacy, but it was like the text ... I wanted the emoji, the wink.

Something!

"I have some good news," Rory said, bringing me out of my Fisher bubble.

"Yeah? What's that?"

"Things are going well here. And I'll be home early. Next week."

"That's ... great."

Rory laughed. "Don't sound so enthused. I thought you'd be excited. I felt bad leaving right after we reunited after so long. Once I get home, we'll have all the time we want to do whatever you want. And I have so much to tell you. So many things have been left unsaid for too long."

I wasn't sure what that really meant.

"Have you met any friends at church yet? Or work? Hailey is sweet, isn't she?"

"Yeah, I like her a lot."

"Any boys at church that have caught your attention?"

"Uh ... no." My face wrinkled. "And let's call them guys not boys. I'm not dating twelve-year-olds."

"Sorry. Guys. Young men. And there's no need to rush into anything. You are so young. Love can be incredibly messy and confusing. Find *you* first."

"I'm not lost."

"Reese, you know what I mean."

"I actually like working for Fisher."

"Well, sure. But there's not a lot of room for advancement unless you're going to actually learn to build stuff."

"He's going to teach me some things."

"Oh, he is? Like ... he's going to teach you things about construction?"

"I think so. I asked him if he would."

There was a pause before she replied with a "Huh

... okay. He's a talented guy. I'm sure he's the best one to teach you things."

I couldn't have agreed more.

"Hope you're being smart around his crew. He's employed a lot of single guys who I'm sure will find you quite appealing, but they need to remember you're eighteen."

"Which means I'm an adult."

She sighs. "Yes, but guys with five to ten years on you are not in your best interest right now unless you meet them at church. Alcohol. Sex. Drugs. I just don't want you getting in over your head before you reach twenty. I'd love for you to find a group of friends close to your age."

"You don't need to worry about me."

"I know. I'm not. I'm sure Fisher is keeping a close eye on you whether you like it or not."

"Yes, he's ... all over me." I bit my lips together to hide my grin.

"I knew it. I had a feeling he'd be a big brother to you."

That comparison nauseated me a bit.

"Anyhoo, I'll let you go. Let's talk again this weekend when we have more time. Maybe video chat so I can see your beautiful face."

"Sounds good."

"Bye, sweetie."

"Bye." I slid my phone onto the counter and stared at the staircase leading to *him*.

I wasn't sure if my mom's call was bad timing on

her part or good timing on God's part. And what happened next? Was I supposed to go upstairs to continue what we started? Ending where? In his bed, sans my virginity?

Why did he have to be twenty-eight and my mom's friend/landlord? Why did he have to be twenty-eight with way more life and sexual experience than me?

I grabbed a pre-made salad from the fridge and ate it with a handful of wheat crackers. Then I changed into jogging shorts, tennis shoes, and a tank top. I assumed Fisher was eating dinner or taking a shower, but as I trekked around to the front of the house, I was proven wrong.

Shorts. No shirt (of course). Bare feet.

He used a hose and spray nozzle to water some plants and flowers by his front door. Shirtless Fisher was not a good idea for me. My body still hadn't recovered from his hands on my legs, his thumbs dangerously close to the top of my inner thighs.

"Going for a jog?" he asked.

"Walk." I didn't stop. Stopping was a bad idea.

"Want company?"

Bad idea.

"Okay." I turned with a little too much bounce to my step, too much enthusiasm in my voice, and way too big of a grin on my face.

Rory was coming home in one week. And I didn't know what that would mean for Fisher and me. I wasn't in his head. I could guess that Rory wouldn't like the idea of me having a physical relationship with

a man ten years older than me. And if I was being
honest with myself, I wasn't sure how I felt about it
either.

Him ... I knew how I felt about him, but I couldn't
turn off all common sense, ignore the logistics of our
situation. What I wanted and what made sense were
not the same things.

"Let me put on some shoes." He shut off the hose
and disappeared into the house via the front door.

When he returned with only shoes, still no shirt, I
had a mild panic attack. When he grabbed my hand
and grinned, it escalated to a moderate panic attack.

"So Rory's coming home in a week," he said as we
strolled down the street, my fingers laced with his.

Every new touch brought a new sensation. Holding
hands wasn't kissing, yet it felt equally as intimate. I'd
held his hand before, during the storm prayer, but this
was different. That was an awkward clasp; this was
more.

"Were you eavesdropping?"

He chuckled. "No. She called me after she called
you."

"Oh. Well ... what did you say?"

"I said you'd be excited to see her." He glanced
down at me for a second.

"No." I kept my gaze in front of us. "What did you
say about us?"

"I told her you have a fantastic mouth and a silky
tongue that tastes like heaven, legs that bring me to my
knees, and a truckload of attitude."

"Oh my gosh ..." I stopped and turned toward him, yanking my hand away from his.

He narrowed his eyes. "What? I didn't tell her about the bathtub incident or that you stole beer from me."

"Fisher!"

His brow relaxed as that stupid smirk appeared. "Stop being so gullible."

"Ugh! Jerk!" I hammered my fists into his chest.

He grabbed my wrists and held me to him, held my hands to his chest. "I'm not saying a word to her."

I stared at his chest as my fists relaxed, as my palms pressed to his firm muscles and tan skin. Another new and intimate feeling. "I ... I don't think ..." My gaze inched its way up to meet his. "I don't want her to know about ..."

Rolling his lips together, he nodded several times. "Yeah. I don't either. She wouldn't be very happy with me."

Grunting a laugh, I glanced to the side, "Then what's the point of this?"

"I don't know." His honesty bled through his words. It was a brief moment when I didn't feel that Fisher was a decade older, a decade more mature, a decade more experienced.

Maybe connecting with someone didn't have boundaries or timelines. I liked the idea of him feeling as drawn to me as I felt to him. It made me feel like we were equals in this, whatever *this* was.

"So we just ..." I wasn't sure if the thoughts in my

mind reflected my true emotions or if I needed to say them to ease his burden. "We just stop when she gets home. Like it never happened."

Twisting his lips, he studied me for a few moments before returning a single slow nod. "Like it never happened."

CHAPTER THIRTEEN

Our "It Never Happened" agreement put a damper on the rest of the evening. We walked. He kissed me goodnight, but it wasn't like the kiss in the kitchen. And that was it.

Friday morning I got a text from Fisher as I was buttering a piece of toast, freshly showered with wet hair, but dressed sans shoes and socks.

Fisher: I'm leaving early for a meeting. You can work in the office if Hailey has stuff for you or you can have the day off.

Immediate let down.

I dropped the butter knife and sprinted to the front of the house without any shoes on just as Fisher started his truck. "Stop!" I smacked my hand on his window.

He jerked his head to the side and started to roll down his window, but I opened his door instead.

"Didn't you get my text?" He squinted.

"Yeah, but didn't you get the memo that Rory's coming home soon?" I stepped up, forcing him to wrap his arm around my waist to keep me from falling out of the truck as I planted my face an inch from his.

He grinned. "Your hair is still wet."

"So?" I whispered, my gaze sliding along his face from his eyes to his full lips so close to mine. "Are you going to kiss me?"

Wetting those full lips, he lifted his right shoulder into a half shrug. "I was thinking about it."

My foolish grin showed all my teeth. "Don't think."

Fisher lifted his other hand and cupped my face, ghosting his thumb along my cheek. "I never do when I'm with you."

A soft breeze blew my wet hair into my face and his, but it didn't stop him from kissing me.

"Now, if you don't get out of my truck," he said releasing my lips, "I'm going to want more."

I giggled, kissing along his cheek as his hand moved from my waist to my butt.

"Like that book *If You Give a Mouse a Cookie*, have you read it?"

I nodded, relishing the feel of his scruffy face against my lips. "Fisher," I whispered at his ear, feeling brave enough to tease his earlobe like he had teased mine with his teeth, "are you saying you want my cookie?"

He laughed, threading fingers through my wet hair and bringing my lips back to his. "Your cookie."

Kiss.

"Your muffins."

Kiss.

I giggled against his mouth.

"I'm going to want the whole fucking bakery."

Kiss.

I wanted his crude and dirty mouth. The kisses ... I wanted *all* of his kisses. His laughter. And the way he looked at me like I was the bane of his existence in the most beautiful way.

"Well..." I stepped down, rubbing my lips together to relish the taste of toothpaste, coffee, and the naked fisherman "...you have work. And the bakery is closed."

"Killjoy." He adjusted himself. Again, it made my grin double. "Are you going to work?"

Twisting my lips, I slipped my hands into my pockets. "I figured I would. I haven't called Hailey yet."

"Take the day off."

I frowned. "And do what?"

"Take a bath in my tub."

I giggled. "I just showered."

"Roll around in my bed naked."

Another giggle.

Our banter felt a little wrong—the way *we* felt a little wrong. And that wrong felt perfectly right in that moment. I knew the upside down version of my world wouldn't last long, so I didn't try to fix it. I just let it be whatever it was meant to be.

A little wrong. A little right.

Just ... us.

"Bye." I took one step back, then another.

Fisher shook his head, but his smile made the bigger statement as he shut his door and put his truck into drive. I pressed my fingers to my lips and kissed them, blowing it to him. He winked and drove out of the driveway.

"Oh, naked fisherman ... this is going to hurt." I crossed my hands over my chest to comfort my heart. Who was I kidding? I knew I was already too invested in him. And even if I also knew I would have to let us end when Rory returned, it still hurt. Even if Fisher didn't share the same emotions, I knew he would always be my first love—that really good kind of love where my brain had no say. The kind with no logical explanation. The kind that took a special place in my heart as *first*.

God willing, I would go on to love another. Have a family. And die in the arms of my husband. But ... *first* would always be Fisher Mann.

<hr />

HAILEY WASN'T FEELING WELL, so I went to work. I delivered lunch to the roofers.

"Thanks. You must be Reese." A guy with black hair and a major suntan smiled at me; it made his teeth stark white.

"Yes." I handed him the sacks of food and slipped my hands into the back pockets of my jeans.

He inspected the sacks and smiled a little. I

ignored his smirk, his unspoken observation. "I'm Jeremiah. Hailey was telling me about you." He peeled his eyes from the big sacks filled with little sacks.

Jeremiah was hot. That wasn't really up for debate. I could see why Hailey thought I'd like him.

"Funny, she might have mentioned you to me as well." I tried to control my grin.

"I missed her party. I heard you were there ... alone."

"Yeah, I was."

He glanced over my shoulder. "I'd better get to eating my lunch. Bossman's here."

I twisted my body and squinted at the white truck and *Bossman* climbing out. Aviators on. He sipped something red from the straw of a big plastic cup from a convenience store.

"Boss," Jeremiah said.

"Jeremiah," Fisher said in a fairly neutral tone.

"Can I get your number from Hailey later?" Jeremiah asked me as if Fisher wasn't hearing every word. "We could hangout this weekend if you don't have plans. My parents have a place near Breckenridge."

Fisher stepped right next to me. My attention shifted between the two men. I anticipated Fisher saying something, but he didn't. Instead, he sipped his drink like a ten-year-old who just got his favorite beverage and couldn't stop nursing it.

"I ... uh ... have plans already. But thanks." I pressed my lips together so Fisher didn't think I was flirting with Jeremiah.

"Maybe another time?"

I didn't know how to reply, so I nodded just before Jeremiah took off with the bags of food for the crew.

"What are your plans?" Fisher asked, taking a two second break from his straw.

"What are you doing here?"

"Working." He shrugged, taking a longer break from his drink. "What are you doing here?"

"Delivering lunch."

"Did you bring me lunch?"

I shook my head. "I can get you lunch. What do you want?"

"You."

On a nervous laugh, I glanced around to see if anyone heard him. "I don't think I know what that means."

"I think you do." He brushed past me to the crew sitting along the side of the house in the shade, eating their lunch.

I didn't move, mostly because I wasn't sure if he wanted me to head back to the office or get him lunch ... me ... which ... yeah, I had an idea of what that might have entailed. But it wasn't on the menu. However, just thinking about it, made me feel an unfamiliar need, a foreign feeling between my legs, and the recently new wet feeling that wasn't a bladder issue.

It had to be better than men getting untimely erections. After all, I could hide it. Still, I *felt* like everyone who looked at me somehow knew.

As Fisher chatted with his crew, inspected their

lunches while shaking his head, I thought long and hard about the definition of sex and temptation. I tried to make a case for sex being only intercourse. That left a lot of options.

"Let's go." Fisher strutted toward me, sipping his red drink.

"What is that?" My nose scrunched.

"Fruit punch and iced tea." He held it out for me.

I eyed the guys eating their lunches, making sure they weren't watching us before I took a sip.

"Don't do that." Fisher grimaced, taking his drink and crossing the street toward his truck.

"Do what?" I followed him since I was parked behind him.

"Lick your lips like that."

I chuckled. "I didn't lick them *like* anything. Why?"

"Because I've been dealing with a fucking hard-on since you climbed into my truck this morning."

Fisher ... so uncensored.

He had no idea—or maybe he did—how much it thrilled me to know that I could slowly unravel him in that way. It made me feel powerful, yet incredibly weak at the same time because I had no clue what to do with my accidental sorcery.

"Do you need a formal apology?"

Fisher opened the door to his truck then rubbed the pads of his fingers over his mouth like he was trying to wipe off his smile before I saw it.

"Say it." Everything I didn't want to hear or see

three weeks earlier had become my obsession, my new education, my real-world path to enlightenment. Fisher thought something, but he didn't want to say it. He didn't think I could handle it.

"Nothing."

I took the four long strides to get from my driver's door to his. With my hands on my hips, feeling way more confident than I should have been, I tipped my chin up. "Say. It."

"It's not for your ears." He eyed me, pushing back with as much confidence—probably more.

"That's code for it's inappropriate. Since when has that stopped you before?"

On a small, controlled chuckle, he shook his head and focused on something over my shoulder, avoiding eye contact with me. "You offered an apology. I was going to say apologies were just lip service. Then I thought …" He dragged his teeth over his lower lip and met my gaze.

"You thought?"

"I thought lip service wouldn't be the worst thing for my problem."

It took me a few seconds … then I got it. My eyes widened, brows sliding up my forehead.

Fisher was a little *extra* that day.

If someone wouldn't have coined the term oral sex, oral *sex*, I would have been able to make a better case for it. Why couldn't it have just been oral or something else like … tonguing? I needed a line, a line I wouldn't cross. And I was okay with moving the line a smidge if

I could rationalize something. I couldn't go there ... not yet.

Oh the hypocrisy ...

"Nothing that ends in the word sex. I just can't."

His eyebrows jumped, one slightly higher than the other. Fisher's expressions were so sexy. How did I expect to not perform any act ending in the word "sex" when the man before me was the definition of sex?

"So ... everything else is on the table?"

What was I missing? I knew it would come back to bite me in the backside. Still, I nodded while chewing on the corner of my bottom lip and wringing my hands together.

"Meet you at home." He turned and climbed into his truck.

"Wait ... you're done for the day? It's only one?"

"I am now." He shut his door and started his truck.

CHAPTER FOURTEEN

REGRET MULTIPLIED the closer I got to home.

Home ...

Was that my home? Was my grandparents' house my home? Did I truly have a home? I wasn't sure I'd ever felt so emotionally and physically displaced in my life. Saying I was at a crossroad was an understatement. "Finding myself" was not right either.

Fisher was getting his mail as I slowed to a stop. How could he so casually get his mail and thumb through it? I barely made it home without wrecking Rory's car because my hands were shaking so much. I climbed out and heaved my bag onto my shoulder, taking cautious steps toward the house.

Fisher kept his head bowed at his mail. "I can hear your teeth chattering. Are you cold?"

I clenched my jaw to stop the chattering. "No."

"Having second thoughts about your offer?"

That felt like a direct challenge to my age, my

maturity, and my sexual experience. Did he want me to back out? Was this another lesson?

"No." I infused as much confidence as I could muster, which was very little.

"You know ..." He continued into his garage, and I followed, leaving a good ten feet between us. "When you've had sex, things aren't so awkward and scary. I'm not implying you should abandon your morals." He held open the door for me, and I removed my boots and set my bag next to them. "I'm just saying it becomes a little more thrilling and less scary. You know what to expect. You know the end game and why you should want to experience it."

"I take it..." I padded my feet into his kitchen and slowly walked around the island, dragging my fingertips along the countertop "...you've had a lot of sex?"

He tossed one piece of mail onto the counter and discarded the rest in the pullout recycling bin. "I'm twenty-eight and single. Yes. I've had a lot of sex."

His words formed a tight knot in my stomach. It wasn't that I didn't expect that to be his truth; I just didn't expect him to be so forthcoming about it.

"How old were you when you first had it?"

"Sixteen."

I nodded, staring at my fingers tracing the lines in the granite instead of him eyeing me from the opposite side.

"What..." he laughed a little "...do you see happening? Do you think I'm going to tie you to my bed and do weird things to you?"

My gaze shot up to meet his, and I didn't blink once. "That hadn't occurred to me."

"Then what occurred to you on that long drive home?"

I shrugged. "I don't know."

"Liar."

"Stop calling me a liar. You can't read my mind."

"Do you touch yourself?"

"Jeez ..." My head bowed to hide my embarrassment.

"I'll take that as a no." He walked to the basement door and opened it. "Go touch yourself. I'm going to take a shower and touch myself. Then we'll have dinner and see how the evening progresses."

Oh ... my ... gosh ...

He was serious. I didn't know what was most unsettling: the idea of him giving me a homework assignment to masturbate or him confessing his own intentions.

I laughed, a little too loudly. "I'm ... I'm not going to ..."

"Touch yourself? Why the hell not?"

Swallowing hard, I shook my head. I felt like the world's biggest prude. And that shouldn't have bothered me. I had my faith. I *did* have morals. And if I gave in and handed him my virginity, what would I have to give my husband on our wedding night. Those were the words I'd heard from my grandma and people at church so many times. Except my grandma took it one step further with a cringe-worthy analogy.

"Therese, if you don't have that to give your husband, it's like borrowing a used sanitary napkin from a friend. You don't want to be a used sanitary napkin, do you?"

So there it was ... not having my virginity on my wedding night was not only disrespectful to my husband and to God, it was gross and had the potential to spread disease. And I bought it. Not only did I buy it, I repeated it to my friends to help remind them of the importance of staying virgins.

Making the virgin walk of shame, I sulked toward the stairs, stopping and glancing up at Fisher.

"Have fun." He gave me a tight smile.

I blinked several times. "I can't do this."

"Why not?"

My head shook in frustration. "B-because I don't want to make myself feel good; I want *you* to make me feel good! I want to feel like I felt last night, like I felt this morning."

He pinched the bridge of his nose and closed his eyes. "Fiiine ..." When he opened his eyes, he blew out a long breath. "But *I* need a shower before that happens again."

"Why?"

"Jesus, Reese ... because. Okay? Because. Can it just be okay with you?"

"No!" I covered my mouth after I yelled my answer.

He growled and grumbled. Things were worse

than I thought. Fisher was mad at me and the rest of the world, but mainly me.

"I want to be the reason you ... well ... you know."

"Done." He gave me a slight nudge, forcing me down the first stair. "I will think of you the whole time. Happy now?"

I deflated. "You don't deserve my dreams, naked fisherman." Turning, I descended the stairs and headed straight to my bedroom, where I wasn't going to touch myself regardless of what Fisher did in the shower.

Plopping onto my bed face-first, I turned my head toward the window and stared at the mountains, thinking I should just go ... just take a drive alone.

"Happy Meals? Really, Reese. You got Happy Meals for my crew today?"

"They didn't complain."

"Not to you. I hope you got the toys you needed, the toys you're no longer collecting."

I didn't respond.

"So ..." his voice got closer to me. "Naked fisherman?"

"Shut up." I didn't turn toward him, even though I knew he was next to my bed.

"Tell me about your dreams."

I sighed. "Sorry. They're mine. Get your own."

The other side of my bed dipped. I turned my head toward Fisher next to me on his back, hands folded on his chest as he stared at the ceiling.

"Take your shirt and pants off," he said.

"What?"

He closed his eyes. "Just ... take them off. Nothing more, just your shirt and pants."

I didn't move.

"Do you trust me?"

"Not really."

He grinned a tiny grin, but he didn't open his eyes. "Well, try ... just this once."

Sitting up slowly, I removed my shirt, eyeing him to see if he was peeking.

He wasn't.

I had to stand to shimmy out of my jeans, leaving them on the floor next to my shirt—leaving me in a white bra and panties.

Fisher's eyes fluttered open, and I held my breath, holding back the urge to cover myself. "You're truly beautiful."

My skin turned pink all over. "Thank you," I whispered, fighting the insecurity to ask him if he thought I was as beautiful as Teagan or the million other women he'd been with while I was just a young girl.

"Come here."

After a few seconds of hesitation, I crawled onto the bed close to him.

"Straddle my legs."

Biting my quivering lower lip, I straddled his jean-clad legs. The level of intimacy made it nearly impossible to breathe.

"Higher."

I scooted higher.

He sat up, shrugging off his shirt, and I jumped as

143

his hands found my hips, his fingers grazing my butt. Our noses nearly touched.

"I'm going to kiss you. And touch you." His voice was just a whisper, a warm breath over my lips. "And you're going to do whatever you need to do to feel ... *good*. And if you get scared, I want you to close your eyes and know that I've got you. You're not too young or too anything. You are you. And I just think that you're ... beautiful."

"Fisher ..." I leaned forward and pressed my lips to his.

We kissed, unhurried, almost lazily.

My hands navigated his chest and back, every muscle, every bend in the terrain of his body. Fisher feathered his calloused hands over my bare skin, sending goose bumps spreading across it.

Our kiss deepened, a soft moan breaking the silence. It took me a few seconds to realize it was me, not him. Fisher's fingers slid up my inner thighs. I stiffened, eyes wide. He blinked a few times and slowly kissed me again. When I closed my eyes, I let go ... finding trust in the man who "had me." His fingers teased the leg of my panties. My right hand found his hair as my left hand clawed his back.

I was so scared. A good scared. The kind of scared I felt climbing a steep hill on a rollercoaster. As he flicked his tongue against mine, a single finger inched beneath the crotch of my panties.

I fisted his hair as my breath hiked.

"Beautiful ..." he whispered against my mouth, along my jaw, and down my neck. Over and over.

Beautiful ... Beautiful ... Beautiful ...

Fisher. The first man other than my father to call me beautiful.

That finger? It moved a fraction of an inch, and I jerked. His finger, his entire body, stilled except for his lips at my ear, his breath whispering, "Make it feel good ..."

Fear shook me. My faith. My fragile beliefs. I held my breath for few seconds like I did at the top of that rollercoaster hill. Then I kissed him. He didn't kiss me.

I. Kissed. Him.

My pelvis moved just enough to rub my clit against the pad of his idle finger. I rocked it a little more until it touched me lower, where I was wet between my legs.

And not once did he move.

I kissed along his jaw and neck, feeling safe, feeling the slow building of my confidence as a woman.

My hips rocked a little harder until I realized what I was feeling ... what I was rubbing ... wasn't so much his finger. It was his erection hard against me. The denim scratched my inner thighs, but I didn't care.

"Fisher ... m-move ..."

"Move what?" he asked with so much control I thought I might die of my own impatience.

"E-everything. Just ... move."

His strong hands claimed my hips again, only this time, they gripped me a little harder, and he moved me over him.

He did it for me, and it felt so addictive I couldn't formulate a coherent thought.

He did it for him, and his breaths grew more labored, his kisses more desperate.

I wanted nothing more than to know what it would feel like for him to be inside of me. "Fisher ... I ... I think I want you to take off your jeans."

He reclined back onto my pillow and grinned as I leaned forward, resting my hands on his chest, my hair falling around my face and his.

"You don't ... not yet." His eyelids grew heavy as his pelvis lifted from the bed.

Giving more.

Taking more.

Proving just how *extra* he was that day.

We weren't having sex. But *we were* ... having sex.

It was wrong. But it was right.

My head spun in dizzying circles as up became down and down became up, and nothing made sense, nor did I really want it to make sense.

And when it happened, that all-consuming, mind-numbing sensation, I gasped and hissed a "Yesss."

Vulnerable.

Out of control.

Fear crept into my conscience. I didn't want him to know how scared I felt, like a teenager trying to be an adult.

Fisher held my hips still as he pumped his up several more times and released a drawn-out expletive that I never said aloud but found it fitting, and even a little sexy, coming from him. Collapsing against his chest, I buried my face into his neck, a little winded and a lot ... happy. As frustrated as Fisher made me, I felt blissful with him.

Was I a terrible person?

Did I disappoint God?

Probably "yes" on both accounts.

Fisher left one hand on my ass and lifted his other hand to the back of my head, stroking my hair several times. "Nine across. Six letters. The first one is 'S' and the fourth one is 'W.' Hint: It's something I still need."

I laughed, nodding without lifting my head from his neck. "Are you trying to speak my language? It's kinda sexy." Lifting my head, I kissed his jaw. "Yes. You can *shower* now."

THINGS I NEVER TOLD FISHER ...

After he left me to take his shower, I sat in the corner of my own shower and cried. It was more than I could handle.

My faith.

My thoughts.

My beliefs.

My desires.

My emotions.

They all took different paths. I felt pulled in so many directions, each feeling equally right and equally wrong for many different reasons. As strong as I felt my faith was, there wasn't a day that passed when I didn't question it. Question Him. His existence. His role in our lives. And our interpretation of His words.

What happened with Fisher didn't feel wrong. We weren't hurting anyone. We weren't harming anything. We were two souls enjoying our physical bodies. Why did it have to be a form of immorality?

The rest ... the guilt ... the lecture I could recite on my own? It felt awful. Was that the point of life? To walk a line of righteousness and feel guilty and sinful for occasionally stepping off the line? Why give us freedom of choice if there was only one right choice?

After drying my hair and applying a little makeup, I slipped on a tank top and a pair of shorts before climbing the stairs. Did I need to knock?

I knocked.

"It's not locked."

I grinned, slowly opening the door.

Wearing only a pair of shorts hanging low on his perfect hips, wet hair, lean, cut body casually resting against the kitchen island with one ankle crossed over the other, Fisher glanced up from his phone. "Hey."

"Hey." I closed the door and fidgeted with the hem of my tank top.

"My parents invited us to dinner."

"Us?" I narrowed my eyes. "You told them about us?"

With a slight shake of his head and a tiny grin, he set his phone on the counter and crossed his arms over his bare chest. "Is that a problem?"

"I ... well ..." I felt everything inside of me tremble. Age didn't matter, but it *did* matter.

"They know you're Rory's daughter. They know you work for me. And they know we were going to grill tonight since neither one of us has plans."

I didn't know we were grilling. "They don't know about ..." I pressed my lips together. What was I supposed to say? That we had sex? We didn't. That I got off on him? That. I *did* do.

"No. I left that part out, but if you feel obligated to tell them, that's your prerogative."

"No." I inched my head side to side. "I don't feel a particular need to tell them or anyone."

"Are you ashamed of me?" He cocked his head to the side.

I padded my bare feet to him and collapsed into his naked chest, pressing my face directly over his heart and inhaling his clean scent. "I don't know what I am." I kissed along his pec muscles as he snaked his arms around my waist.

"So we go as friends. My sisters will be there. Nieces and nephews. No big deal."

My head jerked up. "Your whole family?"

"Not everyone, but most of them. Why?"

"No reason."

"Think you can keep your hands off me for one night?"

"Depends ... will you wear a shirt?"

"Yes." He grinned.

"Then I'll be fine." Taking a step back, I slipped my hands into the front pockets of my shorts.

"Is this solely about my body?" He narrowed one eye.

"Of course. Your personality is just okay, and as a boss, you're kind of grumpy." I put on my best mask and tried to act mature. Cool. Controlled. On the inside, I hadn't stopped reeling from what took place on my bed.

Was Fisher too experienced and mature to let his thoughts linger on something as trivial as what we did?

"I'm ignoring your bullshit. Just like this is the only day that I'm going to let your Happy Meal catering slide."

"I did it to finish off the collection for my mom. I'm done. And if you're upset that I spent your money on them, then I'll pay you back. Are you happy now?"

Wearing a smirk, he cocked his head to the side. "I don't believe you're done. I don't believe it's for Rory anymore. You've allowed this to become your hobby, your addiction. It's cute. Really. But I can't have you stealing toys from some of the Happy Meals. It's going to cause fights with my crew if everyone doesn't get a toy."

"Kiss my backside, Fisher." I narrowed my eyes.

"Your *ass*? You want me to kiss your ass?"

Rolling my eyes, I shook my head.

"Turn around."

Releasing a nervous laugh, I eased back a step. "It

was a joke because you were giving me a hard time over the Happy Meals."

"Yes." He crooked a finger at me. "But now I want to kiss your ass."

"Stop it." I giggled through my nerves.

"Come here. I'm not going to chase you this time."

Gathering up my bravery like collecting the contents of a spilled purse in the grocery store aisle, I turned and bent over, resting my hands on my knees. If he wanted to kiss my backside, then I would let him. No big deal. Nothing to be nervous about.

"Oh, Reese ..." He drew out my name while kneeling behind me.

I wasn't sure why he needed to kneel behind me.

Bend down and kiss it. Whatever. Just do it and be done.

But my thoughts were simpler than his.

"You're a walking wet dream."

"What are you doing!" I jumped.

"Kissing your ass," he said in his calm voice while curling his fingers into the waistband of my jogging shorts and slowly pulling them down to expose my *bare* backside.

I grabbed one of his arms to stop him.

"I'm not kissing your shorts."

Fisher ignored my hand gripping his forearm as he exposed one side of my butt. With my other hand, I gripped the front of my waistband and held on for life so he couldn't completely remove my shorts *and* panties.

He kissed my bare butt slowly at first. Then, he kissed it harder with a lot more suction.

"Fisher ..." I squeezed my glutes. "You're going to leave a mark."

"Mmm ..." He licked the spot that he kissed so hard. "No mark."

As I started to relax, he gave a quick tug and pulled down the other side, totally exposing my entire backside. And before I could protest, he kissed that side and ...

"Ouch!"

He. Bit. Me.

He bit my ass, and I knew there was no way it wasn't going to leave a mark, his freaking dental records on my *ass*!

Lapping his tongue over the area several times, he chuckled. "Now I've left a mark."

It wasn't funny.

Then he kissed it.

"Why did you do that?" I said, a little breathless and completely stunned.

"Because..." his hands pressed to the front of my thighs as he kissed my backside everywhere "...I wanted to."

Beneath the shock, I felt turned on. It felt good. And that confused me. Sex was black and white for me. This was murky and confusing. It wasn't sex, but it was sexual. It was intimate. And I knew it would have to stop soon because Rory was coming home.

My hands relaxed and the front of my shorts and

panties immediately dropped a couple of inches from the tension at the back. Fisher stilled his motions when he realized what I did. I don't know why I did it or what I expected to happen next. I just ... I liked him touching me even when it felt a little wrong.

So I stood there, waiting for him to deliver more kisses, waiting for his hands to move from the front of my thighs to ... That was just it. I really didn't know what I expected or wanted from him. I guess I wanted him to teach me something.

Something new.

Something intimate.

Something a little forbidden.

With my heartbeat tripping over itself, looking for a normal rhythm, I started to turn toward him. He gripped my legs tighter and rested his forehead on my lower back.

"Don't." He sighed. "Just ..." He blew out another harsh breath, and I felt his forehead rolling side to side against my back. "Fuck ... we ... can't." He pulled up my panties and shorts. "Rory's coming home soon." He stood behind me and kissed the top of my head. "I'm going to get dressed. Go put on jeans. We should head to my parents' house now."

CHAPTER FIFTEEN

"My hair is going to be a mess." I tugged off my helmet after he pulled into his parents' gravel drive in Coal Creek Canyon. They lived in an A-frame house shrouded in pine trees with not a neighbor in sight.

He took my helmet and my jacket as I ran my fingers through my hair. After a few seconds, I glanced up at Fisher smiling at me with a hint of something in his eyes.

"What?"

He shook his head. "You're killing me."

"Why?" I continued to comb out my hair.

"Because I want to do very naughty things to you right now, but little kids are staring out the window at us, so I have to keep my hands to myself. And it's really fucking hard."

I paused my hands.

"Stop blushing," he said. "They can see you."

I talked through gritted teeth and a fake smile. "I

can't exactly control it when you say things like that to me. Why? Why did you say it?"

He glanced at the window and the peering eyes for a second before turning toward me. "Because for forty-five minutes, you've been wrapped around me, and I now know what your face looks like when you come, so it's all I thought about."

It thrilled me to know it wasn't just me. That he wasn't as cool and collected as I thought. Fisher was far from unaffected by me.

Where was the switch? In one week, we were going to have to turn off the switch to *us*.

"Thank you," I whispered, glancing down at my feet.

He laughed. "For what?"

"For being strong for me."

"What are you talking about?"

I glanced up, giving the window crowd the quickest of glances. Aching to take the two steps between us and wrap my arms around him. "I wouldn't have stopped you, had you asked me. And then in the kitchen ... I wanted ... more." I shrugged one shoulder while pressing my lips together to hide my guilty grin.

Recognition flitted across his face. His smile died, turning into something more somber. "Don't thank me. It wasn't easy. And I can't promise to always be that strong."

Clearing my throat, I changed the topic. "We should go inside before your family suspects there's something going on between us."

"We don't have to worry about that. There's no way they'd suspect that." He turned and headed toward the house.

"Wow. That's a bit harsh." I jogged to catch up to him.

"TGIF!" A woman, I assumed his mom, opened the door. I was never part of a family that got that excited over Friday. I may have been a little envious in that moment.

"Hey, Mom. This is Reese. Reese, this is my mom, Laurie."

"Hi, Reese. So glad you decided to join us. Come on in. There's food and drinks out back."

"Thank you so much." I followed Laurie and Fisher through an open great room. Three young kids hopped down from the sofa where they'd been spying on us. We passed the kitchen to a sunporch and door to a covered deck where everyone else congregated.

I wanted Fisher to take my hand or put his arm around me. I felt naked in front of these strangers without some physical connection, a grounding of sorts.

"Hey!" The greeting from everyone on the deck was just as exuberant as Laurie's.

"Hey." Fisher turned, waiting for me to stop hiding behind him. "Everyone, this is Reese, Rory's daughter. Rory is my tenant, for anyone who hasn't met her. Reese is also working for me this summer. Reese, this is the crew. Pat, Shayla, Teena, Arnie ... blah blah blah ... let them introduce themselves. And don't ask me to remember the names of the rug rats running around here."

"Oh stop." Laurie shook her head. "He knows everyone's name. Grab a drink, Hun, there's a cooler with pop and water and another cooler with beer and wine. We have burgers and brats on the grill."

"Thanks." I smiled at Laurie and looked around for Fisher. He was already down the stairs, playing a bean bag game with the kids.

Sink or swim for me.

"Beer? Wine?" The woman I believe he nodded to as Shayla, held open a cooler for me.

Did I look older, or did they not care?

"Actually, I'll just have some water for now."

"No problem." She opened the other cooler and handed me a bottle of water. "So ... I'm Shayla. Sorry Fisher is so clueless when it comes to manners. I'm his big sister. And Teena ... chasing the girl in just a diaper down there is his other big sister. Our dad, Pat, is manning the grill."

"I sure am," Pat said while lifting the lid.

"My husband Darren couldn't make it, but Ryan..." she ruffled a blond guy's hair as he sipped his beer "...is here, and he's Teena's husband."

"Don't forget your other brother," Laurie said as she collapsed into a padded chair that rocked and swiveled.

"Oh, yes ..." Shayla rolled her eyes. "Arnie is the baby of the family. He's the one with dark hair and ridiculous blond tips and ... a crazy number of tattoos on his arms and legs."

"I can hear you," Arnie called from the opposite side of the bean bag game as Fisher.

I giggled at his response. "The baby, huh? How old is he?"

"Twenty-two, but he doesn't act a day over five."

"Still hearing you," he yelled, tossing a bean bag with one hand while holding a beer in his other hand.

"So, are you in college?" Laurie asked.

"No. I'm not ruling it out someday, but for now I'm just working and getting reacquainted with my mom."

"Oh? Have you been separated from her? Divorce?"

I nodded. "Yes. Divorce. And my dad died three years ago. And ..." I drew in a deep breath. "My mom sorta just got out of prison."

"Oh ... wow. That's good. Or bad." Laurie cringed. "Good that's she's out. Bad that she went. Just ... ignore me." She pressed the heel of her hand to her forehead.

"It's fine. I've had to learn to just own it as part of my life. It's still awkward, but maybe now that she's out, I can eventually stop feeling the need to mention it."

"Champions!" One of the young boys yelled, high-fiving Fisher.

Arnie climbed the stairs, shaking his head. "Cheaters. They're all cheaters."

Arnie was basically a slightly smaller version of Fisher, but with tattoos, wilder hair, and a piercing through his nose. Fisher would have looked better in tattoos because he had more defined muscles, but Arnie had a boyish grin and his own level of sexy, bad-boy appeal.

"My brother's been holding out on me," Arnie said while easing into the chair next to me.

"Stop it." Shayla rolled her eyes. "I'm fairly certain Fisher didn't bring Reese here for you to hit on her."

"What?" He smirked. "I'm not hitting on you, Reese."

I laughed a little.

"Unless you want me to hit on you, then I'm totally hitting on you."

"Arnie ..." Laurie eyed him with a motherly warning.

"Kidding." He winked at me (just like Fisher) before taking a long pull of his beer.

"Are you in the construction business too?" I asked.

Arnie shook his head while rubbing his wet lips together. "No. I'm in a band."

"A band?" I couldn't hide my surprise. "Seriously?"

"Fisher never mentioned his brother is a famous rock star?" Arnie acted offended.

"You're not famous." Shayla had to give her verbal jab.

"Fisher and that hot doctor came to a concert last week. That's how proud he is of me."

Teagan. He took Teagan to see his brother perform. Yet he hadn't mentioned anything to me about it being his brother's band.

"Food's ready," Pat called.

Arnie stood. "Ladies first."

I couldn't hide my smile as he held out his hand to me. So I took it and stood.

"I perform again tomorrow night. You should come. I know the lead singer." He gave me the most confident grin. "Front row seating."

"Rory's not going to be okay with you hitting on her daughter."

I glanced back, not noticing that Fisher had gotten in the food line behind us.

"Rory loves me. She'll be thrilled to know that I'm inviting her daughter to one of my concerts. I'll text her just to make sure." Arnie pulled his phone out of his pocket.

"Put your phone away, dickhead." Fisher playfully grabbed the back of Arnie's neck and squeezed it.

Arnie wriggled out of his hold. "You and that doctor should come and bring Reese with you. We can grab food and drinks after. A double date with my big bro."

"Now that actually sounds like a good idea." Teena butted in on the conversation while wrangling her toddler on the way up the deck stairs.

I didn't look at anyone, just my feet because they couldn't tell how uncomfortable I was caught in the middle.

"Teagan and I aren't dating anymore."

"Dude, that was short-lived. She was effin' amazing. What did you do?"

"What makes you think *I* did anything?"

"Just a hunch." Arnie continued to prod Fisher.

"Angie's in town for the summer. You have to call her, Fisher." Shayla took a seat with her plate of food as I smiled at Pat when he handed me a plate and nodded to the choices of meat next to a dozen different salads and bags of chips.

"Angie's here?" Arnie and Laurie said at the same time.

"Fisher, call that woman, right now. You know I've imagined you two getting married ever since you were six years old." Laurie accidentally stomped all over my heart.

"Angie's in town. It's a sign, Bro." Arnie filled his plate behind me. "Bring Angie and Reese tomorrow night. Don't even try to make up some excuse. It's *Angie*. You're totally in, right Reese?"

Feeling zero hunger by then, I returned a tight smile to Arnie and nodded slowly. What else was I supposed to do?

"It's official ... almost." Arnie set his plate on the railing and plucked Fisher's phone from his pocket.

"What the f—" Fisher held his tongue with the kids around. Then, he stomped down the deck stairs after Arnie.

"Ha! I knew it. Same predictable code and ..." He ran from Fisher. "You still have her number!" A few seconds later, Arnie slowed and held out one hand, signaling Fisher to stop as he used his other hand to hold the phone to his ear.

I couldn't hear him, but I could see him talking while Fisher rested one hand on his hip and hung his head.

"It's on!" Arnie tossed Fisher's phone to him and strutted back toward the house.

If I read Fisher's lips correctly, he called Arnie a "stupid fucker."

"You'll love Angie," Shayla said as I sat next to her. "The love of Fisher's life since grade school. He's been too stupid to just marry her, so she's now living in California. She comes back here a lot because her mom is disabled and her dad passed away several years ago."

Just great ...

Eighteen-year-old me, with no real-life goals, had known Fisher for just over three weeks, and I was supposed to compete with "the love of his life?"

"Why did she move to California?" I asked despite my better judgment.

"Aside from Fisher not proposing?" Teena sat in the chair across from me after Ryan took the squirming toddler. "She's a biologist. Wicked smart."

I had to give Fisher credit; he knew how to attract smart, successful women—until me. Well, I was smart, but how much success could I have claimed at eighteen, even if I had enrolled in college courses?

"Take my seat, Fisher. I have to check on Isaac." Shayla vacated her spot.

Fisher sat next to me with his plate of food and a beer. I force-fed myself, chewing slowly, swallowing hard, and keeping my head down. That day, being eighteen sucked. I hadn't grown out of my foolish heart. It wasn't enough for me. Fisher's attraction to me wasn't enough. I wanted his heart to be mine and only mine. But maybe that wasn't how his brain or his heart functioned.

"Fisher, did you bid on that job in Aurora?" Pat asked as he removed his apron and sat down to eat.

Their conversation lasted for a long time. Enough time for me to eat as much as I could and not look like I was tossing half of my food in the trash. When I did take my plate into the kitchen, I also looked for a bathroom—an escape.

"Oh, hey ... I was looking for the restroom," I said to Shayla when she startled me as I turned the corner from the kitchen to the small hallway.

"Isaac is using the restroom. He could be awhile." She grimaced. "There's one downstairs."

"Okay. Thanks." I pivoted and headed downstairs. Nobody was in the basement filled with furniture, a big TV like the one in Fisher's basement, a ping-pong table, a wood burning stove, and many collages of photos on the wall. I inspected the photos, smiling at young Fisher and his family that I envied so much.

"I wondered where you went. I was afraid you forgot there are bears and rattlesnakes."

I glanced back at Fisher. "I was looking for the bathroom, but I got sidetracked with all of your family photos."

He nodded, looking at me, not the photos. "About tomorrow night—"

"It's fine, Fisher." That lie made my chest hurt, but it wasn't a pain I could show him. "Your family clearly adores Angie. And you must too. And Arnie seems really excited about the four of us going out." I shrugged. "I have no other plans, so … why not?"

"It's not a date."

Turning back toward the photos, I dug deep for a little more confidence. "It's fine if it is. Rory comes home next week. You said it yourself. Your parents would never believe you were … interested in me. And now I know why."

"You don't."

"No? Well, it doesn't matter."

"No. It doesn't." He took ahold of my wrist and pulled me into a dark bedroom, closing the door behind us and flipping on the light.

I waited for Fisher to say whatever it was he needed to say. He didn't say anything for many seconds, maybe a minute or more. It was just silence and the anguish on his face. Finally, he scrubbed his hands over his face and blew out a long breath.

"We don't have to wait any longer," I filled the silence with whatever I thought might make him a little less stressed because he seemed *so* stressed out. "It can be over now. Maybe it's stupid to act like one more week matters. Maybe I shouldn't have been in your bathtub that night. Maybe hiding from everyone is more trouble than it's worth. And now this Angie person is back, and that would suck for you to miss out on an opportunity because we decided to do...” I shrugged “...*whatever* for one more week.”

He narrowed his eyes. “You want it to end? Now?”

“Yes.”

Gah! Stupid, untimely tears rushed to my eyes.

“Liar.”

Clenching my jaw to lock down all emotions on the verge of breaking the dam, I shook my head.

He cocked his head to the side and pressed his hand to my face, brushing his thumb across my cheek to the corner of my eye, giving it just enough pressure to release one tear and then another. “Let’s go,” he whispered.

“Where?” I sucked in a shaky breath as my strength wavered.

“Home. Rory comes home soon. And I don’t want to share you with anyone else tonight.”

“F-Fisher ...” I sniffled. “You can’t have my heart.”

He smiled and nodded several times while bending down to kiss the corner of my mouth. “I know ... I’ll add it to the list.”

Kiss.

“What list?”

He opened the door and shut off the light. “The parts of Reese Capshaw that I can’t have.”

I opened my mouth to respond, but I had nothing. Not one thing.

“We’re taking off,” Fisher announced as we stepped onto the deck.

"Already? I made pie and there's ice cream." Laurie looked a little surprised.

"Reese has a tummy ache. Maybe one of the salads sat in the sun too long."

What the heck!

I had to have looked just as surprised ... and mortified.

"Oh dear! I'm so sorry." Laurie pressed her hand to her chest.

A string of "that's too bads" and "feel betters" followed from everyone else.

"Take an antacid..." Arnie made a drinking motion with his hand "...and you'll be good for tomorrow night."

Fisher ignored him, and I ... well, I ignored everyone because I still hadn't fully processed what just happened.

"Well, thanks. Goodnight," Fisher said, resting his hand on my back in the platonic region to guide me to the front door.

As soon as he closed the door behind us, I spun around. "Are you kidding me? Did you really just tell your whole family that I have a *tummy ache*? What am I? Five?"

He shrugged, shouldering past me to the driveway. "Kids were around. I couldn't say you had the shits."

"Fisher! Why did you do that?"

"Because we needed an excuse to leave." He handed me my helmet.

"Why didn't you tell them *you* have a tummy ache? Why embarrass me like that?"

He fastened his helmet and grinned. "I haven't had so much as a sniffle for years. I'm kind of a freak of nature like that. They never would have believed it had I said it was me."

"Well ... well ... maybe I haven't been sick in years. Did you even think about that? Maybe I'm a freak of nature."

"Oh." He chuckled while throwing his leg over the seat. "I have no doubt that you're a special kind of freak of nature. Get on."

I was the one grumbling by that point as I climbed onto the back of his bike.

By the time we got home, I was still fuming.

"I'm going to bed ... I have a *tummy ache*." I tossed my helmet on the ground along with the riding jacket and marched my way to the basement door. After kicking my shoes off, I ran up the stairs and locked the door at the top. We were done.

CHAPTER SIXTEEN

Fisher: I'm sorry.

Fisher: Are you going to stay mad at me forever?

Fisher: I'll call my family and tell them it was a lie. That I just wanted to be alone with you.

I ROLLED my eyes at the last text. He wasn't going to tell his Angie-loving family that he wanted to be alone with me.

My phone rang. I didn't want to answer it, knowing it was him. But when I spared a quick glance at the screen, I realized it wasn't him. It was Christina, my only friend from public school who kept in touch with me.

"Heyyy!"

"Hey, Reese! What's up with you? It's been forever."

"I know. It has. Where are you? Last I heard you'd moved to South Carolina."

"We did, but my sister's getting married in a week, so I'm staying with her to help her survive the chaos."

"Amelia's getting married? Wow!"

"Yes. And she's getting married in Colorado Springs. And I heard you're in Denver. I'm in Denver for the weekend. We *have* to get together."

"Yeah, I'd love that. I have no plans ... well ..." I thought about Arnie's concert.

"If you're going to say you have plans with a guy, that's cool. My boyfriend's with me. We should all go out."

"It's ... um ... actually, I was invited to a concert tomorrow night. Local band. I know the lead singer. His brother is my landlord and my boss."

"Oh ... that sounds perfect. Where? When?"

"I'm not sure yet. Can I text you the info in the morning?"

"Absolutely. Gah! I can't wait to see you!"

"Me too. I'm so glad you called. We'll talk in the morning."

"Sounds great. Bye."

I pressed *End* and groaned because I didn't have Arnie's number. I didn't know the time or location of the concert. After a quick internet search for "Arnie Mann band in Denver," I found everything I needed and quickly texted Christina before going to bed early and praying the naked fisherman stayed out of my dreams.

The next morning, I dressed and headed out for a walk. Fisher's truck was gone. It didn't surprise me.

Hailey told me it wasn't unusual for him to work on Saturdays.

After my walk and breakfast, I grabbed my crossword puzzle sketch pad and sat on the screened-in porch. After an hour or so, the roar of an approaching lawnmower grew louder. I looked up to shirtless Fisher mowing the lawn. He didn't see me at first. And I liked that. Even if I wasn't sure I liked him anymore, I liked things about him.

His body.

The concentrated look on his scruffy face when he was focused on a task, especially if it involved tools.

In the middle of me contemplating the things I did like about him, Fisher glanced up and our gazes met. He paused for a moment then continued mowing.

Weed eating.

And he finished the afternoon by pulling weeds on his hands and knees in the landscaping. I slipped inside and filled a tall glass with ice water and took it out to him.

"You should hydrate. You're pretty sweaty." I stood beside him and held out the glass.

Fisher lifted onto his knees and sat back on his heels, sweat and dirt covering his naked chest and back. "Thank you." He pulled off his work gloves and took the glass from me. In one breath, he guzzled the whole thing and sighed while handing it back to me.

"I ... uh ... I forgive you. I just wasn't ready to say it last night when you messaged me."

He wiped his arm over his forehead. "I figured."

"My friend called me last night. She's in Denver for the weekend with her boyfriend. Her sister's getting married in Colorado Springs next weekend. Anyway ... she wanted to get together, so I suggested Arnie's concert. Do you think he can get us two extra seats?"

"I didn't figure you'd want to go."

"I didn't. But I want to see my friend, and she's really excited about it, so ..."

Squinting against the sun, he nodded. "I'm sure Arnie can make it happen."

"Are you taking ... a date?"

Fisher glanced away and shook his head while offering a little chuckle. "You mean, am I taking Angie?"

I nodded, tapping my fingernails on the glass and doing my weird rolling back and forth on my heels thing.

"Arnie invited her. It's virtually impossible for me to *not* take her at this point."

I lifted my shoulders. "It's fine. I was just asking. Should I uh ... drive? Or are we all going together?"

"She messaged me last night. She'll pick us up at six. I said I needed to verify that you were going, but now that you are ... I'll let her know."

"You're not driving?"

He shook his head. "I have a work truck and a motorcycle. You've seen all the shit in my truck, and I don't think all of us can fit on my motorcycle."

"Yeah. Of course. Well ..." I took a few steps backward. "I'll be ready at six."

As soon as I stepped into the house, I rifled through my clothes and found nothing ... nothing to wear on a date. Or double date ... triple date? I didn't know. But I knew Christina would be dressed in something trendy and on point. I hadn't met Angie, but I had to anticipate someone from California bringing her own brand of style.

"You suck," I berated myself ... my wardrobe. In the next beat, I was out the door with my purse and car keys.

Buzzing past Fisher, I hopped into the Outback and sped down the street in mad search of something to wear. Just under two hours later, I returned with a new outfit, shoes, and a smaller handbag.

With under an hour to get ready, I shaved everything ... and I hadn't shaved everything ever. Then I slathered lotion on all my shaved areas, dried my hair, curled it, and applied makeup the way my mom used to apply makeup.

Smoky eyes.

A bit of pink high on my cheekbones.

And red lips.

I made a final inspection in the mirror as I stuffed the essentials into my new clutch. My dad had to be turning over in his grave. And God? I could only imagine.

White shorts that barely ... just barely covered my backside making my legs look even longer. A floral, sleeveless spaghetti strap top. And nineties inspired platform shoes with straps around my ankles.

After a quick glance at my watch, I made my way up front. There was no car in the driveway aside from Fisher's truck, so I stood under his covered porch and waited, clutching my purse in both hands.

"She's running a few minutes late. You can wait inside."

I turned toward Fisher's voice.

Well, dang ...

He was freshly showered with dark jeans that looked fairly new, gray leather sneakers with thick white soles, and a faded gray tee that molded to his chest and shoulders. His biceps looked twice as big, and the veins in his arms did weird things to me. Veins weren't supposed to be sexy.

"O-okay ..." I gulped.

He eyed my legs for a long moment before meeting my gaze as I walked toward the door. "I have a feeling someone will get beat up or arrested tonight."

"Why would you say that?" I stopped just inside his front door.

"Because you're eighteen going on thirty."

"Don't talk like a parent, Fisher."

He shut the door and leaned against it, crossing his sexy arms over his even sexier chest. "Fine. Every guy that sees you is going to get a hard-on. And I promised Rory I'd keep an eye on you."

"I'm sure Angie doesn't want you keeping an eye on me."

He narrowed his eyes at my chest, ignoring my Angie comment. "For fuck's sake ... are you wearing a bra?"

I glanced down. "No. I can't wear one with this top."

"Then go change tops and put on a bra."

"Again ... too much parental talk. I don't need you to dress me."

"And I don't need my horny brother seeing your nipples."

Glancing down again, I shook my head. "It's a dark shirt. You can't see them."

"I can see their outline ... I can see they are erect."

I slowly ran the pads of my fingers over them to push my nipples in so he couldn't see them anymore.

"Just ... fucking stop ..." He pinched the bridge of his nose.

"I pushed them in."

"Jesus ... you're a walking wet dream. Just stop touching yourself." He adjusted himself in his jeans.

And just like that, my nipples popped out again. It took him all of two seconds to notice.

"I'm going to kill Rory for leaving you with me." He took a step forward and grabbed the back of my hair, clenching it in his hand and forcing my head to the side as he sucked and licked my neck.

"F-Fisher ..." I clawed his biceps to steady myself. He wasn't kissing my red lips and smearing my lipstick. I gave him a little credit for that, but he still seemed to be teetering on the verge of control as his other hand slid up the front of my shirt.

I gasped when his rough hand palmed my bare breast. He groaned, his thumb circling my nipple.

"Oh my God—gosh ..." I stumbled over using the Lord's name in vain.

His hand moved to my other breast, giving it the same torturous treatment.

"We ... should ..." I couldn't catch my breath to complete a sentence. I thought we should stop, but my words never got that far.

He whipped me around so my back hit the door, releasing my hair before lifting me up, guiding my legs around his waist with one hand while shoving my shirt up to my neck with his other hand.

"Ah! Oh ... oh ... god!" I lost all ability to censor my words when he covered my breast with his mouth, sucking and biting it relentlessly.

Then ... the doorbell rang.

I froze. Fisher rested his forehead between my bared breasts, breathing a little harder than usual. His hands dropped to my legs, but he didn't unpin me from the door.

"Fuck ..."

The doorbell rang again.

He eased me to my feet, my shirt dropping back into place. I gazed up at him in shock. *What just happened?*

"Just a sec," he said loud enough for Angie (I

assumed) to hear him and stop ringing the doorbell. He seemed ... frustrated?

"I-I'm ... going to go put on a bra and a different shirt," I said softly. I needed to change into dry panties as well, but I didn't think he needed to know that.

Fisher said nothing, but he bit his lips together and nodded slowly. He also didn't give me much space, so I had to awkwardly squeeze past him, retrieve my clutch from the floor, and run to the basement door.

After I put on a bra and a boring tank top, I ran back up the stairs then paused. I wondered if it would seem weird ... me exiting on the main floor? So I made a big production to go around the side of the house.

A woman with curly jet-black hair to her shoulders and a well-defined body turned toward me and smiled. She wasn't as tall as me, but she had *more* in all the other departments. If I won the battle a few minutes earlier, I was sure to lose the war with Angie back in town.

"Angie, this is Reese Capshaw. Reese, this is Angie Flynn."

"So nice to meet you. Cute top." She nodded to my Life is Good top with a huge sunflower on the front of it.

Cute. I was cute.

She was killing it in a red dress and heels.

Trying to not completely deflate, I rummaged through my emotions for a friendly expression and nailed it to my face. "Thanks. Nice to meet you too.

Fisher's family had so many amazing things to say about you."

Fisher eyed me from a few feet behind her, eyes a little squinted as if he wasn't happy with me for saying that.

Angie twisted her body to look at him. "Aw ... your family is the best. They really feel like my family after all these years."

Fisher lifted his eyebrows, lips curled into a reluctant smile as he gave her a nod.

"Well, let's go. You can drive, babe." She tossed Fisher her keys. "I don't know where we're going."

Babe ...

I slithered into the back seat behind Fisher's seat as Angie climbed into the passenger's seat of the white, compact SUV.

"Are you in college, Reese?" Angie asked before we pulled out of the driveway.

Yay ... this line of questioning.

"Nope. Just working for Fisher this summer." I didn't have the energy to make myself sound any more promising like, "I'm taking a gap year," which insinuated I'd be starting college, only a year later.

Angie won. Rory would be home in less than a week. There was no need to try.

"Fisher is the most talented human I have ever met. He's always been good at everything. Such a natural. But what's it like to work for him?" She reached over and squeezed his leg, his upper thigh.

I glanced up in the rearview mirror and caught his gaze on me. Totally unreadable.

"Fisher's an okay boss." I glanced out my window.

Angie laughed, moving her hand from his leg to the nape of his neck. "I can see that about you. I bet it's your intensity. Such a perfectionist, huh, Fish?"

He didn't respond. I felt sure he had some expression to give her, but I didn't want to see it.

Babe ... Fish ...

Lucky for me, Angie shifted the conversation to her mom and that gobbled up the rest of the drive to the venue—where I couldn't get out of the SUV quick enough. Lucky for me, Christina and her boyfriend were waiting at the door. I ran to her, anything to get away from the fated love birds.

"Eek! Reese!" She gave me a huge hug.

"It's so good to see you. I've missed you so freaking much." I released her and glanced at the handsome guy with the richest dark brown skin and black hair I had ever seen.

"Reese, this is Jamison. Jamison this is my BFF since ... gah ... forever. She left me for church school, and I've never forgiven her." Christina winked.

I wondered if she had told Jamison about the fate of my parents and *why* I was forced to leave her for "church school."

Sensing someone right at my back, I turned. "Oh ..." I gave Fisher a tiny smile, but there was no way I was looking at Angie. "Hey, this is my friend Christina and her boyfriend Jamison. Guys, this is my boss, Fisher and ..." *What? His girlfriend?* "Angie."

"Nice to meet you," they all seemed to chime at once.

"So ... where's your rock star boyfriend?" Christina nudged me.

"Fish, you didn't tell me Arnie and Reese were a thing," Angie wrapped her arm around Fisher's arm and gave him a pouty face.

I wanted to vomit.

"He just met her yesterday and invited her and us to his show. I'm not sure that qualifies as 'together.'" He brushed past us to the box office and claimed our tickets.

"But you can and should tell everyone he's your boyfriend." My BFF winked at me while taking Jamison's hand and following Fisher and Angie into the venue.

It wasn't a big venue, more of a dive bar with a stage. I was surprised tickets were required at all. But there was a table right by the stage reserved for us.

Christina didn't even take a seat; she sat on Jamison's lap while Angie pulled her chair so close to Fisher's chair she might as well have perched onto his lap. I sat off to the side, by myself.

"Can I get everyone drinks?" the waitress asked.

Angie ordered a martini. Fisher got a beer. Jamison ordered beer too and had to show an ID. Then Christina ordered a glass of wine and sure enough ... she had an ID too.

"And for you?" the waitress looked at me.

"Water. Thanks."

"I can go to the bar in a sec and get you something," Christina whispered in my ear. "I can't believe you don't have a fake ID."

"I'm good." I gave her a tight smile. "Really."

Fisher eyed me every two seconds, and I knew this because my gaze kept drifting to him as well.

Shortly after our drinks were served, the band came onto the stage while the bar erupted into loud clapping, hooting, and even a few screamers behind us.

"Whoa ... you are *so* getting some of that tonight," Christina said loud enough for Fisher and everyone else to hear. "He's hot, Reese."

Jamison poked her in the side and gave her an eye roll. Angie laughed. I shifted my gaze to Arnie, and Christina was right ... he was hot under the lights. Tattoos. That wild, blond tipped hair. And a guitar hugging his body.

My phone vibrated, and I pulled it from my handbag.

Fisher: You are NOT getting any of that tonight.

When I glanced up, his head was still bowed to his phone.

Reese: Sure thing, BABE! (eye roll emoji)

He lifted his face from his phone and frowned at

me. I turned my attention to the stage.

After the final song, Arnie took off his shirt and tossed it to *me*. I grinned as the women in the venue went crazy, including Christina, despite her boyfriend right next to her. Arnie nodded for us to make our way backstage.

Christina and Jamison headed through the gated off area along with Angie while Fisher stayed back as if he was simply letting everyone else go first.

Except me.

He slid his finger though the belt loop at the back of my shorts to stop me. Then he leaned down and whispered in my ear, "Tell Arnie to do his own fucking laundry."

I barked a laugh and shook my head, glancing back at him. He grinned and gave me a quick wink, making me want to turn around and throw my arms around him. I wanted to pretend it was just us at the concert, and we were going out with Arnie and some other woman Arnie had invited along with my friends.

That wasn't the reality.

He let go of my belt loop, and we squeezed through the opening between two security guards, where Arnie and the rest of our group waited for us.

"You were amazing. I can't believe Fisher hasn't been bragging about you." From the corner of my eye, I could see Fisher frown as I gushed to Arnie.

I could also see Angie's arm slide around Fisher's waist the way Teagan had once laid claim to him. Would it ever be me doing that? I wondered.

"Thanks, gorgeous." Arnie took my hand and pulled me toward an exit. "Let's grab some food. I'm starving." He seemed high. It had to be a real adrenaline rush playing to a roomful of screaming fans.

"Don't you need your shirt?"

"Nah. That's for you. I have another one in my vehicle."

Making a quick glance backward, I made sure everyone else was following us. Yep. The two couples arm-in-arm. Three happy faces and a grumpy naked fisherman.

I rode with Arnie in his Escalade with the others behind us. He didn't make me the least bit uncomfortable, which surprised me. We talked about his band and where he'd played, along with his future gigs across the U.S. opening for some bigger bands.

We ended up at a fancy European restaurant, and I felt so underdressed. I would not have, had I left on my nipples top. Even Arnie slipped on a nicer button-down over his white tee.

"Have you been here?" he asked, again taking my hand and leading me toward the entrance as everyone else pulled into parking spaces.

"I have not."

"You'll love it. The food is phenomenal. And the atmosphere is even better. Big crystal chandeliers. Checkered floors. It's a little dark." He gave my hand a squeeze. "And a little sexy."

"Sounds ... cool," I squeaked the words because my level of comfort started to decline. Even if I wasn't *with* the guy I wanted to be with, I was glad that Arnie and I weren't alone.

"I don't know if we can afford this," Christina joked as we gathered just inside the door. But I didn't think it was entirely a lie.

"I know the owner. And it's on me. No worries." Arnie puffed out his chest and grinned.

I didn't have to look at Fisher to know his eyes were rolling around in his head at his brother's need to flaunt.

As soon as we were seated, Christina stood. "Ladies' room?" She eyed me.

I nodded.

Out of courtesy, we gave Angie a quick questioning glance, but she didn't even look our way. She was too busy drooling over *my guy*!

As soon as we slipped into the posh ladies' room, Christina grabbed my shoulders. "Oh my god. Arnie is so into you. Seriously, what if he makes it really big? You could tour with him. Live the life of a rock star's girlfriend."

"I don't see us being that serious." I laughed it off.

"Well, everyone sees the way he's looking at you, so there's no doubt about what he wants to do with you." She turned and fixed her hair in the frame-lit mirror.

I didn't say anything, but I must have had a slight grimace on my face because she glanced up at my reflection and narrowed her eyes. "I know you went to that church school, but ... you've had sex, right?"

"Well ..." I rubbed my lips together, thinking of the right answer.

"Oh my god. *Well* is not a yes. It's a no." She whipped around. "Reese! You're a virgin?"

If I didn't have a true grimace before, I definitely did after she yelled that. I surveyed the room, praying we were the only ones in there, and it appeared that we were.

"I'm waiting until I'm married. It's no big deal."

"No. If it were no big deal, you'd be all over that rock star out there. I have a boyfriend, but Arnie makes me want to not have one ... for just one night."

"When..." I bit the end of my thumbnail "...when did you have sex for the first time?"

"A week before my seventeenth birthday. Tate Hoover. Remember him?"

"You had sex with Tate Hoover? The kid who rarely talked and played trombone?"

"Yes." She shrugged. "He was nice. And had strong lips from all the trombone playing. Also, his rhythm was perfection."

I covered my mouth and snorted. "Oh my gosh."

Christina smirked. "So ... you haven't had sex. What have you done? I know you've kissed a guy. Maybe two, yeah?"

I nodded slowly. "And uh ... recently I had a date, a couple of dates with someone. *Not* Arnie. And we did some stuff."

She lifted a perfectly drawn eyebrow. "Elaborate on *stuff*."

My cheeks felt warm just thinking about it. "We kissed ... a lot. And I ... well ..."

"Oh my god, just spill. Did he go down on you?"

I shook my head.

"Did you give him head?"

Another head shake.

"Did he finger you?"

My lips twisted.

She grinned. "So he's had his hand in your panties?"

I nodded. I liked the yes and no questions best.

"Have you seen his cock?"

Biting my lower lip, I shook my head.

"Touched it?"

Head shake.

"Hand up your shirt?"

Nod.

"Mouth on your breasts?"

Nod.

"Has he made you orgasm?"

Nod.

"Oh ... then you're close. You're basically going through all the motions. Just do it. I don't really think you get extra points from God for being a virgin."

I rolled my eyes. "I disagree."

"You've been brainwashed for three years. Of course you disagree."

"I haven't been brainwashed."

She shot me a look, a look like she didn't believe me or couldn't believe *I* really believed it either.

"How's your mom? I heard that's why you're in Denver."

"I don't know. I've spent less than three days with her. She's out in California doing some training. She comes back at the end of the week."

"So you've been living alone?"

"Well, sort of. She rents the basement of Fisher's house. So I'm in the basement alone, but he lives on the main floor."

"Living with your sexy boss, huh? Rough life. Too bad he has a girlfriend. And he's a little old for you."

I took the chance to mess with my hair in the mirror. "You think ten years older is too old? I mean ... I'm just asking because I know people who are married who have ten or more years between them."

"Yeah. I suppose. I couldn't imagine dating someone ten years older than me right now. Jamison is four years older, and sometimes I feel like we have to find things in common because he's just at a different place in his life. Ten years would be even crazier. Speaking of Jamison, we'd better get back out there. You didn't actually have to pee, right?"

"I'm good."

"Everything fine?" Jamison asked Christina as we sat back down at the table.

"Totally. Sorry we took so long. I had to cool Reese down. Her date tonight has her overheating."

Oh no. No. No. NO! Why did she say that?

Arnie lit up, more than a little pleased to hear that. Angie nudged Fisher and grinned like she needed to urge him to be excited to hear that. But Fisher's stony expression didn't give that same happy vibe.

And what was I supposed to say? No. I wasn't attracted to Arnie? That would have been a slap in the face to the guy who got us front row seats and was paying for dinner at an expensive restaurant.

So ... with a shy grin, I sat down and didn't confirm nor deny it.

The alcohol flowed nonstop over the next two hours. The food was ridiculously good. And the company wasn't bad. Aside from my glass of ice water, I felt like a real adult on a date with the wrong guy.

With every sip of wine, Angie got more handsy with Fisher, and that made me remain idle when Arnie rested his arm on the back of my chair, squeezed my leg playfully, and whispered things in my ear. Some things I couldn't understand because he'd had too much to drink, but other short phrases included things like "you look so hot tonight" or "I can't stop staring at you."

Those little things seemed to feed Fisher's need to drink more too. By the time Arnie lazily signed for the meal, Jamison and I were the only sober ones at the table. I was glad he was being responsible for my friend.

"I'll order a ride," Fisher mumbled as he pulled his phone out of his pocket.

"Good idea, babe." Angie hugged his arm and rested her head on his shoulder.

"I can drive." I shrugged.

"Yesss ..." Arnie stood and held out his hand. "You

can drive them home." He nodded to Fisher and Angie. "Then you can drive me. And I'll get you home in the morning." He smiled like it was a genius idea.

"Fuck no ..." Fisher spoke up, and I froze. Where was he going with his objection? Would he vomit the truth in his inebriated condition? "I told Rory I'd watch her. I can't watch her at your house."

"Babe." Angie pinched his cheeks. "I don't think you can watch anyone ..." She giggled. "Except me."

I grabbed Arnie's key fob from his hand. "Let's go. We'll figure it out."

Just outside of the restaurant, Christina hugged me. "Bye, my bestest friend ever. I hope you get some yum yum tonight." She giggled.

"Bye." I shook my head as Jamison rolled his eyes at her drunkenness.

I was able to just click "Home" on Arnie's navigation since no one was with it enough to give me his address. It took fifteen minutes to get there. I hopped out to make sure he made it to his door okay.

"Stay." He put his hands into prayer position. "Please."

"I have to take them home. But I had fun. Thank you so much."

"Fine." He sighed. "Goodnight, hot girl."

Just as I started to laugh, he grabbed my face and kissed me. It was hard, but rather still. Not a lot of movement.

"Goddamn ... you taste good." He opened his door and stumbled inside.

As soon as the door shut, I wiped my mouth and descended the walk to his Escalade. When I climbed into the driver's seat, I could feel Fisher's gaze on me from the back seat with Angie draped across his lap sleeping.

"What's Angie's address?"

"Just go home," Fisher said.

"It's no problem. I can take—"

"She's staying with me tonight, and we'll get her vehicle tomorrow. Just go."

I think I would have preferred an actual kick to my gut than to hear his anger. Maybe it was the alcohol. Maybe it wasn't. Either way, I couldn't talk past the lump in my throat all the way home.

"Let's go. Can you walk?" Fisher asked Angie.

"Carry me, babe," she said in a sleepy voice.

As I shut the driver's door, he lifted her from the back seat and kicked the door shut, wobbling a bit as if being reminded that he, too, had plenty to drink.

"Ninety-three-eleven is my garage code," Fisher said.

I typed it in and led the way to open the door to the house, wondering who this woman really was in his life. How did she come and go like they were still together?

Touching him.

Calling him "babe."

Batting her eyelashes.

I didn't get it.

"Can you find your feet?" he asked her as he eased

her from his arms.

Angie wobbled a bit on her heels before stepping out of them and wobbling a bit more as she made her way down the short hallway to his bedroom. "Don't make me wait," she said, unzipping her dress and letting it fall to the floor a few feet from his door.

I lost sight of her as she reached to unhook her bra.

Fisher rubbed his temples, closing his eyes. "Thanks for driving."

A naked woman awaited him in his bedroom just hours after he sucked my breasts while pinning me to his front door, and "Thanks for driving" was his response?

"I'm going to church in the morning, so someone else will have to get Arnie's vehicle back to him." My emotions teetered on the edge of a complete break-down. I knew Fisher would deal with Arnie and his vehicle, but I felt the need to act as unaffected as possible by what he was likely getting ready to do with his childhood sweetheart. And talking about the Escalade was better than screaming at him because that's what I really wanted to do.

"Of course." He moseyed to the kitchen sink to get a glass of water, taking it down just as quickly as he did earlier that day when I brought him water while he was mowing the lawn.

I opened my mouth to say goodnight, but I couldn't do it. I didn't want him to have a *good night.* So I opened the basement door and just as quickly closed it behind me before the tears released.

Just as I reached the bottom of the stairs, the door opened. My fingers made swift moves to wipe my cheeks.

One step.

Two steps.

"What do you need?" I asked.

Three steps.

Four steps.

"There's a naked woman in your bedroom. Better not keep her waiting." I turned on the light in the family room and slipped off my sandals, keeping my back to him as I used the back of the sectional to steady myself while balancing on one foot and then the other.

"If it's not you, then I don't give a fuck who's naked in my bed." He slid his hand around my waist and pulled my back to his chest.

Gripping his arm with my hands, I drew in a slow breath.

Angie was upstairs.

"You're drunk," I whispered.

He chuckled, burying his nose in my hair. "I'm over the legal limit; I'm not drunk. There's a difference."

"Well, *babe* ..." I peeled his arms away from me and put a few feet between us. "Why are you not married to that woman upstairs? Your family adores her. I mean *adores* her. And she obviously thinks the two of you are in some never-ending relationship. Why is that? Are you? Is she your endgame, but for now you're screwing around with other women until you're ready to commit? Because you guys are not broken up. She doesn't just show up out of nowhere and fall back into *your bed*."

Twisting his lips, he cocked his head a fraction. I made him think. Really think.

"You have the best tits. Not too small, but not too big. And I could suck on your nipples all day. They are nothing short of perfect."

Never mind. I didn't make him think at all. I ignored my blush. He brought it out of me with a look, and when he talked dirty to me, it took over my whole body.

"You're drunk." I crossed my arms over my chest.

"No." He grinned holding up two fingers then three. Then back to two. "Scouts honor. In the morning, I will still find your tits to be the best thing I've seen or tasted in a very long time. If they were on Yelp, I'd leave a five-star review of them."

"Stop." I bit my lips to keep from grinning.

"I will not stop. I haven't even started talking about your legs." He took two steps toward me, and I retreated to keep the distance.

"Angie is beautiful. I'm not blind. I'm sure her ... *breasts* are Yelp worthy, and her legs are incredibly toned, along with her arms. Her silky hair and skin. And she's successful. Age appropriate. And she's naked in your bed. So you might have to explain to me why you're down here with me."

Fisher deflated, a long breath releasing from his nose as his shoulders dropped an inch. "She wants a husband and a houseful of babies. A dog. Two cats. And a minivan."

"And you don't?"

"Not yet."

"So ..." I glanced up at the ceiling and laughed, but it didn't really feel funny. "You *are* looking for someone to mess around with until you decide you're ready for wife material. That's awesome, Fisher. Rory comes home in a few days. What's the point? I'm not having sex with you. And why are you so anti-family? You're twenty-eight. Do you know how many men have a family by the time they're your age?"

"No." He prowled toward me again, this time without stopping. "And neither do you. So what's *your* point? You're eighteen. The whole point of your life should be to live in the fucking moment without caring if everything you do makes complete sense."

"Stop." I shook my head, running out of space to escape him as my butt rammed into the pool table.

"I don't want to stop. Do you? Do you really want to stop?"

"I don't know," I whispered. I didn't love the taste of beer, but I thought I'd like it if I tasted it in his mouth. So I kissed him, and he kissed me back. I was right ... beer tasted best on Fisher's tongue. Every well-sorted moral thought in my head jumbled, like the wind catching a neatly stacked pile of papers and scattering them everywhere.

No page numbers.

No sense of meaning.

Just a big, unimaginable mess.

That was what Fisher Mann did to me. He messed with my thoughts.

And that was why I didn't protest when he removed my shirt ... and my bra.

I didn't protest when he unbuttoned my shorts and dropped to his knees in front of me to slide them down my legs, along with my panties. My eyes glossed over with an unfamiliar feeling, like everything he did entered my bloodstream—a drug that robbed any sense of control or objection my brain might have otherwise formulated.

Lifting one leg and then the other, he freed them from my shorts.

"Fisher ..." Everything inside of me felt heavy and slow. My dry mouth panted slowly.

Was he going to put his mouth between my legs?

Was I going to stop him if he did?

All these things I didn't know for sure. Part of me wanted him to stop because I wasn't sure I had the will power to do it myself. But a bigger part of me indulged the curiosity that seemed to have the greatest power over my decisions in that moment.

What were his plans for us? Sex? Oral sex?

He kissed my hipbone and moved a little lower ... and a little lower yet. My heart thundered so loudly in my chest, sending blood whooshing past my ears with such force, I could barely hear him when he did speak.

"Do you want me to kiss you here?" He brushed his lips lightly over *that* part of me.

"I ... I ... don't know." Harsh breaths rushed past my lips as I rested my hands on the side of the pool table to steady myself.

"No?" He left a tiny kiss *there*, before navigating up my body, resting his hands on the pool table next to mine while he flicked his tongue over my nipple before standing straight and shrugging off his shirt. "We'll go until you tell me to stop?"

My lazy gaze worked its way up his body to meet his gaze, and after a few seconds, I nodded. I didn't really know my limit that night. Sex didn't feel right, but stopping felt a little wrong and even a little impossible. All I could do was let him continue and hope that I'd find my limit, that stopping point.

Fisher grabbed my face and kissed me, our tongues mingling as my nipples brushed his chest. And I needed more. My fingers teased his abs just above the waist of his jeans, and he moaned into the kiss. Then my brave and completely inexperienced fingers moved lower, tracing the outline of his erection, and his hips thrust forward into my touch as he moaned a little louder ... kissed me a little harder ... and lifted me onto the edge of the pool table.

It was wrong. I thought. I maybe even knew. But I didn't want to take responsibility ... not yet. The feeling ... the drug he became ... was too strong.

After rocking his hips into me a couple of times, he moved his mouth to my neck, sucking and biting as he unbuttoned his jeans. Things started to feel ... real. Very, very real.

My heart managed to beat even faster. Anticipation soared in my head, making me dizzier.

Stop.

Don't stop.

Gah!

I was so conflicted—those scattered pieces of paper all over the floor without anyone to pick them up and sort them to make sense again.

Fisher's hand tangled in my hair as his mouth returned to mine and his erection, covered only by his underwear, wedged between my legs.

The friction.

The wet feeling.

The heat.

I wasn't ready for sex, or maybe I was. I just didn't know. And as much as I knew, I really knew we needed to stop, I wasn't ready to tell him to stop. It wasn't sex, right? We weren't having actual sex. As much as I wanted more to happen, without actually having sex, I didn't know how to articulate it because I wasn't exactly sure what *more* meant. I only knew I wanted to at least feel him against me, really against me.

My hand rested on his hip, my fingers teasing his underwear's waistband. Sliding one finger beneath it, I slowly inched my way to the front. Just before touching him *there,* putting just enough pressure on the waistband to expose the head of his ... *cock? Penis? No ... Dick?*

Fisher stopped kissing me, and with quick breaths escaping past his parted lips, he glanced down at my finger still curled around the waistband. It was my first glimpse at a man's ... head. That head.

"I need to get a condom," he whispered.

I shook my head slowly. We weren't having sex. I felt fairly certain of that. I just wanted ... well ... I wasn't sure. I wanted to see him and feel him, but not actually have sex. "I want ..." I swallowed hard. "I just want to feel you."

"God ... feel me, Reese." He grabbed my hand and slipped it down the front of his underwear, closing his eyes as his tongue swiped along his lower lip. He released my hand.

It took me a few seconds to move my hand, to gently wrap it around him. He was warm and hard, yet smooth and long. I slid my hand up slowly.

"Fuuuck ..." He dropped his chin and opened his eyes again, watching me touch him, his abs tightening even more than seconds earlier.

My gaze flitted between my hand and his gaze, like I wasn't fully aware that I was the one giving him that pleasure. Me. Not Teagan. Not the woman upstairs in his bed.

Me.

I felt like a queen. A goddess.

The head was even smoother ... and wet ... and a little sticky.

"Reese ..." He closed his eyes, squeezing them shut as if in some sort of agony. "Let me get a condom."

"No. I ... I just want to feel you."

"Fuck ..." His mouth landed on my neck and

shoulder again, his hand grabbing my breast with a little bit of desperation. "You *are* feeling me, and it's killing me."

"No. I want to feel you ..." I pushed down a fraction on his erection, forcing his underwear down a little more and positioning him extremely close to the center of my spread legs. "Here. I want to feel you here, but ... just ... on the outside."

"Reese ..." He rested his forehead on my shoulder and dropped his hand to the edge of the pool table again as we both focused on my hand bringing him so incredibly close to me. Taking the tiniest of steps closer, the head of it touched me there.

"Stop." My breath hitched.

The warmth and silkiness felt out of this world.

After hearing him gulp a loud swallow, I rubbed it against me. It felt so good. Everything about him felt good ... maybe even right, from his lips at my shoulder to his right hand on my knee, gently pushing it out to spread my legs a little wider.

With micro movements, he dipped his hips forward a fraction of an inch, hitting my clit, then back. Forward again. Back again.

It wasn't sex.

It wasn't sex.

It wasn't sex.

That chant played on an endless loop in my head.

"God ..." I closed my eyes and said a quick apology prayer for using the Lord's name in vain, but I somehow ignored the obvious apology for sitting naked on the edge of Fisher's pool table while we rubbed his cock along my ... area.

His movements sped up a bit, becoming ragged like his breathing.

"Fisher!" I gasped, digging my fingernails into his shoulders as he stilled.

He stilled because the head of it went in the wrong direction. It went in ... a fraction. Fisher was inside of me, literally a quarter of an inch, at the very most. But still ... he was there. And he could have moved. He could have jumped back. But he didn't.

I could have moved. I could have scooted back that quarter of an inch. I could have pushed him away. But I didn't.

"I'm so—" He started to apologize. I thought. I wasn't sure. Things were a little foggy at that point.

"No. Don't ... move." I think I meant to say "don't apologize," but I didn't. I had bigger issues than that. I didn't want him to move toward me at all. But ... I also didn't want him to step back. I liked him there. Too much. And if he would have moved forward and pushed farther inside of me, I know I would have let him, but the regret might have been too much. Yet the thought of him stepping away felt nearly as excruciating.

"Reeeese ... I can't fucking stay here." His breaths were little staccatos along my cheek as he dragged his lips from my ear to my mouth and bit my lower lip kinda hard.

Because I couldn't make up my stupid mind, and

he was running out of patience, I grabbed *it* and moved it up to my clit again. That time I didn't let go. I made sure every time his pelvis rocked forward, it didn't go inside of me.

But I wanted it to go there. And that was a part of my brain I couldn't control. I couldn't pray away those thoughts. I wanted to have sex with Fisher Mann nearly as much as my lungs wanted oxygen.

"Lean back." He pressed a hand between my breasts.

I couldn't lean back without letting go of him. And if I let go of him, *things* were sure to happen.

Fisher saw the concern on my face and shook his head. "I'm not taking your virginity ... tonight." He smirked.

I didn't trust him. Then again, I didn't trust myself. So I moved forward with another bad decision. I had a whole stack of them that night, and I leaned back onto my forearms. Fisher rested his hands on my knees and spread my legs wider.

"If you let me put my mouth on you..." his gaze landed between my legs "...I could make you scream."

Biting my lip, I shook my head at least a half dozen times.

Oral *sex*.

Nope. It had sex in the name. So I had to pass.

As if God were applauding me at that point for showing restraint.

Fisher leaned forward, rubbing me in the perfect spot with his erection, again and again, as his mouth found my breasts. As the pressure built, I shifted my hips, but not on purpose.

"Fuck!" He stilled again. And again, he was inside of me, a little. A little more actually, but only maybe a half inch this time. "You can't move like that." He breathed heavily.

I wanted it.

In that moment, I made the decision to ... go to Hell maybe. But I wasn't going there a virgin. I was going there with the naked fisherman inside of me.

"Fisher ..." I rested my heels firmly on the edge of the pool table and lifted my hips a tiny bit.

"Fuck. Fuck. Fuck! Stop!" He grabbed my hips and pushed them back down to the pool table. "I don't have on a condom."

"Then get one."

He closed his eye and shook his head. "They're upstairs."

With Angie.

"Fisher ..." I tried to lift my hips again.

Again, he shook his head and held me down while pulling the head of his erection out of me. Then he used one hand to give me an orgasm while using his other hand to give himself one—the result of it landing on my stomach. That part was sort of weird for me.

"Damnation is in your future, little girl." He pulled up his underwear and jeans before sauntering to the kitchen to grab some paper towels.

"Then you're going with me."

He shook his head. "Only after Rory murders me."

CHAPTER SEVENTEEN

I STILL HAD eighty percent of my virginity. It took some complicated math to come up with that. It also meant I still had an eighty percent chance of going to Heaven—one hundred if I followed the once-saved-always-saved philosophy. That was probably the best way to go at that point.

My guilt held on with more permanence than what I'd hoped, but my remorse declined a bit since the dry humping in my bed incident. That brought me to tears afterward. The pool table? No tears. I think I was in shock that I wanted to go all the way. *Fisher* stopped me. The crude, naked fisherman. I never imagined that. He said we'd go until I said stop. I never said stop. If anything, I had my own little cheering section in my head chanting, "Go! Go! Go!"

Creeping along the side of the house, I made my escape the next morning. A little Sunday morning gospel to cleanse my soul.

Tiptoeing along the side of Fisher's truck, I hid from sight in case he was watering his plants.

"Off to confess your sins?"

I jumped and glanced at the garage with both doors wide open and Fisher bent over his weight bench working his triceps.

No shirt, of course.

"Um ..." I cleared my throat, eyeing Arnie's Escalade. Did it mean Angie was still there too? "Yes. I'm going to church." I tightened my grip on the clutch purse I'd used the previous night and took slow steps into the garage.

"You look nice." He eyed me in my simple white romper and silver Birkenstocks.

"Thanks. Is..." my gaze signaled to the door to the house "...Angie gone?"

"Nope," he replied with a strained voice as he continued his workout. "In the shower."

"Oh. Did you ... sleep on the sofa or in a spare room?"

"No. It's my bed. Why should I have done that?"

Swallowing hard, I clenched my teeth and shrugged with stiff shoulders. My entire body tensed with anger. "No reason." I managed to eke out the words. "Later." I pivoted, holding my breath—holding *everything* that tried to pry open my lips to be set free.

"You want to know if I had sex with her, huh?"

My feet stopped in place, but I couldn't turn around. "No."

"No? Really? Well, we did. Full penetration.

There's really nothing better than being buried balls deep in a woman. No holding back. No fragile hymens. No guilt. Just raw fucking."

Tears stung my eyes before I had a chance to flinch at his vulgarity, and I forced my feet to make speedy, gigantic strides out of the garage.

"Not so quick." I heard the *thunk* of weights hitting the rubber mat, and in the next breath he grabbed my arm and whipped me around to face him. "It's a joke." He shook his head and grinned as his other hand blotted the wet corners of my eyes.

"It's a terrible joke," I whispered past the lump in my throat.

"Probably. But Rory comes home in a few days." He blew out a long breath. "And *you* said it would stop then. You said you didn't want her to know. So if we're a few days from ending whatever this is ... then you need to get ahold of yourself."

That confirmation? The one that said his feelings toward me were *way* different than mine were toward him? It sucked.

Jerking my hand away, I finished wiping my eyes before a new round of emotion made its way to the stage. "I *have* ahold of myself. I'm just not emotionally dead like you are. Not because I'm eighteen. It's because I'm a good person with real emotions, and that will never change. So excuse me if the idea of you screwing someone immediately after consuming me like some tasteless appetizer is a little disheartening, but it's only because I don't offer myself up to just anyone like you obviously do."

Fisher's head jerked backward. "First..." he held up a finger in my face "...you didn't really let me taste you, so the tasteless reference is unfair. And second..." he held up another finger "...if you're insinuating Angie is *just anyone*, then you need to check your facts again."

My face scrunched into my most menacing expression, which probably only made me look constipated. "You are ... you're ..." My hands balled into tight fists.

He smirked.

Gah!

I hated him for smirking at me when there was nothing funny about anything we were discussing.

"For a cruciv—cruciferous whatever that made-up word was you called yourself, you sure lack in vocabulary when the pressure's on."

My hate grew. First his smirk, then his stupid fumbling of the word cruciverbalist. I didn't want to smile. It wasn't okay for him to steal my anger with his intentional or unintentional humor. Yet there I stood, with my hands still fisted and an unavoidable grin climbing up my face.

"You're so stupid. Never again do you get to reference my age since you just called me a botany term denoting cabbage family plants. *Not* the same thing as cruciverbalist—one who constructs or is good at solving crossword puzzles." I added an eye roll for good measure.

"Broccoli. Cabbage. Cauliflower. I know. I'm not as

stupid as you think I am. Again, you just don't get my humor."

"I'm going to church." I turned on my heel and continued toward the Outback.

"Say hi to the virgins for me."

"Jerk," I mumbled—but not without grinning because Fisher Mann was so ... *extra.*

"Welcome back. It's good to see you again." A somewhat familiar face greeted me as I took a chair in the Sunday school classroom. "It's Brendon."

I nodded. "Yeah. I remember." I didn't really. "Thanks. We missed you at the singles' Bible study on Wednesday night."

"I wasn't feeling well. Headache." The hardest part about having a church family was the accountability which led to truths they didn't want to hear or lies they happily swallowed while God knew. He always knew. Like earlier that morning during the sermon, I wasn't thinking about the words echoing through the sanctuary. My mind replayed the previous night. With my Bible open on my lap and people all around me responding to the day's gospel with "Amens," I squeezed my thighs together and thought about Fisher between my legs while silently saying my own kind of Amens.

"Well, I hope you're feeling better now." Brendon sat next to me.

"Much better. Thanks."

"Would you like to have lunch with me today?"

Brendon wasn't terrible looking. He had a great smile, and he was taller than me which was always a bonus. But ... there was Fisher.

And ... there was Rory coming home in a matter of days.

"Just lunch." Brendon chuckled as if he could read my mind. "I don't have that many friends."

"Okay. Lunch would be great. I could use a friend too." If Fisher had Angie in his bed ... in whatever capacity ... I could have lunch with a male friend.

After class, we raced to the parking lot to beat the crowd and congestion of vehicles trying to maneuver out of the tight spaces.

"Shoot. I'm trapped." Brendon frowned at his car blocked in a parallel parking spot at the west end of the lot. He barely had two inches in the front or the back to maneuver. "Guess I'm waiting for the crowd after all."

"Leave it. I'll drive and drop you off after lunch."

"You sure?"

I nodded.

He followed me to my car and gave me an extended glance over the top of it as I unlocked the doors. "How old are you?"

"Eighteen." I unlocked the car and slid into the driver's seat as he got in on the other side.

"Really? Wow. I thought you were older."

"How old are you?"

"Twenty-four."

I wouldn't have guessed that. Maybe twenty. "You look young for twenty-four." I smiled, giving him a quick sideways glance as I backed out of the parking space.

"Good thing this isn't a date. I'd feel a little weird with you being eighteen."

"I'm an adult," I said my new and thoroughly recycled mantra.

We settled on a Mediterranean restaurant and a large booth near the open kitchen.

"We're just a few blocks from my house. I've passed this place many times on my walks."

"You live in this neighborhood?" He narrowed one eye. "With your parents? It's just ... a really nice neighborhood. I couldn't afford to live here by myself or even with a houseful of roommates."

I sipped my water then shook my head. "I live with my mom. And she rents the basement of a house. So I can't afford to live here and neither could she if it weren't a basement rental situation."

"I see. Makes sense. So what are you doing this summer? Getting ready for college?"

"I'm taking a gap year." There it was. My go-to. "But this summer, I'm working for a construction company doing random things in the office or delivering lunch to the crew."

"Sounds..." he smirked "...fun."

"It's interesting. Fun? Probably not."

"Do you like your boss?"

"What?" My head snapped up from the menu. "Why would you ask me that?"

"Uh ..." His eyes rolled quickly to one side and then the other. "Just making conversation."

I relaxed my defensive posture. "Sorry. Yeah. He's nice. He's actually my mom's landlord. It's his house. He lives on the main level. And he was kind enough to offer me a summer job."

"That's a cool situation."

I nodded. It was cool. And sexy. And my newest obsession.

"So ... what do you do?" I asked. "I assume since you're twenty-four, you must be out of college, if you went."

"I went." He nodded while studying his menu. "I just graduated from law school, actually."

"Can you be a lawyer at twenty-four?"

He laughed. "If you graduated high school a year early. Yes. You can."

"Wow. Brainy."

Brendon set his menu down and shook his head. I was pretty sure that was a blush on his face. "Good memory. That's all."

"Photographic?"

He shrugged. "Maybe. I've never been officially tested. I can read quite quickly too. My dad died when I was in fifth grade. And my mom spent all of her time working to put me and my sisters through school, so we didn't spend a whole lot of time figuring me out. And we didn't have a lot of money, so I spent more time reading than watching the single television we had in the house. No cellphone until I earned money to buy my own and pay for a plan. No computer outside of the ones we used in school. No video games. Pretty boring, huh?"

I felt an instant connection to Brendon in that moment. "Well, my dad died too. Three years ago. Then I moved to Texas to live with my grandparents until I graduated. I didn't have a phone either until I bought my own ... which my grandparents didn't let me do until I was eighteen. So I've literally had a cell phone for less than a year. Now who's boring?"

"Really?" Brendon smiled as if my confession, albeit a little sad and pathetic, made him feel some joy.

"However, we did have a computer in the house. I had one from the school that we could bring home. So it's not like I didn't have internet access even if it was monitored for appropriate content." My nose wrinkled.

"No internet porn for you."

That made my face heat a bit. Just the word porn did that. "No." I returned a nervous laugh. But I had seen porn. Once ... okay twice. My friend Kat lived with her dad, and her dad worked nights so he was always sleeping during the day. Kat thought it was fun to check out her dad's browser history on the computer; he wasn't only paying bills and ordering socks from Amazon while Kat and her younger brother were at the Christian academy. Worth noting too ... he taught the teen's Sunday school class at church.

"Have you taken the bar exam?"

"Nope. I've taken a job with a law firm here in Denver, and they're adamant about helping me study for it. But honestly ..." He winked. It wasn't a Fisher wink, but it was still adorable in its own way. "I've got this."

Confidence.

Man ... what I wouldn't give to have had even half of his confidence. And direction. That was it more than anything. A sense of direction imparted a certain level of confidence. I didn't know if gap-year kids had as much confidence.

We ordered food and chatted for over an hour. Brendon's mom lived just outside of Chicago. And his two younger sisters still lived there too.

"Enough about me. Tell me about your mom? Why were you living with your grandparents after your dad died?"

"My mom had some ... *issues* after the divorce. So my dad had custody of me. Then my grandparents stepped in after he died because my mom was still not able to take care of me."

Why did I lie? I didn't know. Out of all the people I should have been honest with, Brendon was at the top. He was a Christian, which meant he would not have judged me. (Yes, I realized that thought held zero actual truth.) He wasn't trying to date me, so I had no need to impress him. And I'd been upfront about my mom's situation with so many other people before him. I don't even remember making the conscious decision to lie to him. My mouth started moving, and it took a bit for my brain to process the automated lie.

"So how is it now ... with your mom? Are things weird?"

"Well, that's hard to answer. I no sooner arrived and she left for L.A. to do some salon training. She'll be home in a few days."

"You must be excited about that?"

Was I excited? Rory home equaled things ending with Fisher.

"Sure." I smiled, but it barely bent my lips.

After he bought my lunch, in which I argued because it wasn't a date, we climbed back into the car and started to pull out of the parallel parking spot and into traffic.

"Show me where you live."

"Why?" I laughed through some uncontrolled nerves. My goal that day was to avoid going home for as long as possible.

Brendon shrugged. "Sunday afternoon drive. It's a great neighborhood. And when you mentioned you lived close by, it piqued my curiosity."

Scraping my teeth along my bottom lip a few times, I nodded slowly. "Okay. We can do a drive-by."

It took less than three minutes to get to the house. I slowed down, but not much. "That's it, right there."

"Wow ... wait ... slow down. The view from the back has to be spectacular."

"Yeah, it's fine."

"Reese." He laughed. "Seriously, are you not going to stop? Can I see the back of the house?"

"Not a good idea." I slowed down a little more. Arnie's Tahoe was gone and the garage doors were shut.

"Why? Because you don't really live here?"

"What?" I stopped the car. "Of course I live here. You think I'm lying?"

He smirked. "There's only one way to find out."

"Gah. Fine!" I pulled along the side of the street and hopped out. "Let's go in back."

Brendon followed me around to the back of the house.

"Happy now?"

Slipping his hands into his pockets, he nodded. His blue eyes bright and the gel in his hair reflecting the sunlight. "Not unless we go inside."

"Are you serious?"

"Are *you* serious?" He shot back at me.

I couldn't hide my smile, so I rolled my eyes and led him to the door. "See?" I said as the key fit the lock and I opened the door.

"Yeah, I see. You weren't lying." He followed me into the basement. "This is huge. And really nice. When you said you were living in a basement, I think it conjures images of dinky spaces with no light, cobwebs, and a growling furnace. This is by far nicer than any place I've ever lived." He milled around the space, running his fingers along the edge of the pool table. "You play?"

I had used the pool table, just not for pool.

"A little."

"Then let's play." He grabbed two sticks and handed one to me.

Midway through our game, the door upstairs opened and footsteps followed. Brendon shot me a narrowed-eyed glance. Of course, he had to be thinking ... who would be coming down the stairs? Surely, I locked the door. Right?

Wrong.

You didn't lock the door when you secretly hoped your landlord would sneak down with a condom so you didn't have to stay stuck at an eighty-percent virgin status.

"Hey," Fisher said coming to an abrupt halt at the bottom of the stairs.

"Hey," I said. "What's up?" I pretended that his uninvited trip downstairs was no big deal.

Was he coming downstairs to take the rest of my virginity? I thought a million things along that line.

"I'm Fisher." He ignored me and made his way to the pool table with his hand held out for Brendon.

"Brendon." My non-date friend shook Fisher's hand. "You have an amazing house."

"Thanks." Fisher shot me a quick glance.

I bit my lips together for a second before realizing we were suspended in silence. "Fisher built this house. He's really amazing."

"It's great, man. Really incredible." Brendon rested

the end of his pool stick on the floor and leaned into it casually.

"Thanks," Fisher said once again while shooting me another glance, this time with his head slightly canted and an unusual look in his eyes. "I think that's the first time you've complimented me on my skills."

My eyebrows shot up my forehead. "Oh? I don't know about that. Did you ..." I dropped my pool stick on the ground with my fidgety hands, and it made an embarrassing *clank*. "Uh ..." I quickly retrieved it. "Did you ..." I totally forgot what I was going to say or ask.

"Did I ...?"

"Uh ... need something?"

The smile that swelled on Fisher's face was almost too much to handle without wearing more absorbent panties. "Yeah, I needed something, but it can wait until you don't have company."

Brendon's cool expression morphed into something a little more uncomfortable like he sensed a third-wheel feeling.

"Was it about work?" I made an effort to normalize the situation.

"No," Fisher said slowly, as slowly as he shook his head, as slowly as he made me weak in the knees.

"Did you hear from my mom?"

"No ..." He dragged out another long, torturous no.

"Oh ... I know. Duh. I was going to show you where water's getting into the back room."

Fisher lifted a single brow. I ignored him, handing Brendon my pool stick. "Be right back." I marched to the back room with Fisher right behind me. As soon as he shut the door, I turned.

"Who's your friend? Your introduction skills are not up to par. I know his name is Brendon and he likes my house. Care to elaborate now?"

"No. Why did you come downstairs?" I took one step then another toward him, my hands itching to touch him, my eyes disappointed that he was wearing a T-shirt. "Did you bring a condom?"

A half grin formed on his sexy, scruffy face. "No. Give your innocence to Brendon. I'm not in the business of pissing off my friends. And if I were you, I'd look for a new church. The sermon has already worn off. You're looking for sin just hours after crossing the threshold of the church's doors."

"Who's your *friend*?" I fisted his shirt, telling my unwise heart to ignore his comment about giving myself to Brendon or his rambling about finding a new church.

"Rory." He kept his hands to himself and eyed me with caution.

"Rory is your tenant."

"And my friend."

"So you thought she'd be good with you only inserting the tip?" I could barely say those words without burning up.

"You're a temptress. A typical church girl playing the innocent role. You should be truly ashamed."

"Fisher?"

He waited a second to respond, but when his gaze fell to my lips, I knew I had him. "What?"

"Are you going to kiss me?"

"I was thinking about it."

"Don't think."

Wetting his lips as his grin hit full capacity, he said, "I never do when I'm with you." Then he slid his hand to the back of my neck and kissed me. The knuckles of his other hand brushed my cheek. His touch so gentle —too gentle. It felt different. And maybe it was just my foolish heart hoping for more, but it didn't feel like a purely physical moment.

"Send your friend home," he murmured over my lips. "I want you all to myself."

"I can't. I have to drive him." I pulled back, releasing his shirt as he released my neck.

"Did you pick him up at church?"

"His car was pinned in, and we wanted to go to lunch before the crowd flooded the parking lot."

"A date?"

I started to respond but stopped just as quickly. "Why? Do you have a problem with me dating him?"

Say yes, Fisher. Just please say yes.

He twisted his lips, like his silence twisted my heart. "No."

Fisher ... why?

"Well, it wasn't a date." I shoved his chest, forcing him to move out of my way. "But thanks for reminding me how little this means to you."

"Reese ..."

I opened the door, tipped my chin up, and plastered a smile on my face. "Sorry. Problem solved. Now ... where were we? Was it my turn?"

"Yes." Brendon handed me my pool stick as I ignored Fisher's exit from the utility room.

"Nice meeting you, Brendon. You two have fun."

I clenched my jaw, trying to hide my slight wince at his words while keeping my back to him.

"Thanks. Nice meeting you too."

It was really nice that they got along so well. Brendon didn't want to date me because I was too young for him. And Fisher didn't want my virginity because he wasn't in that business anymore. I felt a little rejected.

After Brendon won three games in a row, I drove him back to the church.

"Thanks for lunch. Again, I would have paid for mine."

He opened his door. "It was my pleasure." Pausing for a second he narrowed his eyes and lifted his gaze to mine. "What if..." he pressed his lips together, again pausing for a second "...our age difference didn't really matter? What if we did this again, but we called it a date?"

"A date?" I echoed in a soft tone just before taking a hard swallow. "I ... well ... maybe we can discuss it next weekend after church."

"Discuss it?" He laughed a little. "Wow, you really take dating seriously. Since we both have cell phones now, how about we exchange numbers and discuss it this week before church next Sunday?"

I thought about Fisher. Then, I thought about Rory before nodding. With his number and several social media follows, he grinned and closed the door. At any other time in my life, I would have been thrilled to have met Brendon. He was closer to my age. Employed. And he attended church. I also felt certain that he wasn't a crude talker.

On the way home, I gave myself a pep talk. It involved ignoring Fisher until Monday morning. Eating dinner alone. And going to bed early with a book or my current crossword puzzle.

So much for pep talks ...

The second I climbed out of Rory's car, I marched straight to his front door and rang the doorbell. A few seconds later, he opened the door, eyeing me from head to toe before stepping back and silently inviting me into his domain.

"So ... you won't take my virginity." It felt weird having that conversation because he'd said something so eerily similar to me. "What will you take from me?"

With a contemplative expression that seemed to border on the painful side, he whispered, "Let's start with your clothes."

I wondered ... I wondered *so hard* when he made the decision to draw a line. He knew as well as I did that Rory wouldn't be okay with anything we had done together. It wasn't just me pushing lines and bending rules to serve my own needs and desires; Fisher did it too.

I just didn't know why. He could have had Angie or Teagan or a million other women meeting his sexual needs.

Why me?

Why seek something you know you won't conquer ... out of choice?

So many thoughts stirred in my head, but they didn't stop my hands from sliding my shoulders and arms out of my romper, letting it drop to the floor.

That confused and painful expression remained affixed to Fisher's face until he met my gaze. Then it vanished, leaving the Fisher I knew all too well.

Cocky.

Confident.

Unapologetically crude.

"Shoes."

I slipped out of my shoes.

"Bra."

Reaching both hands behind me, I unhooked my bra and let it slide down my chest and arms. He focused on my bare breasts, on my erect nipples.

After the bra landed on the floor at my feet with my romper, I reached for my panties.

"No." He inched his head side to side. "Leave them on. Turn that way. And walk slowly to my bedroom."

There I was, following Fisher off the side of the mountain. Did he know I would do anything for him? Did he know what that meant?

Turning, I feigned confidence and made the slow walk down the hallway to his bedroom.

"Stop."

I stopped because he told me to stop.

"Turn around."

I turned around, centered at the threshold to his bedroom.

Fisher took his time making his way to me, slowly peeling off his shirt, leaving him in bare feet and exercise shorts. When he reached the doorway, he pressed his hands to the wood frame. "Put your hands below mine."

Eyeing his hands for a few seconds, I pressed my hands to the frame. "W-why?"

"Because." He kneeled in front of me. "Your knees will want to give out soon." Sliding his hands to the back of my legs, he moved my hips toward his face, stopping with his mouth just above the waist of my panties. "Can I kiss you here?"

I couldn't speak. Swallowing and breathing heavily became a full-time job. Fisher pressed his mouth to my skin and glanced up at me.

I nodded.

He kissed lower. "Here?"

I nodded, gripping the wood with anticipation. My knees were already weak.

His lips descended another inch or more. *There.* He was right there. A whooshing sound—a thumping that matched my ever-escalating heartbeat—made it hard to hear anything else.

"Here?"

I barely heard him, but I still nodded.

Fisher pressed a soft kiss over my panties. Then his grip on my legs tightened, and he kissed me a little harder, sucking some of the thin cotton into his mouth. Biting it. And tugging it. Exposing part of my flesh.

Again, he kissed me hard. Sucked. Bit. Tugged.

My panties were no longer covering much. I fought the gullible thoughts tripping over themselves in my head. Thoughts of love and happily ever after's. Some men showered women with poems and flowers. Maybe oral sex was Fisher's way of expressing his love. Sadly, my panties between his teeth wasn't exactly something I could photograph and share with my friends on social media.

#relationshipgoals

#myfirsttime

#LazySunday

#LickIt

We weren't going public with our relationship anyway because it was ending soon.

"I'm going to fucking devour you," he said just before his mouth covered my bare flesh.

Just before his tongue parted me.

Just before he hummed.

I was ...

Terrified to have his mouth there.

Elated because it felt so good. Too good. Sinfully good.

Confused because it wasn't sex, but it was sex.

Surely, the look he gave me fell under Rory's testicle removal threat. Did he think about that? Even once?

All the blood in my body made its way to the exact spot his mouth was on me. And it made it impossible to think or breathe. And yes, it made it really hard to keep from falling to the floor beneath my shaky knees.

"Fisher ..." I found a tiny voice to speak one word as my body teetered to the side, my whole forearm resting on the frame as my other hand claimed a large handful of his hair and my knees bowed inward.

It was *wrong!* I knew it. I just didn't have the mental or emotional capacity to stop it. A prime example of why giving in to temptation was a bad idea. There were points of no return, and I had breezed past mine the second he opened his front door.

Fisher was unrelenting and hungry. He seemed famished. Then he seemed ... impatient, ripping my panties down my legs. I released his hair and reached for them, as if they were my last line of defense, even if they weren't covering anything whatsoever at that point. Did keeping one item of clothing on make it less wrong?

Oops ... I didn't even remove my panties. He accidentally tripped and his mouth just landed there.

Fisher's hands guided my legs to spread wider before he resumed his *oral* navigation and, in general, driving me to the edge of passing out or using really bad words.

"This is so wrong ..." I mumbled.

In the next breath, he was gone. Well, his mouth was gone.

Fisher stood and chuckled, resting his hands on my hips to guide me backward to his bed while he kissed my neck. "Do you want to stop?"

The back of my knees hit the bed, and I plunked onto my butt.

"We can stop right now."

Resting back on my elbows, I shook my head. "I just don't want it to be wrong."

"Well ..." He twisted his lips. "Sorry. I can make it good, but I can't make it right in your head."

"I want ..." I bit my lip and searched for the right words. "I want it like last night."

He squinted one eye. "No fucking way."

Swallowing, I frowned. "I want to ..."

Feel like we're having sex, even if you won't actually have it with me!

"I want it like last night or ... more," I said with defeat to my voice. At that point, I was already dirty. Would finishing the job before taking a spiritual shower really have made that much of a difference?

"Despite you being naked on my bed, despite you incessantly wetting your lips while staring at my erection ..."

Busted!

I cut my gaze straight to his, grinning with admission that he caught me gawking at his tented shorts.

"I'm not taking your virginity. I had a little talk with myself about it, and we—me and my moderately well-honed conscience—decided to pass on the offer. I don't feel worthy of it."

"Worthy of it?" I coughed a laugh. "You mean to tell me you've never taken someone's virginity?"

"I didn't say that." He grabbed my leg, forcing me onto my back while he brought my foot to his mouth and kissed the pad of my big toe.

"Why? You can't say that and not have an explanation. Why was it okay then?"

"Because it wasn't some crowned jewel. It wasn't a prized possession. There was no hesitation. No chanting 'this is so wrong.'"

I frowned.

"I can't give it back, Reese. If or *when* you have second thoughts or regret, I can't give it back to you."

"So you'd rather borrow someone's used sanitary napkin?"

Dropping my foot to the bed, he ran a hand through his hair. "Um ... what?"

I sat up and crisscrossed my legs, covering my breasts in my cupped hands. "My grandma used to say that not having your virginity to give your husband was like borrowing someone's used sanitary napkin on your wedding night."

Fisher blinked slowly for several silent seconds. "I ... I don't even know how to respond to that. Were you ... raised in a cult? What the fuck? Who says that?"

I winced, feeling a little defensive. It wasn't that I believed my grandma, but I didn't like him insinuating that she was crazy or some cult member.

"Listen ..." He sighed and took a seat next to me on the bed with his legs dangling off the end. "I haven't walked in your shoes. So I don't know what's been planted into your brain. I liked what just happened in the doorway. It's that simple for me. I liked it. I'd like to do it again. And I don't want to feel guilty for being a consenting *adult* with you. My opinion should mean nothing to you. So while I'd like to tell you to spend more time touching yourself than worrying about going to Hell, it's not my place."

After letting his words resonate for a moment, I released my breasts and stood on my knees, swinging one leg over his lap. "Fisher ..." I laced my fingers together behind his neck while positioning myself so his cock (covered by his briefs and shorts) was pressed between my legs again, much like the previous night.

"What are you doing?" he whispered, eyeing my mouth while his hands gripped my hips.

"I like how you feel between my legs, naked fisherman."

"Fuuuck ..." He closed his eyes for a brief moment, gripping my hips tighter while pushing me down a fraction—pushing into me a fraction.

Cock.

Briefs.

Shorts.

"Yes ..." I closed my eyes.

"Don't say that," he said with a strained voice and lines of tension along his forehead.

Thrust.

Thrust.

Thrust.

He prodded me like he, too, knew that point of no return was a mile behind us in a foggy rearview mirror.

My hands ghosted down his back. His hands gripped my butt.

Thrust.

Thrust.

Thrust.

I spread my legs wider, allowing him to push into me a fraction more.

Thrust.

Thrust.

Thrust.

Each move a little harder.

Each breath a little more ragged, just like his next words.

"I." *Thrust.*

"Want." *Thrust.*

"Inside of you." *Thrust. Thrust. Thrust.*

"So fucking bad."

I did too. And while I knew it would be different, that it would be painful the first time, I still wanted it. I wanted it with Fisher. Instead, we were dry humping harder than two people had probably ever dry humped. I swore his cock, briefs, and shorts were halfway in by that point—like a clothes condom—and soaking wet from me ... and maybe a little from him too.

"Fisher!" I seethed when he ducked his head and

bit my nipple and tugged it like he was trying to rip it off.

Thrust.

Thrust.

Thrust.

"No." He released my nipple and grabbed my hand when I reached between us, sliding my hand down the front of his shorts and briefs. "Not a good idea."

I kissed his neck. "I promise I won't. I just want to feel you."

He groaned or grumbled, clearly warring with the decision to stop me or trust me to not cross the next line.

Releasing me, he rested that hand on the bed behind him, chin dipped, watching me slide down the front of his shorts and briefs.

"Make it feel good," he whispered while a grin stole his lips.

My teeth scraped along my bottom lip as I gathered up as much confidence as I could find. My hand wrapped around the top half of his cock while I rubbed myself along the bottom part. It was so much better than the scratchy fabric.

That day, the naked fisherman taught me how to make it feel good for me and for him at the same time while keeping that eighty percent of my virginity.

I knew it was wrong. I just started to care a little less about its wrongness.

While Fisher showered, I ran downstairs to get my computer. I had several important searches to do.

Is oral sex as morally wrong as intercourse?

What does the Bible say about masturbation?

Can a woman get pregnant if a man ejaculates between her legs without penetration?

That last search sent me into a frenzy. I peed.

Prayed.

Jumped into the shower and put the handheld head between my legs to rid myself of any residual semen.

Prayed again.

Checked my phone for my monthly cycle app to see if I was anywhere near ovulation.

Prayed again.

Dressed.

Sprinted up the stairs.

"YOU CAN GET PREGNANT WITHOUT PENETRATION!"

Fisher closed the refrigerator door, popping the top of a beer and taking a swig, eyeing me intently the whole time. "I'm a guy. I can't get pregnant."

"Ugh! Shut up! I'm talking about me."

Totally relaxed, he perched himself atop one of the barstools. "I came on my own fucking stomach, not anywhere on you. Sperm might be fast swimmers, but I don't think they jump from one person to another."

"Fisher! I rubbed against you. My..." I motioned between my legs "...I rubbed against you. And it ... *you* ... might have dripped. What if all of it didn't go onto your stomach? What if a drop or two mixed with my ... you know? And you can have SEVEN HUNDRED

AND FIFTY THOUSAND sperm in one drop of semen. Did you know that? Because I didn't."

Still, he didn't seem the least bit phased by my concern. "I think the odds are greatly in your favor of *not* getting pregnant. That would be quite the story." He chuckled before taking another swig of beer.

"No." I shook my head a half dozen times. "That would not be quite the story."

"Are you ovulating?" He stole some of my fire.

No. According to my app, I wasn't ovulating. But ... abstinence was the only certainty. And while we abstained from intercourse—well, full, bare penetration —we didn't abstain from possibly mixing bodily fluids.

It was like he read my mind ... my next train of thought.

"I would have thought you might have been more concerned about STDs than a rogue drop of semen. I know I'm safe with Virgin Therese, but you know I've been with other women. Yet you never asked me. Kinda stupid on your part, don't you think?"

I deflated. I had been stupid. Young and so very stupid.

"I haven't had unprotected sex ... except what just happened with you, since I was last tested. You're safe. So at least if you're pregnant, you'll have one less thing to worry about," he said.

"Not helpful."

Fisher grinned. "It's a little helpful."

"I'm not ovulating."

"Well, that's a relief. I was really worried about it."

"That can't happen again."

He set down his beer and held up his hands in surrender. "I'm pretty sure you knocked on my door. And I guarantee you I wasn't going to get you pregnant with my face between your legs."

My jaw flapped a few times, but nothing came out.

"Maybe you should think about getting on birth control."

"What?" My head jerked backward. "I'm not having sex."

"Reese." His smile vanished because he was being twenty-eight and I was being ... younger. A lot younger.

Stupid.

Naive.

Childish.

I wasn't stupid. I was scared and disappointed in myself. It was easier to act shocked and offended by his comment than to admit my part in what we did.

"It just ..." I admitted my wrongdoing with the change—the defeat—in my tone instead of saying the actual words. "It can't happen again."

With a quick half shrug, he reached for his bottle of beer. "Agreed."

"What if ..." I cleared my throat. "Hypothetically, what if I were pregnant?"

"No." He grunted. "No. We are not doing this. If you come back to me in a few weeks with a positive test, we'll have this conversation. But I'm not having it now."

"Why?"

"Because I'm not."

"I think it's irresponsible to not at least have a plan."

"Me too. If I had a vagina, and I wanted to play peekaboo with the head of a guy's dick, I'd plan ahead and be on *birth control*."

Wow.

That hurt.

Fisher wasn't just cold about it; he was cruel. Aloof, like he didn't care about me.

"I'll see you in the morning, unless I'm driving to the office and we're not together."

We're not together.

It was funny how I managed to say exactly what was on my mind, just in a different context.

"We're together."

That hurt too because I knew he meant it completely in the work sense. He let Angie go. He let Teagan go. Why did I think I would be any different?

"Goodnight."

CHAPTER EIGHTEEN

I CALLED Christina while making a sandwich, even though I wasn't hungry because the previous twenty-four hours with Fisher had been unbelievable.

"Miss me already?" she answered.

"I need to talk. In person. Where are you?"

"Thirty minutes outside of Colorado Springs."

"Ugh!" I viciously cut through my sandwich.

"What is it? Just tell me."

"Do you have me on speaker?"

"No, why?"

"Because I'm out of control, and I ... I don't want anyone else to know. But I need advice because I'm losing my mind."

She chuckled. "Okay. Take a breath. Tell me what's going on. Does it have to do with Arnie or the other guy?"

Arnie.

I'd forgotten about Arnie and the made-up other guy, who wasn't actually made-up at all.

"The other guy. He doesn't want to have sex with me because I'm a virgin, so we've been doing everything *but* having actual sex ... intercourse ... you know what I mean. Anyway—"

"Whoa ... wait. Back that shit up. He doesn't want to have—"

"SHH! Don't say it out loud. I don't want Jamison to know I'm having issues in that department."

"Okay, fine. So he doesn't want to try your ... cooking. That's insane. Why not?"

"Because he's worried that my *cooking* is too important to me. So he wants someone else to try my cooking first because he said he's not in the business of trying my cooking."

"Maybe he's never tried a woman's cooking ... like her first official dinner, and he's nervous about it."

"No." I took a bite of my sandwich and chewed it a few seconds. "He's tried other women's *first dinners* because it apparently didn't matter to them."

"Well, does your cooking matter to you?"

"No. Yes. Gah! I don't know. I mean ... can't it somewhat matter to me yet still be okay for him to try it before anyone else does? I'm not asking him to ... open a restaurant for me."

Christina laughed. "I love this conversation. So you go out to eat a lot, and you both enjoy that and mutually want to eat out, but he just won't try your cooking?"

"Right. But, Christina ... I'm not on the pill. And we've been doing things that are risky, but again, not penetration. And I casually asked him what he would do if I ended up pregnant, and he changed. Like his whole demeanor changed. He refused to discuss it with me unless I find out that I am pregnant ... which I highly doubt I am."

"Uh ... Reese, why would you even think that if you ... if he didn't try your cooking?"

"Because he ... you know. And I ... you know. And what if there was a mixing of ... ingredients ..."

"A mixing where?"

"Just ... never mind. It doesn't matter. I'm not near my ovulation time."

"Kudos to you for knowing that."

"I use an app."

"Oh. That's smart. So what do you need from me? I'm obviously no help. Sorry, bae."

"Well, I guess I want to know what you think I should do? He obviously is just in it for the physical part. And I want to have sex with him ... but he won't, despite his total disconnect to the emotional part."

"And you're sure you want him to?"

"Yes. No. I don't know. I know that I wouldn't say no, even if I'd be filled with regret."

"Call Arnie. He'll take it. Probably won't even care if it's more than a one and done. Then you can ... *cook* for anyone without this being an issue."

I didn't want to *cook* for anyone but Fisher.

"Thanks." I sighed. "I'll figure it out."

"Okay. Call me if you need anything, even if I'm not much help."

"Will do."

"Good morning." Fisher walked out of the garage with a mug of coffee in his hand just as I rounded the corner to his truck.

Dang! He looked hot that morning.

Jeans.

Tee.

Work boots.

Wet hair.

Scruffy face.

The same as other days, but different too.

Just ... hotter.

"Morning." I couldn't maintain eye contact with him. Looking at him without thinking about him naked presented itself as the world's most impossible task. Truth? There was a reason I'd thought of him as the "naked fisherman" since the day we met.

"Coffee's still hot inside if you want a cup to go." He opened his door as I opened my side.

"I'm good. Thanks."

As we pulled out of the driveway, he shot me a brief glance. "How was your weekend?"

I tried and failed to hide my grin. As if he didn't know ...

"Fine. How was yours?"

"Not too bad. Mowed the lawn. Went to my brother's concert. Did a few loads of laundry. Oh ... and I got a damn good hand job last night."

My head whipped in his direction. "I didn't give you a hand job."

He sipped his coffee while focusing on the road. "Your hand *did the job*. That's pretty much the definition of a hand job."

My words fell flat before finding an actual voice to go with them. I didn't give him a hand job. I held his cock while I pleasured myself. I held it to prevent it from going inside of me. I wasn't ...

Or was I?

I cleared my throat. "What am I doing today?"

"What's your *job* today? Hmm ... let me think on that. What do you want your job to be today?"

On a nervous laugh, I shrugged. "You're the boss."

"Oh, my choice? I like that."

"I think we should stick to construction stuff."

"As opposed to?" He spared me another lightning-fast side glance.

"I think you should teach me something today."

"Fine. After we make our morning stops, we'll grab lunch and go to my workshop."

"You have a workshop?"

Driving with one hand casually draped over the top of the steering wheel and his other hand holding his coffee, he smiled. "Of course. I was there until just before midnight last night working on wardrobe drawers."

After we ... did what we did, he left. And I had a breakdown on the phone with Christina. Once again, my actions showed my age. Fisher didn't have time to call a friend and overanalyze what had happened between him and the girl from the basement (it wasn't a glamorous label, but it wasn't inaccurate either) because he was a *real* adult with a job and responsibilities. He didn't have his virginity to babysit 24-7. Sex was—not a life-changing choice that required copious amounts of prayer, guilt, overthinking, and dramatization.

We made the morning's stops. I followed him like a good puppy. He asked Hailey to deliver lunches so we could head to his shop after grabbing lunch for ourselves.

"Is this a joke?" I asked as he pulled into the McDonald's drive-thru.

"Lunch. Not a joke." He rolled down his window. "Do you want the Hamburger Happy Meal or the Chicken McNuggets Happy Meal?"

I narrowed my eyes at him.

"I'm doing the hamburger because I'm not overly trusting of chicken nuggets."

I didn't trust *him*. So ... I softly murmured, "Hamburger."

"Drink? I'm splurging on a chocolate milk."

"Juice," I said in the same cautious tone.

He ordered our Happy Meals and pulled to the window.

"Use the change to pay for as many orders as you

can behind me." He handed the guy a hundred-dollar bill.

Fisher was a pay it forward (or in that case backward) kind of guy. Why? Why did he have to be so ... *extra*?

"That's kind of you," the guy at the window said, handing Fisher the bags.

As we pulled onto the main road, Fisher tapped the bags. "Aren't you going to see if the toys are something you don't have?"

I shook my head.

"Why?"

"Because it's no longer my hobby. Rory can get them if she wants them."

"You got all the current ones when you picked up Happy Meals for my crew, didn't you?"

Rubbing my lips together and keeping my gaze locked on the dash, I returned a single nod.

Fisher chuckled.

Ten minutes later, we pulled into the driveway.

"I thought we were going to your shop."

"We are." He grabbed the bags and hopped out of the truck.

I wasted no time following him. In his garage, he grabbed the side of a gray cabinet and pulled on it.

"What the heck?"

He grinned as a light turned on to a stairway leading downstairs, below his garage.

I slowly made my way down the stairs as he closed the cabinet or door behind us. At the bottom, there was a huge space, a second garage, but this one was filled with piles of wood, partially finished cabinets, saws, and walls of hanging tools.

"We're in the basement."

He nodded, wiping his hand across a small high-top table in the corner that had two tall barstools.

"But how do you get here from the basement?"

"Hidden passage, of course. Sit." He nodded to the other barstool and set the Happy Meal bags on the table.

I didn't sit. Not yet. I milled around the shop, feathering my fingers over pieces of wood and cabinets sanded to perfection.

"Is there anything you can't do?" I made my way to the table, and he pulled his burger, fries, and sliced apples out of the sack.

He grinned, but he didn't meet my gaze. "You."

I climbed onto the stool, eyeing him, begging for him to look at me, to give me more than that one-word answer.

He didn't.

We ate in silence for at least five minutes. In that time, he ate every bite of his lunch, and I ate two bites of my burger and maybe three fries because I was too distracted by him.

His secret shop.

His insane talent.

And that comment.

Me. He didn't think he could do me.

"Do you want to cut, sand, or nail?" He wadded up his wrappers and shoved them back into the bag.

"Nail," I said without flinching.

He rubbed his hand over his mouth as if he could wipe the tiny grin from his lips, but the knowing glint in his eyes couldn't be missed. "Let's sand. No sharp blades and no nails. We've made one urgent care trip since Rory left town. Let's not have to make another."

I used a french fry to trace my lips slowly.

Fisher snatched it from my hand and ate it. "Knock that shit off. You're on the clock."

"Okay, Boss." I hopped off the stool and followed him to the opposite side of his workshop.

"These are nearly finished, but if you feel a few of the areas, you'll notice they could use just a light sanding." He rubbed his hand across the front of a drawer then took my hand and moved it where his had been. "Feel that?"

I nodded. "Light." He handed me the sandpaper. "Very lightly. Just until it's smooth."

I sanded it. Felt it. Sanded it more. "Like this?"

Fisher feathered the pads of his fingers over it. "Perfect."

My spine grew two inches with his compliment.

We spent the afternoon in his workshop. I didn't graduate past sanding with the finest sandpaper, but that was okay. Just watching Fisher do his thing was a gift. He wore his safety glasses as he cut the pieces of wood, his gaze so focused on the task. He had no idea that his most intent expression involved him wetting and rubbing his lips together. It was nearly too much.

"Time to call it a day." He tore off his safety glasses and glanced at his watch.

"This was fun. Thanks for letting me see you in your element." I brushed my hands together, removing a light dusting of residue from sanding.

"Anytime."

"Don't say it unless you mean it." I smirked. "The last time you said 'anytime,' I took you seriously and ended up in your tub when you brought your date home."

His lips twisted as he returned a slow nod. "Mmm ... yes. You did."

"Well ..." I jabbed my thumb over my shoulder. "I'm going to take a shower."

Fisher kept nodding slowly, his backside leaned against one of the workbenches, his hands slightly tucked into his front pockets.

Basically ... irresistible.

"Rory comes home this week," he said.

"Yeah," I whispered.

"I'm sorry if I did anything that made you feel—"

"No!" I didn't mean to cut him off so quickly. It was a knee-jerk reaction. "You ... you haven't done anything wrong. You didn't make me feel anything but ... good."

Make it feel good.

"And..." I couldn't help my grin "...a little crazy."

He stared at his feet. "So we're ... good? Friends.

What happened, happened and we move on. No big deal?"

The biggest deal of my eighteen years—well, the good kind of big deal. It was hard to top Rory going to prison and my dad dying for life-changing, catastrophic events.

"Friends," I said just above a whisper. "No big deal ... we're ... good." Someone needed to use some sandpaper on my heart because it felt rough and splintered.

———

THE NEXT MORNING, I woke up to a text from Fisher.

You're with Hailey today, drive your mom's car.

He'd sent the text an hour before my alarm went off.

Hailey had me enter bids into the computer and deliver lunches. Then she had me file—my least favorite job.

"Can I ask you something personal?" I asked her.

"Sure," she said slowly without a glance up from her computer screen.

"Did you like sex the first time you had it?"

Her fingers stilled, and her gaze lifted to meet mine. "Did you just have sex for the first time?"

"No."

"Have you had sex?"

"Not really."

Hailey laughed. "Oh my god, 'not really' is not an answer." Her smile faded when she realized I wasn't finding anything that amusing. "Sorry. My first time ... god ... I don't remember much. Isn't that pathetic? I don't recall it being great. But I didn't have the most considerate man—boy actually—exerting any effort to make it great. He didn't know it was my first time until it was over."

"Was he mad?"

"Mad? What do you mean?"

"That it was your first time and you didn't tell him?"

"No." She chuckled. "Why?"

I shrugged and shook my head.

"You know you can tell me anything. Right? If you have guy problems, I'm your girl. I've had every guy problem imaginable. Cheaters. Married men. Assholes. Narcissists. Stalkers."

My eyebrows peaked as I stopped filing. "Seriously?"

"Oh yes. You name it. I've probably experienced it or have a friend who did."

"Have you been with older men?"

"Yes. Well ... how old? I don't date grandpas, even if they are rich."

"I don't know ... five ... ten years older?"

"Sure. You like an older man?"

"Maybe."

The office door opened and Fisher stepped inside, again sipping one of his big red drinks from a straw.

"Hey," he said to Hailey or me. Maybe both of us. "How's it going today?"

"We're about to clock out, Bossman. After I get done giving Reese some dating advice."

I ducked my head and focused hard on the papers in front of me. Why did she say that?

"Oh yeah? What advice is that?" He slid behind me and opened the desk drawer to my right, dropping a set of keys into it.

His proximity raised the temperature in the room a good ten degrees.

"I'm not sure yet; you walked in and interrupted us."

"Sorry." He chuckled. "Do you want me to leave?"

"No. Just do your thing and ignore us. As you were saying, Reese ..."

I shook my head as Fisher lifted some of the papers around me like he was searching for something on his desk. "It's not a big deal. We can talk later."

"Don't let me stop you. Maybe I can be of help. I'm a guy. So I know a lot about them." Fisher found a folder and turned, resting his butt on the edge of the desk.

I felt his gaze on me, but there was no way I could look at him.

"Yeah, ask Bossman. He's a walking example of failed relationships." Hailey giggled.

"Then he's definitely not the one I need to ask," I murmured.

"Reese was asking me about dating older men.

You've dated plenty of women younger than you. What's your take on it?" Hailey asked Fisher.

I didn't want in on the conversation. I didn't even want to be in the same state as they talked about me or my dating life.

"I think Reese needs to find herself a nice Christian who can make her feel good about herself and her decisions."

"No." Hailey drummed her fingernails on the desk. "That's a terrible idea. You're eighteen. You have to *live*. Don't settle for safe and boring."

"I think Rory would love for Reese to settle for that," Fisher added.

"No. Just ... no. Reese, listen to me. You won't regret the bad decisions you make now. You'll only regret the missed opportunities to make mistakes and *live*. You don't need a good guy to give you a home and needy kids. You need a string of bad guys to give you experience. You'll never know what you do want in life until you experience everything you don't want in life."

"Said no mother ever." Fisher shook his head.

"Mothers are hardwired to protect their offspring. If you want advice on canning or ironing, ask your mom. If you want advice on being a woman ... a free-spirited woman ... then don't ever ask your mom. Well ..." Hailey tapped her chin with her finger. "Come to think of it, you could probably ask Rory. She's cooler than most moms."

I glance up at her. "Why do you say that?"

"Just because."

Fisher cleared his throat. "Clock out, Hailey. Have a good night."

"Are you dismissing me? I feel dismissed. Are you shooing me out of here so you can give Reese some lame advice on dating because Rory's made you feel protective of her?"

"Yes. Leave so I can give her some lame advice." Fisher closed the folder and tossed it onto the desk next to my piles of papers.

"Don't listen to him, Reese. Call me later." Hailey hiked her purse onto her shoulder.

I nodded, giving her a tight grin.

After the door closed behind her, Fisher used his leg to swivel the desk chair so I was facing him. "Who are you dating?"

"No one." I gave him two full seconds of my gaze before averting it to the side.

"So why are you talking to Hailey about it?"

"None of your business."

"Am I the guy?"

"There is no guy."

"Yet, you're talking to Hailey about a guy."

"Oh my gosh!" I skittered to my feet to wheel the chair backward a good six feet, hitting the front of Hailey's desk. "I wasn't asking her about dating. I was asking her about sex. There. Are you happy?"

"Why not ask me about it?"

With an incredulous laugh, I shook my head. "Sorry. What was I thinking? I'm sure you're experienced with how it feels to have a penis in your vagina. Does it hurt the first time?"

Fisher excelled at masking his reactions to things, but I had him. I didn't miss his Adam's apple bobbing with a hard swallow. He didn't see that question coming. A month earlier, he didn't see *me* coming.

"I'm not talking—"

"Full. Of. Yourself!" I cut him off, shooting straight up from the chair and planting my fists onto my hips. "You are so full of yourself. What makes you think I'm talking about you? We're over. Remember? And you didn't want my virginity. It was too inconvenient for you. So stop assuming you're some bright star that I orbit."

He narrowed his eyes. "What are you so angry about?"

HIM!

Life.

My dad dying.

My mom missing out on my high school years.

Church school.

The cloak of guilt I wore because of church.

God.

Yeah, I was angry at God too because I didn't understand what kind of god would give me so many emotions, desires, and uncontrolled feelings, then tell me I had to suppress them until I was married.

What if I didn't want to get married yet? Did "good" Christians get married just to remove the sin from sex?

There wasn't anything Fisher could say to make me feel less agitated. His silence showed his maturity and understanding of that, yet it also infuriated me. I wanted him to at least *try* to make a case for himself.

"Why me? And I don't mean it like I have no sense of self-esteem. It's not that. I'm not ugly. I'm not stupid. I'm fun. I have a decent list of quality traits. But you're not ugly either. Or stupid. And you can be fun. But you're also ten years older than me. With *so* many options. I just don't get it. Was I a game? A toy? Were you bored? I know I've asked you this before, but I just don't get it. Why engage with an eighteen-year-old who has no solid direction in her life yet, can't drink legally, and who's a virgin. I just don't get it."

He let my words settle, dissipate, and vanish, replaced with silence. "What did you like about the mountains?"

I shrugged. "What didn't I like? The air. The tranquility. The vastness. Just ... I don't know. When we stopped at that overlook, I just liked how I felt. There. In the moment. It's hard to describe."

"Because you can't."

"Maybe." I tried to think of the right words, but they fell short.

"Well, neither can I."

"It ..." I shook my head. "It still doesn't make sense."

"To whom? How you feel about ... everything— people, places, things, events, good times, tragedies, the past, the future—it only has to make sense to you. In this life, we don't owe anyone anything. No explanation. Feelings are the most personal part of who we are. You're not accountable for your feelings any more than you're accountable for the amount of oxygen you consume. Think for yourself. And don't ever let anyone tell you how to feel."

I frowned. "I think you tried to make me feel bad when I told you I was taught that homosexuality was wrong."

"Well, if you think I was trying to tell you how to feel, then fuck me. But I don't believe our thoughts are always in-line with our feelings. And sometimes we think what we believe we're supposed to think, despite our feelings. When your feelings align with your thoughts, then you're thinking for your fucking self. So if you feel it's wrong to love someone who is of the same sex, then don't let anybody tell you your *feelings* are wrong. But show the rest of the world the same courtesy, and don't tell anyone else how they should feel."

I nodded a few times. He was right. Professor Fisher teaching more life lessons. I didn't know how to distinguish between my feelings and my thoughts. How much of me was authentic and how much of me was manufactured through sermons and lectures?

"How do you feel about me, Fisher?"

With a neutral expression, he lifted his shoulder into a slow-motion shrug. "It's none of your business."

And just that magically, I wasn't angry. Not at Fisher, or my parents, or God. All that seemed to matter was Fisher Mann *did* have feelings for me. My business or not. He felt things for me.

"I'm leaving." I stood and grabbed my backpack.

He nodded twice. "I'm watching you leave."

When I reached the door, I turned my head, restraining my grin for a few seconds. "But is it as good as watching me come?"

Fisher smiled like blowing up a balloon, one centimeter at a time. "Speechless."

CHAPTER NINETEEN

"Hey! Oh my gosh. I wasn't expecting you today." I knew something was up when the basement door wasn't locked.

Rory glanced up from the kitchen counter where her hands furiously chopped vegetables. "Surprise. I got an earlier flight. And since I wanted it to be a true surprise, I grabbed an Uber home. I didn't even tell Fisher I was coming home today ... until about five minutes ago. I just texted him. I'm making dinner for the three of us."

The three of us.

Lovely.

"He said you had just left the office. So ... sit." She nodded toward the barstool. "Tell me everything. I want to know everything you've been up to while I've been in California." With a knife in one hand she used her other arm to give me a side hug and kiss on my head.

She didn't want to know what I'd been up to.

"Just working." I climbed onto the stool and rested my crossed arms on the counter. "I work in the office with Hailey some days and other days I go to job sites with Fisher. Church on Sundays. Evening walks. Crossword puzzles."

"Crossword puzzles? You like them?"

I nodded.

"Your dad did too."

"I know. That's why I construct them."

Her eyes widened. "You're constructing them?"

Another nod.

"Oh, Reese ... your dad would be so proud."

"I think so too. It makes me feel close to him."

"Well, you'll have to let me see them. I used to try to solve your dad's, but I was terrible at it."

"How was California?"

"Amazing. More than amazing! I feel all energized with fun new skills and techniques to use on clients. I go back to work tomorrow. I was thinking we need to get you a car."

"Yeah, I was thinking that too. Fisher gives me a ride some days, but other days, like today, I drive into the office by myself."

"I can ask my parents—your grandparents—for some help to get you a car."

"I can afford a car."

Rory gave me a fake smile of recognition. "Of course. Your dad left you money."

"Yeah. I was going to look for one right away, but

then you left, and I had your car to drive, so there wasn't the urgency. I should go look for one tomorrow. I'll ask Fisher for—"

"Ask Fisher for what?" Fisher said, coming down the stairs.

"Hey, there's my handsome guy." Rory dropped her knife, wiped her hands, and hugged Fisher.

I wondered why she wasn't interested in him. Clearly, she liked him. Maybe the age thing bothered her more than it bothered me.

Fisher sat right next to me. He could have chosen a different stool or even scooted that stool over a few inches, but he didn't. "What do you need to ask me?" He rested his arms on the counter and nudged my elbow. It was so ... weird.

Dare I say it was *brotherly?*

"I need to buy a car."

"And you need to borrow money? How much do you need?"

I shook my head. "No. I have money. I need time off tomorrow to go get a car."

"You taking her?" He glanced up at Rory.

"Not tomorrow. I have to work. I can see about getting off early on Saturday and taking her."

"Why does anyone have to take me? I'll get an Uber and drive my new car home."

Fisher's eyebrows slid up an inch.

"She has money from her dad. She's going to pay cash for it."

He nodded slowly. "What car are you getting?"

"I don't know."

"I'll go with you," he said.

"I don't need you to go with me."

"Oh ..." Rory wiped her hands again and picked up her phone. "I have to get this it's ... a friend. I'll be right back."

I squinted at her odd behavior while she hustled to her bedroom and shut the door.

"I realize this is going to piss you off, but it's just life right now. If you take me with you, you'll get a better deal on a car because there will be a *male adult* negotiating for you."

"That's—"

"Sexist? Not fair? Ridiculous? Yes. Yes, it is. But it doesn't make it less true."

"You have work."

He grabbed my stool and turned me to face him, my knees tucked between his spread legs. "I know the boss. I can get the morning off." He rested his hands on my legs.

I made a quick glance at the closed bedroom door.

"She'll be in there for a while."

I turned back toward Fisher. "How do you know?"

"Because she's talking to Rose."

"Who's Rose?"

"Her friend."

"Were they in prison together?"

Fisher inched his head side to side.

"Oh. Do they work together?"

"Rose is a teacher. She teaches middle school art."

I nodded, twisting my lips. "She's probably a client."

"Yeah, Rory does her hair."

"Once a social butterfly, always a social butterfly. I'm more introverted like my dad." When I allowed myself to look at Fisher for more than two seconds, I realized he was looking at me. It was that more than friends look.

"I wonder how long it will take before I no longer want to kiss you."

Again, I checked her bedroom door while pressing my lips together. "Y-you want to kiss me?"

He grinned while squeezing my legs. "Desperately."

I don't know why I thought Fisher had everything on a switch, including his emotions or his attraction to me, but I did. I thought it. I relied on it.

"We're done. Right?" I punctuated the *right* with serious doubt like I really needed him to answer me because I wasn't sure where any of this was coming from.

"I think that was the agreement."

That wasn't an answer. He threw it back on me. I was the one who first said things would have to end when Rory came home. I said I didn't want her to know about us, but he agreed.

He. Agreed!

"Yeah. It was the *mutual* agreement." I rested my hands on his hands to slide them off my legs, but when my skin touched his, it wasn't that easy.

"How's that leak in the back room?" he asked.

"I don't know. Should we check?"

Fisher grinned and slid off his stool. I followed him to the back room.

Door closed.

His hands in my hair.

My hands up the back of his shirt, fingers digging into his skin.

Our mouths colliding.

Tongues exploring.

My hum mixed with his hum, vibrating our lips.

We didn't have an official last kiss, so who could blame us for needing to officially end things ... with a mind-numbing kiss.

"Reese? Fisher?"

We jumped apart, breathless and a little disheveled.

"Where'd you guys go?"

Fisher ran a hand through his hair, even though it wasn't *his* hair that got manhandled and tangled.

I wiped my mouth and combed my fingers through my hair as he grinned and shot me a quick wink before opening the door.

Fisher and his winks.

"Back here. Reese thought she'd been hearing some dripping noise in the back room, but I think it's just condensation from the furnace."

"Oh. Yeah, probably." Rory lifted the cutting board full of cut veggies and dumped it into a wok.

"Who's Rose?" I asked. "Fisher said you have a

friend who's an art teacher. How did you meet her?" I hopped back onto the chair as he walked behind me to join my mom in the kitchen, but not before letting his fingers tease the skin on my lower back where my shirt had slid up just above the waistband of my jeans.

I jerked, but Rory didn't seem to notice.

"Rose. Um ..." Rory shot Fisher a funny look. Did she see him touch me? "I've actually known her for many years. She was a client of mine when I owned my salon in Nebraska."

"Wow. Really? That's cool. And now she lives here too and is seeing you again?"

Pressing her lips together, she nodded. "Mmm-hmm."

"Nice."

"Very nice." Fisher stole a sliced carrot from the wok, and Rory smacked his hand.

"How have the two of you been getting along?" she asked.

I cut my gaze straight to Fisher, but he didn't give a single glance in my direction. No. He was too cool to act guilty in the slightest way.

"Fine. She's a bit of a handful at work. We've made a trip to urgent care for a nail in her hand as a result of her clumsiness, and she got it in her head that Happy Meals were a good idea for my crew, but other than that ... it's been pretty uneventful."

It took me a minute to unpack his insane summary of our time together.

"You went to urgent care? Why didn't you tell me?"

I shrugged. "It was no big deal. No stitches."

Rory blinked several times and nodded. Then, she smiled. "Happy Meals?"

I rolled my eyes. "It's no big deal."

"It's a gigantic deal." Fisher ruffled my hair.

Ruffled my hair!

Like I was five. What the heck?

"Your daughter carried on your collection while you were in prison. How sweet is that?" He climbed onto the stool next to me.

I ignored him.

"Really? Oh, Reese ..." Tears filled her eyes.

"It's no big deal. And I'm sure I missed plenty of items. It's like making a few crossword puzzles after Dad died."

"A few?" Fisher opened his big, dumb mouth. "More like an entire book full of them."

With a tight smile, I shot him an evil glare.

Rory added a bunch of seasonings to the wok filled with veggies and chicken. "You are the sweetest girl."

I didn't respond with more than a small grin.

"Have you met anyone at church? Any nice boys?"

Fisher rested his elbow on the counter and his head in his hand, staring at the side of my face like he was waiting anxiously for my response—taking his "extraness" to a whole new level.

"I did, actually. His name is Brendon. He's twenty-four, and he just graduated from law school. We had lunch and played pool here. We're planning on doing something again this Sunday." I narrowed my eyes and shot Fisher another glare—a "take that, you obnoxious jerk!"

He focused solely on my lips while wetting his.

Why did he always one-up me?

"Sweetheart, I'm so happy for you. Sounds like quite the catch. A lawyer."

"He *is* quite the catch." I kicked Fisher in the shin because he was mocking me with his overtly enthusiastic gestures while I talked to Rory.

"He's not the best pool player," Fisher said, pinching the hell out of my leg just above my knee.

I had to bite my lower lip to keep from yelping. "You never saw him play," I said through gritted teeth.

"I saw him holding the pool stick. Total amateur."

All I could think was ... "Who are you?"

Really, Fisher was so *so* much extra. Was he jealous? Or was he just trying to pester me, poke the bear? Treat me like a child?

"I knew it." Rory shook her head while stirring dinner. "I knew you two would end up acting like brother and sister."

My stomach turned.

Fisher? He seemed amused.

Gross.

"Let's eat out on the screened-in porch." She spooned stir fry onto three plates and slid two toward us. "Grab whatever you want to drink. Fisher, if you want beer, you'll have to get your own. I didn't get any before I left since Reese won't drink it ..." She walked by me and bopped my nose. "Because she's not twenty-one, and I know she's not a drinker."

She stepped out onto the screened-in porch, and I followed her with Fisher right behind me.

"You sure have her fooled. You drink and give a killer hand job. But we'll keep that between us."

I whipped around, nearly sending my dinner flying off my plate. "I didn't give you a hand job," I whispered.

"Oh, Reese ... you're just adorable. Really."

I narrowed my eyes and growled, taking a page from his playbook.

Fisher glanced over my shoulder, probably seeing if Rory was watching us. "If you growl at me, I'll bite your ass again ..." His gaze cut to me. "And you'll like it."

"I will *not* like it." I turned back around.

Fisher's face landed right next to my ear. "You will if I tie you up first."

My back came to attention as I choked on a little saliva.

What the heck? Tie me up? Who does that?

"What are you two talking about?" Rory eyed us suspiciously as we stepped out onto the porch.

"Just sibling stuff." Fisher grinned while taking a seat.

I chose the chair in the opposite corner of the porch as Fisher sat on the sectional.

"Rose wants to go to a jazz club Friday. Why don't

261

you come, Fisher? She's bringing another friend. A single friend who happens to be an interior designer. Rose thinks she's a good match for you. What do you say?"

"I like jazz," I said.

Rory frowned. "Oh, sorry, sweetheart. You have to be twenty-one to get into the club."

I focused on my plate of food, stirring it with my fork, waiting for it to cool down ... waiting for *me* to cool down.

"Sounds fun. Count me in."

My head snapped up, shooting my gaze right to Fisher. He chewed slowly, giving me a challenging look.

For the rest of dinner, I stay quiet, letting Fisher and Rory catch up.

"I'm going to my room to read before I go to bed. Thanks for dinner." I headed toward the door.

"Okay. Sweet dreams, love," Rory said.

"Don't let the bed bugs *bite*." Fisher leaned back on the sectional, stretching both arms across the back.

I wanted to kill him. He excelled at bringing out the worst in me. Why did I find him the least bit attractive?

CHAPTER TWENTY

THE NEXT MORNING, Rory had coffee and breakfast made for me by the time I dressed, pulled my hair into a ponytail, and brushed my teeth.

"You're up early," I said.

"I'm a morning person. I didn't used to be, but that changed."

In prison.

I nodded. "Thanks." I took a few sips of coffee and grabbed one of the muffins she made. "Gotta go. I'm sure he's already waiting for me." Slinging my backpack over my shoulder, I smiled.

"Have a good day. I'll be home from work around four. If you want, we can grab dinner."

"We'll see. We're supposed to look for a car for me today. So who knows how my day will go?"

"Okay. Bye, sweetheart."

"Bye."

Sure enough, Fisher was in the truck by the time I made it to the driveway.

"Morning." He grinned when I opened the door.

I stared at my muffin as I tried to maneuver my bag into the back without squishing the muffin.

"Here." Fisher leaned over and took the muffin to hold it for me.

I thought about saying "thanks," but then I remembered I was mad at him for his behavior the previous night.

Tossing my bag in the back, I climbed into the seat and fastened my seat belt.

"Hey!" My mouth fell open as I gasped.

Fisher had eaten half of my muffin.

"You jerk! That was my muffin!" I grabbed his wrist with one hand while trying to pry the rest of the muffin from his grip with my other hand. By the time he softened his grip, the muffin looked like a squished ball of dough.

"Oops ..." he stared at the ball in his hand.

"You dumb fucker!" The second that left my mouth, an audible *whoosh* of air filled my lungs a split second before my cupped hand covered my mouth.

Fisher's eyes doubled in size as he eased his head to the side like a dog.

I turned away and crossed my arms over my chest. "Just drive."

Fisher hopped out of the truck. I didn't care where he was going. I officially didn't care about him at all. A few minutes later, he returned with another muffin.

"Are we good now?"

I stared at the muffin in his hand. "What did you tell Rory?" I took the muffin and held it because I was no longer hungry.

Fisher put the truck into *Drive* and pulled out of the driveway. "I told her I took a bite of your muffin. You had a hissy fit and called me a dumb fucker."

"You what?" I whipped my head back toward him.

"Don't worry. She didn't believe me. You have her fooled. You have everyone fooled. Except me. I know you. And you are not the innocent little Christian you pretend to be."

"Well, you're not the nice guy everyone thinks you are."

Fisher shot me a sour expression. "Oh, I'm absolutely the nice guy everyone thinks I am. I've been looking out for your immature ass for weeks."

I scoffed. "You've been *looking* at my butt for weeks, not looking out for it."

"You must think you have a great ass. What if you're the only one?"

I started to scoff again, but I caught myself. Nope. I wasn't going to let him drag me down to his level of cruelty. Once again, he proved how much of a terrible influence he was on me.

My inclination to do what was right.

And my desire to be a kind person.

Fisher granted me some silence, but only for ten minutes. Then he pulled into a car dealership.

"How much are you planning on spending?"

Ugh ...

I'd planned on giving him the silent treatment for the better part of the day, but he had to make car shopping our first stop of the day.

"I don't know. I should probably check with my grandparents. They'll have to release the money to my account."

"Well, it would have been smart of you to do that before suggesting we go car shopping."

I frowned. "I thought it would be smart to know what car I wanted before going to them. They're going to ask me about the car and how much money I need."

"Okey dokey." He pulled into an empty parking space and hopped out of the truck.

I climbed out just as he rounded the front of the truck and held open the door before shutting it behind me and locking it.

He turned, sauntering toward the lot of cars. I leaned my back against the truck door, resting one foot on the running board. A few seconds later, he glanced a foot behind him only to realize I wasn't there. Then his gaze lifted to me.

Turning, he visibly blew out a long breath.

Yes, Fisher ... I don't always wear socks, and I reserve the right to be upset with you even if you are taking me car shopping.

I maintained my emotionless expression, giving nothing away, yet demanding everything.

His booted feet planted right in front of me as he

rested one hand on a hip and tipped his chin toward his chest.

Another sigh.

"Apologize," I said.

Ever so slowly, he lifted his gaze to me, a tiny grin quirking one side of his mouth. "For?"

"Exactly. I'm glad we agree that you have *so* much to apologize for."

"The muffin?"

I nodded.

"I got you a new one."

"But you didn't apologize."

"Actions speak louder than words. I. Got. You. A. New. One."

"And last night? Your obnoxiousness? You agreeing to go on a date like ... ten minutes after sticking your tongue down my throat? Making unnecessary jabs at Brendon, whom you've met once, for two seconds. What about that?"

Twisting his lips to the side, he narrowed his eyes. "Do you want a verbal apology? Or do you want a physical one?"

I wasn't sure where he was going with that offering? A physical one?

"I'm not giving you both. So ... choose carefully."

"Define physical."

"It's something I do, instead of something I say."

"What would you do?"

"I'm not telling you. Just choose."

It was so ridiculous. Why couldn't he simply say

sorry and go on with the day? And why couldn't I just choose the verbal apology? Why was I so curious about his physical gesture?

"Am I a toy to you?"

Fisher's gaze slid down my body and inched its way back up to my face. That answered my question.

"Are you asking if I enjoy playing with you?"

"Are you going to sleep with your Friday night date?"

"And by sleep, you mean?"

"Fisher ..."

"Are you going to sleep with your Sunday afternoon date?" He lifted one eyebrow.

"You know that answer."

Fisher nodded slowly. "I do. But is it because of Jesus or because you gave me a hand job?"

"Are you going to sleep with your date because you have no moral code or because my hand job wasn't good enough?"

Satisfaction lit up his entire face. "So you *do* admit it was a hand job."

"Fisher ..."

"Let's find you a car so we can get to work." He turned ninety degrees and retraced his original path toward the lot of cars.

I followed with my heart dragging behind me, getting bruised and scraped by the harsh road that was Fisher Mann.

"Hey, looking for anything specific?" the salesman asked.

"Something reliable with good gas mileage," Fisher spoke for me.

"Something fast," I said with a serious face.

The salesman gave me a dismissive "hehe" laugh.

"I have a Honda Accord over here. One owner. Sixty-five thousand miles. Good gas mileage. Reliable."

"I'm thinking about an SUV because I'll be making a lot of trips into the mountains."

Again, the salesman gave me a look like I wasn't the one purchasing the vehicle. "Subaru Outback?"

"Sounds good. Let's see it," Fisher said.

I shook my head. "My mom has one. I don't want the same car."

"It's a good car. You can take it into the mountains." Fisher tried to make a case for the Outback.

"I see you have a Porsche Cayenne at the front of the lot."

Both men looked at me like I was crazy.

"Um ... we do. It has close to forty-thousand miles on it, and it's fifty-five thousand, but we could probably get you into it for a little less."

"She's not looking for a fifty-thousand-dollar vehicle," Fisher said, walking down the row with the boring Outbacks and Accords.

"*She* is looking for whatever *she* wants." I crossed my arms over my chest and followed him.

"We'll test drive this one," Fisher nodded toward a Subaru.

"I don't want an Outback."

"It's a Forester." He peered inside the window before reading the specifics on the sticker.

"I'll grab the keys," the salesman said.

"I needed a ride, not a parent. A ride, not a bully. What is your deal? This is my purchase. My decision."

He took a break from the sticker to look at me. "Should we call Rory?"

"No." I tipped up my chin.

"Then we're test driving the Forester."

"Fine. But I'm not buying it."

He eyed the salesman getting closer behind me. "We're not buying anything today, just test driving."

"*We're* not buying anything ever. *I'm* buying it."

"I'll just need to see your driver's license, miss."

I turned and huffed as I dug it out of my wallet.

"You can head north. It's a nice three-mile loop."

I took the key without acknowledging his suggestion or Fisher's satisfied smile.

I wasn't buying it.

And I wasn't coming back with Fisher when I did decide to buy a car. Maybe Brendon would come with me. I felt fairly certain an attorney could negotiate a car deal for me just as if not better than Fisher.

"Left," Fisher said as I pulled to a stop at the lot entrance.

"Shut up."

I didn't give him my full attention, but I also didn't miss his smirk, how much he enjoyed me in my most unruly state.

We drove a mile up the road.

"It's a nice vehicle."

I ignored him.

Another mile.

"You could fit four friends and some camping gear in the back. If you have four friends."

I swerved across three lanes of traffic to an exit.

"Jesus Christ!" He grabbed the dash. "What in the hell are you doing? Trying to get us killed?"

I pulled into the empty parking lot of an elementary school. "Would you just shut up?" I punched the button to my seat belt and climbed out of the vehicle, marching with no purpose other than to get away from him.

Landing at the playground, I planted my butt on a swing, gripped the chains, and hung my head to take a timeout ... a few long breaths to regain my composure.

Fisher's work boots made it into my line of sight, but I wasn't ready to look at him or talk to him or ... acknowledge his existence on the planet.

As I said a silent prayer for him to not say anything, God answered it.

Fisher walked behind me and grabbed the chains close to the seat, pulling me backward and giving me a gentle push forward.

He did it again and again, until I was so high I felt like the younger version of myself taking a deep breath and staring at the blue sky, imagining what it would be like to touch it.

After ... I didn't know. Five minutes? Ten minutes? He stopped pushing me and waited for me to come to a complete stop without forcing it with my feet or anything else. It was hard to explain how that moment touched me. It was stupid, really, but I had never felt so much patience given to me from another human as I felt as Fisher waited for me to come to a complete stop.

Feet dangling in virtual stillness.

The mulch crunched beneath his boots as he appeared in front of me again. Kneeling in the dirty mulch, he slid his arms around my waist and rested his head on my lap.

My poor teenaged adult heart. It didn't care if Fisher was good for me. It didn't care about anything other than the way he made me feel in that moment. I released the chain with my right hand and threaded my fingers through his hair.

"I'm trying so hard..." I whispered, my voice shaky in my chest and wobbly as the words fell from my lips "...trying *so* hard not to fall in love with you."

A few breaths later, he whispered back, "I know."

I didn't know what that meant. He knew I was falling in love with him? Or he, too, was trying to keep from loving me?

It didn't matter, not at that moment. All that mattered was he knew *me*.

Fisher released my waist and sat back on his heels, resting his hands on the top of my work boots dangling in front of him. "What do you want?" He gave me his eyes and a world of sincerity in them.

It shook me.

Maybe because I had never experienced real love in the romantic sense.

Maybe because I was scared.

Maybe because I didn't really know what I wanted.

"The Porsche Cayenne," I said, giving him the tiniest of smiles because I knew what he meant, but I wasn't emotionally ready to answer that question.

Him.

I wanted him, but I had no idea what that really looked like. Me, an eighteen-year-old teenaged adult with no real direction, and him, a twenty-eight-year-old adult with his own house, his own business, and many people relying on him.

We couldn't have been at more different places in our lives, yet ... we somehow found each other. And there was something there.

Something undeniable.

Something real.

Something I wasn't ready for, but I sure didn't want to let it go.

With a painful flash of amusement, he returned the hint of a grin and nodded while standing and holding out his hand to me. "Can you afford the Cayenne?"

I nodded.

"Then get the Cayenne."

Resting my hand in his, I hopped off the swing. He interlaced our fingers and led me back to the Forester. We returned the keys and got in his truck to go to work.

Fifty grand. That's what I needed to ask my grandparents to give me because I wanted the Cayenne because it was sexy and fun—just like the naked fisherman.

He dropped me off at the office. And later that day, he asked Hailey to give me a ride home since he had to play catch up from taking me car shopping.

"Good timing," Rory said, getting out of her Outback right as I climbed out of Hailey's truck. "Hey, Hailey. Long time no see. How are you?"

"Good, Rory," Hailey said with her window down. "How was California?"

"Good, but I'm sure glad to be back here. Thanks for giving Reese a ride home."

"No problem. Talk to you later." She rolled up her window and backed out of the driveway as I gave her a wave.

"Where's Fisher?" Rory asked as we walked around to the back of the house.

"Still working. He took me car shopping this morning, so I think that put him a little behind today."

"Oh, that's right. Did you find anything?"

I shrugged. "I suppose. I just need to talk to Grandma and Grandpa since they have to approve all large purchases and transfer the money to my account."

She opened the door. "So what did you find? I love my Outback. Did you look at Subarus?"

"Um ... yeah, we actually test drove a Forester."

"Nice. Was it in your price range?"

"Yeah, but I saw another small SUV that I liked

too. We didn't test drive it today, but I might another day."

"That's good. You don't want to make a rash decision. It's your first big purchase."

"I know." I unlaced my boots, slipped them off, and tossed my backpack onto my bed. "I'm going to grab a quick shower."

"Okay. I'll start dinner," Rory called.

CHAPTER TWENTY-ONE

I DIDN'T SEE Fisher again until Friday afternoon. He was buried in work, so Rory took me to the office in the morning and Hailey dropped me off after work.

Fisher texted me later that day.

I'll give you a ride home. See you in twenty.

"Fisher's picking me up," I said to Hailey as I sat at Fisher's desk, going through receipts submitted by subcontractors.

"Then, I am out of here. Tell Bossman I had to run to the post office before it closed."

Eyeing her, I grinned. "You don't have to run to the post office, do you?"

She winked. "I have a date. And I'd love a pedicure."

"Have fun."

"Oh, I will. Bye." She floated out the door with a big grin.

Hailey deserved to grin. She had a date. Fisher had a date. Rory didn't have a date, but she had a friend to hang out with on a Friday night. I had my tumultuous thoughts and crossword puzzles to build.

Just as I finished paper-clipping the last of the receipts, Fisher came through the door. His beard was a little scruffier than usual. His jeans a little dirtier. And he wore a baseball cap that looked pretty used and soiled as well.

"Hey," he said, flipping through the pile of notes for him from Hailey on the corner of his desk.

"Hey." I piled everything neatly in the bottom drawer of the filing cabinet then stood and hiked my bag onto my shoulder. "I was surprised you messaged me. Hailey could have given me a ride home."

"I had to knock off early anyway. Rory wants to leave by six."

Eyes wide, I bit my tongue and nodded several times.

"What are you doing tonight?" He filled a coffee mug with water from the cooler.

Missing you. Soothing my aching heart. Hating Rory for inviting you.

"I'm not sure yet. I'm sure I'll find something age appropriate to do."

Fisher finished gulping the water and set the mug on his desk. "I remember being your age and feeling like I wasn't old enough to do anything fun."

"I have plenty of fun things to do." I walked to the door.

"I'm going for Rory. It would seem very odd to her if I didn't go. Before you moved here, I went out to clubs with them a lot."

"Well, you're going. I don't need to hear your reasoning." I sulked to his truck and climbed into the passenger's seat.

On the way home, I didn't say anything. What could I say? Fisher didn't speak either, but he took every chance to give me a quick glance like I was going to give away something in my demeanor or meet his gaze and talk. I had nothing to say about his big date night.

"Whose car is that?" I asked when we pulled into the driveway. But I quickly figured it out.

"Rose's," Fisher said.

On his porch, sat three women. Rory and who I assumed was Rose and Fisher's date. They were all in dresses. All laughing. And all sipping wine like non-teenaged adults.

"Well, I hope there's a DD tonight." I pulled hard on the door handle and hopped out of the truck before he put it in *Park,* slamming it shut with a little extra attitude.

"Sweetie, come meet my friends," Rory called.

I didn't want to meet her friends. Well, I didn't mind meeting Rose, but the interior designer could have sucked my proverbial cock. As soon as those words floated through my mind, I made the decision that I would spend the night in prayer and scripture because I didn't want to be the person thinking someone could suck my proverbial cock. Yet ... that was my situation, and I hated it.

"Hi." I plastered on a fake smile.

"Reese, this is Rose and Rose's friend, Tiffany."

"So nice to see you again," Rose said. "We actually met when you were much younger. Your mom had you at the salon in Nebraska one day when I came in for my appointment. But ... you had a long summer's worth of freckles on your face and pigtails. You've grown into a beautiful young woman."

Fisher stood just inches behind me; I could feel his nearness as Rose made sure we all were reminded of my age. Pigtails and freckles.

Fantastic.

"Thanks." I forced my manners instead of acting like a disgruntled, pouty child who didn't get to go out with the adults on a Friday night.

"Fisher, this is Tiffany. Tiff, this is Fisher." Rose made the introduction, and I stepped aside so I wasn't blocking them from their big introduction.

"Hi, nice to meet you." Fisher nodded and smiled. "I didn't expect everyone to be here so early. I need to grab a quick shower."

"Take your time," Rory said. "We have more wine." She laughed and so did Rose and Tiffany.

Me? Not so much.

As soon as Fisher disappeared into the house, Tiffany's jaw hit the ground. "Oh. My. God ..." She fanned herself. "You weren't kidding. He's just ... smokin'. I should have waxed everything, not just my legs."

The ladies giggled.

Again, I didn't share in their amusement. I definitely wasn't going to laugh about Tiffany's bold assumption that Fisher would see some unshaved part of her body.

Gah ... I hope he doesn't.

Feeling sufficiently nauseous, I excused myself. "I'm going to head downstairs and grab a shower too. Have a fun time."

"I hope you have plans, sweetie. I feel bad leaving you if you don't, but you're just not old enough to get into the club."

Rose and Tiffany gave me sad expressions.

My fake smile jumped to the rescue. "Yeah, I might meet up with some friends from church."

"Okay. Be safe. I'll see you tomorrow. If we're going to be too late, I might just crash at Rose's house. So I don't want you to worry if you don't see me until morning."

Rory crashing with Rose.

Tiffany offering her unshaved parts to Fisher.

Just wonderful. I could not have been more excited for the real adults.

"Sounds good. Goodnight."

I lugged my bag around the house to the basement. As soon as I removed my boots, I ran up the stairs and pressed my ear to the door. When I didn't hear anything, I opened it slowly and peeked into the kitchen. When I didn't see anyone, I slid around the corner and padded down the hallway to the closed master bedroom door. Pressing my ear to it, I listened for Fisher, but I heard nothing. Again, I slowly opened the door. The lights were on in his bathroom, so I stepped inside his bedroom and quietly closed the door behind me.

My bare feet made a silent trek to his bathroom, where I peeked around a third door.

"You don't know how to knock, do you?" Fisher looked at me in his mirror as he stood in front of his sink, ruffling his wet hair, wearing nothing but a bath towel around his waist.

"They're drunk. I hope you're driving." I peeled my gaze away from his reflection and moseyed into his walk-in closet.

"I'm sure I am." He appeared in the doorway to his closet as I browsed around at his hanging clothes, mostly button-down shirts. He must have kept his work shirts in one of the drawers by my feet.

"Tiffany's pretty excited. She thinks you're 'smokin' and she regrets not waxing *everything*."

"Is that so?"

I turned toward Fisher; his shoulder leaned against the door frame and his arms crossed over his bare chest. Of course, Tiffany was planning on *all* things with Fisher. How could any sane, single woman not think like that?

"Yes. That's so."

"Is that why you're in my room? In my closet? To tell me about Tiffany's grooming habits?"

I nibbled the inside of my cheek while running my hand down one of his long-sleeved button-downs. "Pretty much."

"Well, thanks for the heads-up. I'll keep that in mind tonight."

I made my way to him, but he didn't move to let me leave. He uncrossed his arms and took a step closer, so there were no more steps for either one of us to take.

My right hand lifted, feathering along his abs. They tightened even more under my touch.

The tips of my fingers met the top of his towel, pausing there as I lifted my gaze to his. His full lips parted, and the look in his eyes was pure sin.

"Don't have sex with her tonight." I couldn't keep my eyes from averting to the side and then to my feet. I had no right to ask him for that favor. After all, it wasn't like I was offering him anything.

"There's a lot we can do without having sex. You know this."

I wasn't sure what ached more, my fractured heart or my nauseous stomach. My brave fingers tugged at his towel. It fell to the floor. Fisher didn't flinch.

I had no clue what my plan was ... I officially had the naked fisherman in front of me.

Completely naked.

Cock erect.

Eyes hooded.

Tongue slowly swiping his lower lip when I forced my gaze from his cock to his face.

"What now?" He smirked.

I had *no* clue, but my jealous mind drifted to partially waxed Tiffany. She wanted my naked fisherman.

"She can't have you." I tried to infuse confidence into my words, but I think it fell a little short of the mark.

"No?" He canted his head to the side.

"No."

"What makes you so sure?"

I lowered to my knees, *way* out of my comfort zone. Way out of my own league of intimacy. And definitely scared out of my mind. I just … I wanted to be an adult with Fisher. I wanted to be a *woman* with him. And I didn't want some hairless hussy meeting his needs.

"Reese …" His voice held reservation. It was the first sign since I came into his room that he was dealing with his own emotions, his own expectations or maybe lack thereof.

My hands ghosted up his legs and gently took ahold of him.

"I don't expect this from you," he whispered.

From you …

He expected it from other women? Like Tiffany? Teagan? Angie?

As if dealing with God wasn't enough, I felt so much conflict because I had no clue what I was doing. Fisher became his own godlike man in my life. And I wanted to please him, nearly as much as God, who was surely frowning at my behavior ... at what I was about to do out of wedlock.

Before Fisher could talk me out of it, I wrapped my lips around the head.

He closed his eyes.

I continued doing things to him with my mouth that seemed to please him, despite my cluelessness, keeping my eyes on his face the whole time like a guide. That was how I knew what he liked.

What made him breathe heavier.

What made his teeth dig into his lower lip.

What made his hands grip the side of the doorway, knuckles white.

What made him rock his hips ever so slightly.

Dropping one hand, he gently threaded his fingers into my hair. His muscles tightened, even the ones in his face.

At the last second, he took a step back. Gripping his cock in his hand, he dropped to his knees and kissed me, keeping one hand in my hair while his other hand did something ...

I wasn't sure what until his tongue drove deep into my mouth and a loud moan vibrated from his chest and throat, his body making a few short jerking motions.

Then he relaxed, releasing my mouth. I glanced down.

Whoa ... okay ...

He finished ... the ...uh ... *job* on his bath towel.

"Fisher?" Rory called as three knocks tapped his bedroom door. "Are you coming?"

He grinned at me. It was so big and beautiful as he answered her. "Yes, I'm definitely coming."

My cheeks caught fire.

"Give me five more minutes, Rory."

I skittered to my feet and turned my back toward him, breathing heavily and wondering if she heard anything, if she knew I wasn't downstairs.

"I have five minutes," Fisher said just above a whisper as he pressed his naked body to my back and snaked a hand around my waist. His fingers dipped an inch into the front of my jeans.

"You should get dressed," I said in a nervous tone, stepping out of his hold and circling to get out of his closet while tugging on my shirt to fan the heat away from my skin.

He chuckled. "What should I wear?"

I ignored him as I splashed water on my face and pressed a hand towel to it, trying to slow my breathing, trying to not think about my mom and her friends in the other room.

Tiffany ... he was still going on a date with her. I bet she would do more than what I did to him, and she'd probably do it with way more confidence and experience. Fisher stood a few feet from me when I pulled the towel away from my face. He looked painfully sexy in his dark jeans, light blue button-down with the sleeves rolled up, and stark white sneakers.

He looked painfully sexy for someone else.

I was ready to puke.

"Why the face?"

I shook my head.

"Don't shake your head." He glanced at his watch. "I have three minutes left. What can I do to ease your anxiety?"

Don't go.

"I'm not anxious."

Lies ... lies ... lies ...

"Then are we going out there together? Are we letting everyone know that you like to watch me shower and dress?"

I needed a second round of cold water on my face. "I didn't watch you shower."

He smirked. "But you'd like it, wouldn't you?"

"You're a jerk."

Holding that smug expression for a beat, he nodded once. "Probably." Again, he glanced at his watch. "Two minutes. Are you sure there's nothing I can do?"

I rolled my eyes. "What are you going to do in two minutes?"

"Anything you want."

My voice didn't exist. It must have required more than eighteen years to find my voice. To unapologetically ask for what I wanted without fearing embarrassment or rejection.

I wanted him to not go.

I wanted him to stay with me.

I wanted him to touch me and *make it feel good.*

But I wanted him to do it without me having to ask.

"Time's up." He turned, making his way to the bedroom door with confident strides.

I balled my hands and clenched my teeth, fighting for one word, the smallest semblance of a voice.

Nothing.

He shut his door behind him and voices sounded from the other room. I squeezed my eyes shut and pressed my hands to my face, grumbling at myself for a few seconds before heading straight to the door and plastering my ear against it.

"Tiffany was the interior designer of the house you built in Golden last month," Rose said.

"Oh really?" Fisher seemed a little too enthused.

"I was. It's a beautiful home, Fisher. It's my dream to have you build something for me someday."

I rolled my eyes at Tiffany's gushing reply.

"In fact, I'd take this house right here," she continued.

Really? Could she have been any more obvious and needy? It was just ... gross.

"I'd love to see what you did with the house in Golden," Fisher said.

"Oh ... absolutely. I'll call the Jensens. They'd be totally cool with me showing it to you." She laughed. "But I'm sure they know you quite well. I suppose you could call them too. Maybe we can make a date of it sometime."

No. No. NO!

Peeling my ear from the door, I pressed both palms

to it and sank into a squat, my forehead gently pressed to it as I closed my eyes and prayed for God to erase the past month from it.

Take me back to Texas.

And never let me think of Fisher Mann again.

CHAPTER TWENTY-TWO

IT WAS ONE NIGHT. I should have stuffed my face and gone to sleep in a food coma. Instead, I skipped dinner and went for a run. Then I did an hour of yoga.

Shower.

Crossword puzzles.

Bible.

Prayer.

More prayer.

Ear to the upstairs door, listening for any sign of Fisher.

More prayer.

I went all in, asking for forgiveness for my thoughts and for putting Fisher's penis in my mouth. Did God get a lot of penis prayers? It seemed unlikely. Maybe guys with STDs praying for a quick recovery and promising to return to celibacy.

I didn't promise celibacy because technically, I was still celibate. Or so I told myself.

A little before one in the morning, I took my restless self to the screened-in porch, wearing a tee and white panties. Blanket in hand.

Reaching for the light switch, I accidentally hit another switch and strings of globe lights illuminated the porch. I didn't know they were there. How did I miss them?

It was ... enchanting.

I grinned. My first grin since Fisher left me for Tiffany and jazz music. Curling up in the corner of the patio sectional, I took a deep breath of the chilly night's air and closed my eyes. That was all it took for my mind to settle and sleep to find me.

At some point, my eyes fluttered open, a weird feeling that someone was there.

Fisher ...

He stood next to me, watching me sleep.

"What time is it?" I squinted my eyes.

"Two."

"Where's Rory?" I rubbed one eye.

"She stayed at Rose's place to sober up."

I nodded and yawned.

"Why are you sleeping out here?" he asked.

"Because I couldn't sleep inside."

"Why?" He toed off his shoes.

"I ..." I lifted a shoulder, feeling embarrassed about my terrible thoughts. "I don't know."

He sat at the end of the sofa, stretching his legs out, swallowing the entire length. "Come here," he whispered.

I gave his request a moment's pause before crawling toward him with my blanket. Settling my body between his legs and over his chest, I nuzzled my face into his neck.

He still smelled like pine and soap. And not *her*.

I so desperately wanted to ask him if he did anything with her. Held her hand. Kissed her. Promised her another date. But I didn't because I was enveloped in his arms in the middle of the night beneath the glow of several dozen globe lights, and it was pretty perfect.

A few minutes later, Fisher sat up partway, taking me with him, guiding my legs to straddle his midsection. He held the most contemplative expression on his face. I wanted to solve it like one of my puzzles, looking for clues in his eyes, the part of his lips, or his hand brushing the hair away from my face before caressing his knuckles down my neck.

I closed my eyes, reveling in the moment, in the way he made me feel like I was flying. Free of everything that kept me from finding myself, my voice, my place in the world.

When I opened my eyes, he feathered his other hand along my cheek, his thumb tracing my bottom lip. The night air was no comparison to the way Fisher's touch elicited an endless emergence of goose bumps along my skin.

"What are you doing?" I whispered.

His gaze followed the trail of his hand along my

skin for another breath or two before he gave me those intense eyes of his. "I'm apologizing."

From earlier that week ...

The car dealership. The park. His extreme *extra*.

Sorry meant nothing if that kind of touch was his way of apologizing. My soul felt it.

"Fisher?" I whispered.

He seemed mesmerized with my lips—his thumb ghosting along them, eyes drifting from mine to his thumb.

"Are you going to kiss me?"

The hint of a grin moved his mouth. "I was thinking about it."

My hand curled around his wrist, pulling his hand from my mouth as I leaned in a few inches and grinned while my lips brushed along his. "You think too much."

We kissed.

We let our hands explore each other's bodies.

We made out ... the first time I actually made out with a guy.

No sex.

No orgasms.

Just lots of kissing and touching.

Eventually, our hands stilled, our bodies entwined, and our lips eased apart as we fell asleep.

In the morning, I woke first, lifting my head from his chest. One of his hands rested on top of mine pressed to his chest next to my head. His other hand ... it was resting on my butt ... on the inside of my panties.

I wasn't sure when it laid claim to that spot, but I kinda liked it.

That was a lie.

I kinda loved it.

If I was going to Hell, I wanted to go there with Fisher's hands all over me, his lips on mine, and his dirty words in my ear.

"Good morning, Ed." Rory's voice sent me into major panic mode as she greeted the neighbor on her way around to the basement. To us!

"Oh my gosh!" I whisper yelled. "Get up!" I tugged on Fisher's arm.

He squinted, not entirely awake.

"Rory's coming! GET UP!" Had I whispered any louder, she would have heard me.

Fisher stumbled getting up. I pushed him with all my strength toward the door.

"Go! Hurry!"

"Christ, woman ... I'm going already." He walked like a drunk man with his shirt unbuttoned and hanging off one shoulder and his hair matted in back.

As soon as he made it to the stairs, I rushed back to the porch.

"Look who's up early," Rory said in a cheery voice as I grabbed the blanket and kicked Fisher's sneakers under the sofa.

"Yeah, I uh ... slept out here last night. When I discovered the lights, I couldn't resist."

She opened the door to the porch instead of going in through the main door. "Oh, yeah. I should have told you. I guess I figured you'd see them and look for the switch."

I wrapped the blanket around my shoulders. "So ... did you have fun?" I sat back down on the sofa while she took a seat in the rocker.

"We had a great time. When you're older, we'll have to go to all the clubs. There are some really great ones around here. If ..." Her nose wrinkled. She sometimes forgot that I spent the previous three years with my grandparents in a very conservative home and school. "If you're comfortable with it or you want to." Her pained expression softened into the mom I once knew, the face of unconditional love.

The face of absolute comfort. She was my safe place. I was never a daddy's girl, despite my interest in his job and his hobby. I idolized my mom, and I didn't think she ever really knew.

"I want you to be whoever you need to be to feel comfortable in your own skin. I want you to never feel the need to fit in or follow others if it's not who *you* are. Okay?"

Right there. That was my *mom*.

Pressing my lips together, I nodded slowly. And I almost, *almost* told her that my path had crossed with Fisher's path.

Collided.

Crashed.

And I wasn't sure I'd ever find my own way again because I loved him. More than that ... despite my battered and prodded ego ... I liked who I was with him, even if it made no sense. Even if I'd never tell him that.

Did love have to make sense?

"So the club was fun?"

She nodded. "Yes. One of our favorites was playing."

"And Tiffany and Fisher ... did they hit it off?"

"Yeah, I think so. They have a lot in common. They chatted it up during the breaks and at the bar we went to after the jazz club. She's definitely interested in him, but I haven't had the chance to talk to him yet. I'd like to see him find someone. I know he has the eternal heart of a bachelor, but Fisher deserves more."

I wanted to be that more.

CHAPTER TWENTY-THREE

I DIDN'T SEE Fisher the rest of Saturday because Rory took me shopping, then we had lunch. We ended the day at her salon where she gave me a haircut, even though it was her day off, and we both got manicures and pedicures.

It was a good day, one that started with me in Fisher's arms and his hand on my butt.

Sunday morning, I showered and slipped on a striped romper and my Birkenstocks for church.

"Coffee?" Rory asked from her corner of the sofa, robe on, hair pulled into a low ponytail.

"I'm good. They have coffee and a buffet of baked goods at church. You know, you could go with me."

"Mmm …" She wrinkled her nose. "I'm not sure I'm church material anymore."

I giggled, slipping a few items into my smaller purse. "I don't think there's such a thing as church material. All are welcomed in the Lord's house."

"When I think of the Lord's house, I think of Heaven, not a lackluster building with a gymnasium, fitness center, coffee and donuts. Really ... they used to build churches—cathedrals—to make you feel like God himself resided in the building, his spirit woven around the intricate wooden carvings, flying buttresses, and stunning stained glass works of art. Sorry ... I don't think the Lord's house has a basketball hoop ... and I love basketball."

"Fair." I laughed. "I'll see you later. I'm not sure when. I told Brendon we could go out for lunch again after church."

A date. I basically committed myself to another date. But if Fisher could go out and enjoy his time with half-waxed Tiffany, then I could break bread with Brendon after Sunday service.

"You need my keys?" Rory asked as I opened the door.

I forgot to mention that Brendon was also my ride to church since I didn't have a car yet, and I didn't want to take Rory's car with her back in town.

"Brendon's picking me up."

Rory's smile doubled. "That's ... good. Yeah?" She latched onto that like a dog on a rabbit.

"A ride? I suppose it is. I'm still working out some things with Grandma and Grandpa on the money for my car."

It was a flat "no" when I called them last week. They said "yes" to the Accord or the Forester.

"You know what I mean." Rory shook her head.

"Byeee ..." I closed the door and headed up front.

The two men in my world, if I could call them that, arrived at the same time. Brendon pulled into the driveway just as shirtless Fisher finished his morning jog. One of them nearly gave me an orgasm.

"Brandon," Fisher said as my church date rolled down his window.

"Hi, it's uh ... Brendon," *Brendon* corrected him.

Fisher knew his name, and the grin he gave me when his back was to Brendon's window said as much.

"Reese." Fisher stripped me with one look. I think he also took the rest of my virginity with that same look.

I needed to check on the specifics of getting re-baptized.

Clearing my throat and forcing my gaze to stay on his face instead of his sweat covered chest, I smiled, "Morning, Fisher."

"You going to confession?" he asked.

"It's a Christian church. We don't have confession."

"Mmm ..." He winked before heading into the garage. "A shame."

Brendon smiled as I climbed into his car. "You look nice."

"Thanks, you do too."

He laughed like my reciprocating the compliment wasn't necessary.

"Thanks for picking me up. I'm having trouble deciding on a car."

"Oh?" Brendon backed out of Fisher's driveway.

"Yeah, well ... it's that my grandparents don't want to give me the money for the car I want, even though it's my money."

"What car do you want?"

I stared out the window to my right and shrugged like it was no big deal. "It's a used Porsche Cayenne."

"A Porsche?" Brendon choked on his words.

"I want something sporty that can go into the mountains."

"Reese, I think you can find something a little more practical. After all, you're eighteen. Don't blow through your money before you get a chance to make some decisions on your future like going to college. Maybe you'll want a down payment on a house. Maybe you could invest some of the money."

Why did he have to sound so sensible—so parental —too?

During the church service, Brendon shared his Bible with me since I forgot mine. At least I got points for forgetting it because it was by my bed because I'd been reading it—all the parts on sins of the flesh.

In Sunday school, we played games, more like twenty questions to test our morals. I did quite well, just because I'd sinned didn't mean I wasn't aware of my sins. Some of the other people in class were legiti-mately clueless. That meant they were ripe for accepting their opportunity at salvation.

"You choose the lunch spot today," Brendon said as we made our mad dash to the parking lot again to beat the after-church crowd. This time he parked where he couldn't get trapped.

"It's hot today. Let's do something light like a big salad."

"So ... ice cream for lunch?" Brendon shot me a conspiratorial grin over the top of his car just before I lowered into the seat.

"I knew I liked you." I returned the same grin.

We stopped at an ice cream shop for sundaes and spent over two hours there talking about ... everything. It was easy and refreshing.

"I talked with my boss ... well, bosses at the law firm. After I take the bar, I'm going to go on a mission trip for six months. I told them I understood if they can't hold my position, but they were really great. They said I'd have a job waiting when I returned."

"Wow ..." I sipped my second glass of water as Brendon fiddled with his spoon and empty sundae bowl. "A mission trip. Where to?"

"Thailand."

"That's ..." I shook my head. "Great?" I laughed at my own response. "Brave? I don't know."

"Exciting with a dash of scary." Brendon grinned. "I've done small trips to places in Central America, just through my church. But this one is through a bigger organization. It's a bucket list thing for me. I want to feel like my life is useful beyond settling disputes among people wealthy enough to hire an attorney from a big law firm. I just ..." He focused on his spoon for a few seconds. "I just want to stay grounded in my purpose. I want to always feel like I'm taking opportunities to really serve and do God's work. You know?"

I did. And I didn't.

Truth?

I envied Brendon's direction in life. He was focused and driven. He wasn't lost in his journey or stalled along the side of the road like me. I felt certain he didn't stay awake at night worrying if the object of his affection was holding hands with someone else or kissing them.

My priorities were shameful.

"You know ..." he continued. "It might be something for you to consider too. If you're not going to college right away, and you don't really know what direction you want to go, it might be a good way to get a direction. Focus. Perspective. And if it doesn't give you any of that, you'll still have done something great. Made a difference."

Brendon would be a good attorney. He had mad skills at making a good case for things.

"Well..." I frowned "...now I feel like a loser."

He laughed and shook his head. "No. Don't feel like that. Not at all. You're eighteen. You have your whole life to work, volunteer, make a difference. There's nothing wrong with just being young and a little lost."

"Pfft ..." I rolled my eyes. "Says the guy who, I'm sure, was going on mission trips at my age."

With a sheepish grin, he shrugged. "Only because I legit had no life beyond that. Now who's the loser?"

I sighed. "I just don't know what to do."

"Just ... think about it. I'm not saying you have to go to Thailand with me, but I'm not saying it would be a bad thing either." Brendon relinquished a very endearing and maybe even convincing smile.

"I guess I'd feel silly getting an expensive car if I were planning on leaving for six months."

"Practicality wins." He winked.

As handsome and flirty as Brendon was, I didn't care for his winks. Only one man could wink at me and make my insides turn to gooey mush.

"Well, I'll take you home. How would you feel about going out some night this week?"

"Um ..."

He held up his hands. "No pressure."

"No. I ... it ... well, you have my number. I guess text me."

Brendon lit up with satisfaction, a glow of victory. "I'll do that."

He drove me home and pulled in the driveway. Fisher and my mom were on the front porch drinking iced tea ... or maybe beer. I couldn't tell for sure.

"We have an audience," Brendon said.

"Yeah. We do."

"I guess that means I'll have to wait to kiss you another time."

Gulp ...

On a nervous laugh, I nodded. "I guess so. Well,

thanks for the ice cream. It was fun." I opened the door.

"Wait! I messed up when I picked you up. I'm not going to screw this up in front of your mom." Brendon jumped out and ran around the car to open my door.

"Oh." Another nervous laugh. "Thanks." I climbed out of his car.

"Reese, introduce me," Rory called.

Brendon took my hand.

He took my hand!

And we walked to the front porch. A kiss was more than he wanted to do in front of an audience, but he thought hand-holding was okay?

I died a million deaths.

After warning Fisher about Tiffany, after losing hours of sleep from thoughts of kissing or *hand-holding*, my hand was latched to Brendon's right in front of Fisher.

"Hi, you must be Rory. I'm Brendon. So nice to meet you." Brendon released my hand to shake Rory's hand.

Fisher slowly sipped his drink, his eyes saying everything as he focused on my hand that had just been attached to Brendon's.

"The pleasure is all mine," Rory gushed. "Reese told me so much about you."

I did?

I mentioned him and maybe a few things about him, but I didn't go on and on about him. Too late.

Brendon glanced at me, a huge smile on his face. I returned more of a tight grin. What could I say?

"Well, I think Reese is pretty great. We have so much in common. And it's easy to talk for hours."

Rory eyed me. Either she was ready to plan my wedding or she wanted to date Brendon herself. I feared it was the former.

"I'm going to take off. Nice to meet you, Rory. And good to see you again, Fisher."

Fisher returned a slow nod, no smile.

Brendon grabbed my hand again and gave it a quick squeeze, but something crossed his face, like he was contemplating something. Before I could stop it, he leaned in (IN FRONT OF THEM) and kissed my cheek.

I felt like an adulterer.

"Aw ..." Rory rested her hand on Fisher's arm like, *"Look at your sister. She's found a nice boy."*

"Bye," I whispered past the painful lump in my throat. After Brendon pulled out of the driveway, I forced my gaze back to Rory and Fisher.

"He seems perfect, Reese." Rory beamed.

"He's nice." I couldn't hold my gaze to Fisher's, so I stared at my feet, kicking at a few landscaping rocks that were on the paving stones.

"Well, I'm going to run to the store and grab some groceries for the week. Do you want to come with me?"

"Um ... would it be okay if I didn't go? I feel like I've been gone all day."

"No problem. Anything special you want me to get for you?"

"Whatever you get is fine." I risked a glance at Fisher.

He had the most unreadable expression.

"Okay. Thanks for the tea, Fisher."

"Yup," Fisher said in a monotone voice.

I waited for her to go into the house to presumably put her glass in his kitchen and get her purse. Sitting in her chair, I waited for him to say something.

He didn't.

A few minutes later, Rory came back out the front door with her purse over her shoulder. "Text me if you think of anything you do want me to get for you."

"Okay," I murmured.

We watched her get into her Outback and drive down the street.

"I'm sorry. I didn't know he was going to—"

"For god's sake, Reese." He stood, making his way to the front door. "Don't do this. Don't apologize for finding an age-appropriate guy."

I jumped to my feet and followed him. "I didn't find *an age-appropriate guy*. We're just friends."

"Didn't look like that." He put his empty glass in the dishwasher.

"Well, he's mistaken. And I'll let him know that when I see him again."

Fisher turned, eyes narrowed, hands sliding into his back pockets. "Rory likes him."

I shrugged one shoulder. "Then she can date him."

He grunted. "I don't think he's her type."

"Well, he's not my type."

"No?"

I shook my head.

"He should be."

"Are you ..." I sauntered toward him. "Are you jealous?"

"I'm not fucking jealous of Bible Boy." He glanced down at me, hands still planted in his back pockets.

I frowned. "Be nice."

"What if I don't want to be nice?"

"Then tie me up and bite my ass, but don't take it out on Brendon."

It thrilled me that Fisher didn't want to smile, but he couldn't help it. "Did you just say ass?"

"It's a donkey."

"So you want me to tie you up then bite your donkey?"

"I thought *you* wanted to tie me up?" I wasn't sure how to back my way out of the donkey comment.

"I'm open to the idea."

Gah!

What did that mean? I would have handed over my entire inheritance for the chance to read Fisher Mann's mind.

I tipped my chin up. "Maybe I am too."

I wasn't. Not at all.

First ... I had some claustrophobia issues.

Second ... I didn't trust him with my body if I couldn't control my limbs.

And third ... back to the claustrophobia issues. That was a big one for me.

But I sure liked acting brave with Fisher. It was the most exhilarating feeling. Some people bungee jumped or jumped out of planes with parachutes on their backs. My adrenaline rush came from my cat and mouse game with Fisher.

"I have some work to do in my woodshop." He removed his hands from his pockets and brushed past me to the back door.

"Will you teach me something?"

Stopping, he glanced over his shoulder. "If you can listen without distracting me."

"How would I distract you?"

He nodded to my outfit. "Go change your clothes. I don't want to see your bare legs. And you need a thicker bra. I can't teach you shit when your nipples are popped out like that. And wear your work boots."

Biting my lips to hide my grin. I nodded. "Yes, sir."

CHAPTER TWENTY-FOUR

FISHER TAUGHT me how to measure and cut. Glue and screw. Properly use a hammer and level.

An hour later, Rory found us. "There you are. I was looking for you."

I turned away from Fisher's workbench, my safety glasses a little foggy. "He's teaching me things, so I'll be more useful."

Fisher stayed focused on piecing together the drawer he'd just made. "I don't know about useful, but a smidge less useless."

Rory laughed. "Well, I was thinking about inviting Rose over to grill out. Fisher, do you have plans? Tiffany might come too."

"No plans," Fisher mumbled, ultra-focused on the joint he just glued.

I wanted to knee him in the balls. No plans? Another date?

"Reese, do you prefer chicken or steak? Or I have tofu. Rose doesn't eat meat."

As my gaze bored a hole in his temple, I murmured, "Doesn't matter."

"Okay. Does an hour give you enough time to finish up?"

Fisher didn't give her a verbal answer, just a tiny nod.

"Cool. I'll let you know when they're here."

After Rory's feet *tapped tapped tapped* their way to the top of the stairs and the door clicked shut behind her, I rammed the toe of my work boot into Fisher's shin.

"Ouch! The fuck?" He reached down and rubbed his shin.

"Another date with Tiffany? Are you kidding me?"

He seemed too aggravated over his shin and me interrupting his work to spare the slightest glint of regret. "What did you expect me to say?"

"I expected you to say you had plans."

"But I don't. And you're going to be here too. What's the big deal?"

"The big deal is she likes you. A lot!"

"Like Brendon likes you *a lot*?" He shot me a scowl.

"I'm not inviting him to dinner." I parked my fists on my hips.

"Well, maybe you should. Sounds like Rory has lots of food, and the more the merrier. Right?"

"Now you're being a jerk. Such a jerk."

Standing erect, he pulled off his glasses and tossed them onto the workbench. "Oh really. *I'm* being the jerk? What about you?"

"You should have lied." That was my answer. Church schooled, Bible study, virgin me advocating lying. It was a new low.

"I won't kiss her cheek or hold her hand. Are we good now?"

My ego was in overdrive. We weren't good. Well, he was probably good. Twenty-eight-year-olds had a little more maturity and self-control. Achieving good status was probably easier for him.

Teenaged adults, such as myself, struggled with letting the little stuff go and just being ... good.

"I'm *not* good."

"No?" He cocked his head to the side.

I think I knew I was in trouble, but I wasn't sure how trouble would play out.

"Then let's make you good." He grabbed my shoulders and pushed me backward.

I stumbled, but he kept me standing. Squatting in front of me, he untied my work books.

"W-what are you d-doing?" I couldn't hide my nerves.

Fisher didn't answer. His quick hands discarded my boots to the side.

"Fisher ... what are ..." My words caught in my throat. I'd poked the bear a little too hard. Actually, I had kicked him in the shin.

He didn't look at me. He was too busy focusing on my jeans.

Unbuttoning them.

Unzipping them.

Peeling them down my legs.

"Fisher ...we can't ... not here ..." I gave him a weak protest.

What if Rory came back? The door wasn't locked.

My jeans landed next to my boots as he tossed them aside. Still, he hadn't made a single glance upward to see my sheer panic.

As his fingers curled inside the waist of my panties, I grabbed one of his hands. "Fisher, we can't ..."

He stopped, completely still. Eyes homing in on my hand clawing at his hand. Then his lips twisted as he squinted. His head swiveled, surveying one side of the room and then the other.

Leaving me half naked and panicky, he stood and took several steps to a stack of drawers. After opening several of them, he retrieved something and shoved it into his back pocket, and something else from another drawer. Then he turned.

"No ..." I shook my head when I saw the zip ties in his hand. "No ... I can't. I'm claustrophobic. My heart will stop. No ..."

He ignored me while grabbing a couple of dirty rags.

"Fisher ... no!" I tried to pull my hand out of his grip.

"Shh ..." He shook his head slowly, still not looking

at me while he wrapped a rag around one wrist and then a zip tie.

"Uh-uh ..." My head jerked side to side. "No. I said no ..."

"Shh ..." He repeated the process with my other wrist.

With unnatural ease, he lifted me onto the barstool and used two more ties to restrain my hands to my sides by looping them around the legs of the stool.

"Fisher!" I jerked my arms, but they didn't move.

He finally looked at me, holding a stiff finger to his lips for several seconds before kissing me.

I yelped into his mouth, and he swallowed it again and again. His hands peeled my panties past my butt to my knees. He lifted his boot and stepped on them, shoving them the rest of the way off my legs as his kiss grew hungrier. His hands gripped my knees and spread them wide before his fingers teased me.

Made me jump.

Made me moan.

Made me crazy.

He pulled his mouth away from mine. "Tell me no, and I'll release you," he whispered over my lips.

His fingers were making me delirious, drunk, incapable of forming a coherent thought.

"Fish ... Fisher ..." My heavy eyelids closed for a second.

He was relentless.

I was ... I didn't even know. But I wasn't thinking

about my hands being restrained. There wasn't enough blood in my head to acknowledge my claustrophobia. It had all pooled around the sensitive bundle of nerves between my legs.

He dropped to his knees and ...

Oh my ... fuck ... fuck ... FUCKITY FUUUCK!

Ten seconds ... not even, I orgasmed so quickly, and I did it with one of Fisher's hands on my knee, keeping my legs wide open and his other hand over my mouth, muffling my unholy chain of uncensored words.

Fisher's hand fell from my mouth as he sat back on his heels like he did that day at the park and rested both hands on his thighs.

His gaze affixed to the very spot his mouth had been just seconds earlier. I couldn't imagine what it must have looked like.

I eased my legs together, and he lifted his gaze slowly up my body to meet my eyes. And they were filled with tears.

"Are you *good* now?"

I blinked and the tears fell down my face. "A-are you m-mine?" My lower lip quivered.

Fisher owned me. Maybe it was stupid and childish ... maybe it made me a weak woman, but Fisher Mann owned me. And the thing that scared me more than absolutely anything in the world was that he wasn't mine.

He reached into his back pocket and pulled out a pair of wire cutters. After clipping the ties and tossing the rags aside, he bent down and snagged my panties off the floor, sliding them back up my legs and lifting me off the stool to finish pulling them over my butt. Next, he put my jeans back on.

Tug.

Zip.

Button.

Finishing with my boots, he tied them with expert precision like he did the day he bought them for me.

There I stood, limp, my heart lodged in my throat, and an unattended stream of tears on my cheeks. Fisher stood again and met my gaze. He slid my foggy safety glasses onto my head, then his thumbs took care of my tears.

"You know the answer to that." Ducking his head, he kissed me.

Not hard.

Not demanding.

Not like he did when he tied me to the chair.

He kissed me like ... I was his and ... *he was mine*.

"Go get ready for dinner. I have to clean up." His knuckles caressed my cheek. It was my favorite gesture.

So tender.

So endearing.

It made me feel unequivocally special.

I nodded before turning my head so his palm brushed my lips, and I kissed it. "Fisher ..." I grinned.

"Yeah?"

My hand ghosted over his, guiding it so my lips met

his wrist. I closed my eyes for a second, feeling his pulse—that heartbeat that I wanted to claim as mine. I wanted it to beat for me.

"I'm *good*," I whispered.

CHAPTER TWENTY-FIVE

I TOOK a quick shower and put on my nicest sheer blouse and fitted jeans. Then, I plugged in my curling iron and applied a little makeup.

"You about done?" Rory poked her head into my bathroom.

"Yeah." I glossed my lips.

"It's casual. You don't have to get all dolled up."

I shrugged. "Yesterday, it was fun having my hair curled. And with my day job, I rarely get to look *dolled up*. So ... why not?"

I smiled at her reflection in my bathroom mirror.

"You're absolutely right." She took my big comb and ran it through my hair. "It took me awhile, after I was released, to feel like I wanted to make the effort. But sometimes we do. Even if it's just for family and close friends." She grabbed the curling iron and nodded for me to sit on the toilet seat. "Even if it's just for ourselves."

I closed my eyes and hummed as she curled my hair. I loved it. I had always loved it.

"I should have told you to invite Brendon."

My eyes opened. "I'm not sure my feelings for him are the same as his are for me. I think he's great. And we do fall into the easiest conversations, but I don't know if there's more. At least for me. So I just don't want you to get your hopes up."

"Oh, sweetie, I think you're just not seeing it. Oftentimes, the greatest friendships turn into beautiful love stories. So I'm not saying he's your forever, but I want you to always keep your heart open to let love grow. Not everything in life starts with sparks and flies to the sky in a wave of butterflies."

"Were you and Dad friends first?"

"No." She laughed. "Those were sparks."

"Clearly, those sparks worked for you two."

She nodded slowly, hesitantly. "Until it didn't."

Because you went to prison.

I opened my mouth to ask her why. Why was she growing marijuana? Why did she risk everything for drugs?

But I knew Rose and Tiffany were on the screened-in porch waiting for us. And Fisher was upstairs taking a shower.

It wasn't the right time.

"There." She unplugged the curling iron. "You have the most beautiful hair." She loosely ran her fingers through my dark curls to relax them just a bit, giving my hair a beach wave look.

I grinned. "I have your hair."

"Only better." She kissed my cheek. "Let's go eat. Would you mind running upstairs and knocking on Fisher's door? Tell him everyone is here and dinner is ready."

"Sure." I held my enthusiasm inside. Go get Fisher?

Yes, please.

As Rory carried a tray of drinks to the porch, I ran upstairs and opened the door. No Fisher in the kitchen. So I listened for him as I made my way to his bedroom. Just as I reached for the handle, he opened it.

A whoosh of his clean scent nearly made my knees give out on me, not to mention his killer smile.

Jeans. Tee. Wet hair.

He glanced over my shoulder as if to see if anyone else was upstairs with me.

"Dinner is ready. And your date is here."

"Where is here?" He gave me a quick once-over that I *felt.*

"Downstairs on the porch."

Pursing his lips, face so serious, he nodded several times. "Well, get your sexy ass in here." He grabbed my arm and yanked me into his bedroom.

"Fisher!" I yelled a little louder than intended. I wasn't expecting him to do that.

Or shut the door behind us.

Or toss me onto his bed.

Or dive onto the bed after me.

I flinched. "Eek!" I curled my body, not completely trusting him to not squash me.

Like a cat, he landed on all fours, straddling my body. His grinning face hovering over mine.

"Hi, beautiful."

Oh, naked fisherman ... how does it feel to carry my heart in your pocket? Its fate solely dependent on you?

"Handsome." I matched his grin a second before he kissed me.

One leg at a time, he wedged himself between my legs and rested over me on his elbows. Our kiss so slow, almost lazy. Maybe it was the comfort in knowing it wasn't our first, and it wouldn't be our last.

"You smell edible." He kissed my neck while inhaling deeply.

"They're waiting on us," I said with little to no true concern in my voice. I liked the naked fisherman universe too much to care about the mortals on planet Earth or the screened-in porch.

He took liberty with the deep exposed V of my shirt that I left unbuttoned to the top of my cleavage. Then he took more, unbuttoning the next two buttons.

"Fisher," I whispered on a weak breath. His touch never failed to jolt my pulse out of rhythm, never failed to rob my brain of blood and sensible thoughts.

"What is it?" he whispered, a breath before sliding my bra down just enough to expose my nipple.

On a hitched breath, my back arched into his touch as he sucked it slowly, teasing it with his tongue and teeth.

"W-we ..." I tried so hard to be the mature one, but it was a monumental struggle. "We ... have to go to ... dinner."

"Yeah?" he said between kisses, working his way to my other breast.

"Yes ..." I hissed when he trapped my nipple between his teeth and tugged it.

"Cock blocker." He lifted his head and adjusted my bra back into place before buttoning those two buttons.

I giggled. "You can't call me that. I want ..." I bit my lips together before anymore words tumbled from my lips.

"You want what?" He grinned, dipping his face to my neck again. Biting and sucking it. "My cock?"

My fingers played in his hair as my drunk eyes drifted shut again. "Yes," I whispered.

"Well, what are we going to do about that?" He continued his assault on my neck, and I felt certain my neck and face would be red from his scratchy face.

"Fisher ..." I didn't recognize that voice, but it was mine. It was me wrapping my legs around his waist, begging him for ... well, his cock.

He chuckled, coming onto his arms to get off the bed, to get off of me.

My legs locked around his waist and my arms did the same around his neck.

Again, he laughed, standing with me wrapped around him. "I think you said dinner's ready."

"Fisher," I whispered just before kissing his neck

the way he had been kissing mine just seconds earlier. "I ..."

Kiss.

"Want ..."

Kiss. Bite. Long lick up to his ear.

"You."

He pushed my back against the door and grabbed my face, kissing the life out of me. I felt it heaving in my breasts and radiating all the way down to the spot his erection hit between my legs.

"Fuck ..." He pulled away breathless as his forehead hit the door just behind my shoulder. "You are *killing* me."

I grinned, teasing the nape of his neck with my fingers. Killing Fisher wasn't my intention, but I didn't exactly *not* like it either. My confidence feasted on his words.

"When is dinner?" He lifted his head. "Because I already know this erection is going to last more than four hours. I might need a trip to urgent care." He reached for my legs, forcing me to unlock them so he could set me on my feet. "Now, go tell them I'm on my way. In four hours." He sauntered to his bathroom.

"Are you going to ..."

He glanced back at me as I wrinkled my nose and bit my lip. "Rub one off? Yes. Fuck yes. It's the only way I'll make it to dinner."

"Do you want me to—"

"Nope. I've got it." He shut the bathroom door and locked it.

I covered my mouth and squealed into my cupped hands. So much dopamine in my veins. Fisher was the most glorious addiction. And I wanted him. All of him. And I knew what that meant, but I didn't care. I wanted to have sex with Fisher. Lots of naked fisherman sex. And after that? I didn't know. I just knew we'd figure it out a day at a time.

CHAPTER TWENTY-SIX

I RAN from the bottom of the stairs to my bathroom.

"Fisher ..." I frowned at my reflection in the mirror. He totally destroyed my hair. And my face, neck, and chest had a severe case of whisker burn. So I splashed lots of water on my face and reapplied my makeup. Then, I buttoned my blouse to the top and tied a light-weight scarf around my neck.

"Sorry. Fisher was still in the shower, so I had to wait for him to get out so I could tell him dinner was ready." The lies came way too easily.

"Cute scarf," Rose said.

I touched my scarf, making sure it was coving my neck. "Thanks."

"Your mom said you work for Fisher, is that correct?" Tiffany asked as I took a seat on the sectional, the spot where I slept with Fisher. Tiffany sat at the opposite end.

"Yes, for now." I persuaded my lips to curl into a smile for Fisher's date.

"What's it like working for him? He's such a perfectionist. I bet it's intense." Tiffany sipped her sangria that Rory made.

"Yes, what's it like?" Fisher appeared in the doorway, giving me a serious expression as he sat on the sofa, not too close to me, but definitely closer to me than Tiffany.

"It's like working for a man child." I gave him a toothy smile.

Rory and Rose laughed, rocking in the only two rockers on the porch. Tiffany seemed uneasy. Her gaze ping-ponged between me and Fisher.

"Brave girl." She cringed. "I'd never talk to my boss like that."

Fisher leaned forward and grabbed a glass of sangria from the tray. "I'll fire her on Monday."

"Oh, Fisher. Do you want to go with me to the Jensen's this week? I messaged them, and they're out of town this week, but they gave me their door code and said we can stop by anytime."

Fisher sipped his sangria before rubbing his lips together and nodding. "Let me check my schedule and see how my week goes."

"Absolutely. I'm really flexible."

"And by flexible, she means she does yoga." Rose threw Tiffany under the bus.

Rory laughed. Fisher smirked with slight amusement. Tiffany turned as red as the sangria. And I grinned past my clenched teeth.

"I know you won't, but I'm fine with you having a glass of sangria if you'd like to try it, Reese." Rory nodded to the last glass on the tray.

"My mom wasn't near as cool as your mom, Reese," Rose said. "It's the best sangria. Try it."

"Don't push her." Rory shot Rose a look. "She's accustomed to a more conservative lifestyle, and we need to respect that." Rory worked overtime trying to convince everyone, including me, that I wouldn't or maybe shouldn't try the sangria.

"I'll try it." I shrugged.

Fisher leaned forward again and handed me the last glass.

"Thanks," I murmured, giving him a quick glance.

"Nice scarf," he said so only I could hear him.

My eyes narrowed a fraction as I sipped my drink.

"Well?" Rory waited for my response to the sangria.

"It's really good."

"Easy, lightweight," Fisher said, eliciting laughter.

I lifted my foot onto the sofa and kicked the side of his leg.

He grabbed my ankle and held it, nearly making me spill my drink as I tried to break free from his grip.

"Now ... now ... *kids*." Rory rolled her eyes. "I wasn't the least bit surprised to find these two acting like siblings when I got home from California. We have guests. I don't need you two wrestling around on the floor."

Fisher released my ankle, but his touch lingered on my skin. I liked his hands on me. So very much.

Tiffany watched us, a slight catty expression pinned to her face.

"I shut off the grill, but everything is ready. Steak. Chicken. Tofu. And in the foil, there's veggies and potatoes. Want to grab the food off the grill, Fisher?"

"Sure thing." He stood, setting his glass onto the tray.

"Grab the cookie sheet on the counter and set everything on it. Reese can help you."

I didn't waste a second before standing and heading into the house behind Fisher.

"Tiffany keeps scowling at me. Do you think she suspects something? I don't think she likes me," I said as Fisher grabbed the cookie sheet and the grill tongs.

"I've sucked your tits and you came in my mouth today. She probably senses that I'm still craving more of you."

When I didn't respond, because my jaw dropped open, out of commission for a few seconds, Fisher turned toward me and smirked.

"Don't." He shook his head. "You're not allowed to act offended anymore. Tits is not a bad word. I gave you the PG version. Really, you should thank me."

"W-what ..." I loosened my scarf. "What's the adult version?" I glanced over my shoulder to make sure we were still alone and out of earshot. "Oral sex?" I whispered.

Fisher rolled his lips together to hide his amusement, but it hid nothing. He was laughing at me. My age. My innocence ... or what was left of it.

"What?" I narrowed my eyes.

"Could you be any more clinical?"

"Could you be any more crude?"

"Yes." He took a step toward me, also eyeing the gathering on the porch behind me. "I could have said I jerked off thinking about biting your nipples and eating you out earlier in the day."

I did *not* like the phrase "eating you out." It made me shudder. I wasn't an apple. Although, I probably felt like the forbidden fruit to Fisher.

"Did you learn to be so crude? Or is it genetic?"

He shrugged. "It's the Y chromosome."

"No." I crossed my arms over my chest and shook my head. "I know plenty of men who are not crude and filthy like you."

"You *think* you do. Like ... Bible Boy. You think his chivalrous hand-holding and sweet peck on the cheek is who he is. It's not. It's who he's been trained to be. But I promise you, after he got home this afternoon, he rubbed one off thinking about you in the most unholy ways. He's thought about your cunt and your tits *so* many times." Fisher brushed past me.

"Don't say the C word."

"Too late. I already did." He opened the storm door

and shot the ladies his sexy grin before heading out to the grill.

I followed, adjusting my scarf that covered my whisker burn and my embarrassment. I probably had half the Bible committed to memory, yet I managed to fall in love with the son of Satan.

As Fisher opened the lid to the grill, I sidled up next to him. "Have you ever been to church?"

"Yes. I went to a Presbyterian church every Sunday until my parents could no longer physically pick me up and force me to go."

"Do you believe in God?"

He set the meat and tofu kabobs onto the cookie sheet. "Why? Are you on a mission to save me?"

Selfishly, no. I was on a mission to save myself. But I wasn't ready to give up my newest addiction, so I thought God would reward me for making Fisher a little less ... *extra*.

Unfortunately, my religion didn't believe the way to salvation was through good deeds.

Bummer.

"Because ... I'm getting mixed signals. I think you want me to have sex with you, but you also want to do what Jesus would do. Which means I need to marry you to have sex with you, and I'm not marrying you just to have sex with you." He peered down at me with raised brows and a tilted head as if to make sure I understood him.

I did not.

Fisher was the king of statements that could be

interpreted in more than one way. He wasn't going to marry me and therefore we weren't having sex? Or he wasn't going to marry me *just* for sex, but it was possible he would marry me for sex *and* other reasons?

"You want to know the funny part ... even if it's not that funny?"

He closed the lid to the grill. "I'm intrigued now. What's the not-so-funny part?"

"The only thing that stands between virgin me and non-virgin me is you having a condom on you at the right time."

"No." He shook his head. "It's not my lack of preparedness, it's just bad sex. *Deflowering* isn't all it's cracked up to be. And unless you're trying to be biblical about it, it's not a gift. It's a curse. You are not going to enjoy that moment when some guy's dick rams into (pun intended) *virgin* territory. You'll wince, nearly cry, then fail epically at faking an orgasm. No." He shook his head. "I'm not having any part of that."

I blinked slowly several times. Shocked. Speechless. "Uh ... has this happened to you?"

He rolled his eyes and took the tray from me. "Yes. Yes, it has."

Again, I skittered on his heels, desperate for more information. How many virgins had he deflowered? When did he retire from his deflowering job? Did the naked fisherman have virgin phobia? But the most pressing question was ... why was I so eager to give him my virginity? Sex wasn't special to him. He wasn't going to declare his love for me to the world after bad, de-virgining sex.

No rings.

No proposals in the sky.

No "Here Comes the Bride."

"This is super informal. Just grab your food. There's more sangria in the pitcher." Rory turned on music. Jazz. Then she flipped on the globe lights.

I didn't want the globe lights on with Tiffany there. Those were lights for me and Fisher.

"Oh my gosh ... I love the lights!" Tiffany's eyes widened for a second before she sat with her plate of food on the sofa *right* next to Fisher. She might as well have sat onto his lap.

My monkey brain spun in circles like an out of control tilt a whirl. She wasn't a virgin. No "bad sex" with her. No deflowering dilemma.

Fisher leaned over and tapped my plate with his fork, startling me from my self-destructive trance.

"You're not eating. Are you good?"

Tiffany watched with minimal concern as Fisher's question seemed benign to everyone else.

Are you *good?*

I let my gaze remain locked to his for a few seconds. I thought of how I felt when he zip-tied me to the stool, when he said those words "you know the answer to that."

Tiffany thought she was on another date. She flirted with him. She sat right next to him. And I couldn't blame her one bit for finding him irresistible. But ... he was mine.

"I'm good." I smiled.

He rewarded me with a wink. And anyone else could have seen it, and maybe someone did. But he didn't care, and I loved him for it.

After dinner, Rory made a comment about her menstrual cycle.

Rose and Tiffany laughed, eyeing Fisher.

He shook his head and sipped another glass of sangria.

"This is important stuff, Fisher." Rory grinned. "Your wife will thank me someday for enlightening you on the matter."

"She'll thank you for me knowing when it's time to leave the room." He stood. "Like now. I'll just tidy up the kitchen. Have fun with your discussion." He grabbed the empty plates and left the overabundance of estrogen on the porch.

I spent the next twenty minutes listening to Rory and Rose discuss perimenopause. Tiffany was too young to add much to the conversation, but she still laughed and pretended to know.

My ability to pretend ran out five minutes after Fisher left. I could no longer see him in the kitchen. The dishes were clean, but I didn't see him leave.

"Anyone else need anything? I'm going to use the bathroom and get some water," I interrupted.

They shook their heads, mumbling, "We're good, thanks."

It was a quarter to nine on a Sunday night. Didn't they have jobs in the morning?

After I peed, I decided to sneak upstairs to see if Fisher was there, but I didn't make it past the doorway to my bedroom.

"What are you doing?" I asked Fisher, who was sitting on the floor at the end of the bed.

Taking a few more steps in the room and shutting the door behind me, I saw exactly what he was doing.

Solving my crossword puzzles.

I would have been upset had he not been using a pencil.

"Do you like crossword puzzles?" I asked, plopping onto the bed, on my belly with my head next to his. I rested my chin on his shoulder and watched him focus on one of my hardest puzzles.

"I like them better than talking about menstrual cycles."

I giggled. He turned his head just enough to grin at me and press a short kiss to my lips. Then he returned his attention to the puzzle.

"You're not going to get fourteen across."

"Gulping in haste," he whispered the clue.

I smirked, knowing he'd never ever get it.

Five letters.

Second letter was E.

Last letter was Z.

"Move on to the next one." I bit his earlobe and tugged it. "You're going to break your brain trying to figure it out."

"Zip it," he said, and it made me giggle more.

I kissed along his neck, and he cocked his head to the side, giving me better access.

"Xertz," he said, filling in the missing letters.

I jerked my head straight. "How did you get that? You cheated. You used your phone."

Fisher tossed the puzzle and pencil aside before reaching back and grabbing me, pulling me onto the floor.

"Fish—"

"Shh ..." He covered my mouth with his hand while kissing my neck.

I quieted. His hand slid away from my mouth and his lips replaced it. He rolled us so that I was on top of him, my hair in his face, his hands on my butt, my hands on either side of his head.

"Fisher ..." I deposited kisses all over his face. "If I'm yours..." my lips brushed the shell of his ear "...then you have to take the bad with the good."

Bad sex.

I wanted him to take the bad sex that would come with our first time.

"What if ..." He threaded his fingers through my hair, pulling it away from our faces. "What if you're not supposed to be mine?"

Before I could present my most heartbroken frown, a fist tapped my door twice, and then it opened.

There was no time to stand. There was barely time to blink.

"Reese, do you have—" Rose stilled. Eyes wide.

Lips parted into a huge O. "I ... I'm sorry." She backed out of the room and shut the door.

"Rose ..." I flew to my feet and out of my bedroom.

Grabbing Rose's arm before she got more than two steps toward the porch, I pulled her into my bathroom and shut the door.

Closing my eyes for a brief second, I blew out a slow breath. When I opened them, Rose eyed me with concern.

She didn't see us kissing. Our clothes were on. And for a split second I considered pretending that we were wrestling like siblings. But Rose wasn't stupid.

"If you tell my mom ..." I had no clue what came after those words. I didn't actually know how Rory would react, but with a certain level of certainty, I knew it wouldn't be good.

"She'll send you back to Texas and kill Fisher," Rose said without hesitation.

I nodded. That worked. Honestly, Rose knew Rory better than I did. I trusted her prediction.

"Reese, he's *ten* years older than you. You know that, right?"

Another nod while biting my lips together.

"What has he done? Have you ..."

I shook my head at least a half dozen times. "We haven't done ... *that*." It bothered me that Rose jumped immediately to Fisher, as if he had taken advantage of me. Like a predator or child molester.

"It's a terrible idea."

"I know," I whispered, even though I *didn't* know

anything for certain when it came to Fisher Mann. "Please ... *please* don't say anything to Rory. Let me tell her when I'm ready."

"Uh ..." She chuckled. "I don't think she ever needs to know. If you're not having sex ..." She narrowed her eyes as if she was clarifying again that we hadn't had sex. "Then it's nothing more than wasted infatuation. Boredom. And it will and should end soon. Right?"

My answer didn't come out right away because I didn't know the answer.

"Reese, listen, honey ... Fisher is a wonderful man. And he's your *boss*. Rory and I adore him. And for the right person at the right time, he will be quite the catch. But ... and I mean this in the kindest way possible, Fisher is a man whore."

My eyes narrowed.

"He's not ready to settle down. He enjoys dating. He enjoys casual sex. And that's great for women who are in the same place in their lives. Like Tiffany. She's not ready to settle down tomorrow. She's looking for casual and fun. Fisher is a great fit for her right now. But I honestly have no idea what he has to offer you beyond a job. If you're not sexually active, then you need to be smart. You need to remind Fisher that he's your boss, your mom's friend, and that's it. Anything else makes him a guy who is way too mature for you and focused on only one thing ... trying to get into your pants. And your heart will get broken because I know enough about you to know that you are not that girl looking for anything less than the fairytale. Fisher is not anyone's Prince Charming right now. Okay?"

Her words paralyzed me. I couldn't speak. I couldn't piece together a string of thoughts that made sense. A man whore? That seemed extreme. And he didn't want into my pants. Or did he? Was it the game? Was I his toy?

"If you want me to talk to him—"

"No!" I shook my head. "Please, just let me handle it. Don't tell Rory or anyone for that matter. I'll ... handle it."

CHAPTER TWENTY-SEVEN

FISHER WAS GONE, upstairs I assumed, by the time Rose and I exited the bathroom. Rose suggested she and Tiffany leave. I didn't know what she was going to say to Tiffany, but I felt confident that it might be a "Fisher is a man whore you deserve better" speech.

"Night, sweetheart." Rory poked her head into my bedroom a little before ten as I reorganized my puzzles after Fisher rifled through them, solving the hardest ones.

After Rory's bedroom door clicked shut, I texted Fisher.

Reese: Hi. Rose isn't going to tell Rory or anyone.
Fisher: We leave at six in the morning.

I deflated at his cold response.

Reese: Are you mad?

I waited over fifteen minutes for a response.

Nothing.

So I decided to sleep on it. Things would be better in the morning.

Or so I thought.

When I reached the driveway the next morning, Fisher was already waiting, and it wasn't six yet.

"Morning," I smiled, hopping into the truck and tossing my bag in the back.

"Morning." He gave me a forced smile for less than a second and put the truck into drive.

I gave him time. Five minutes. Ten minutes.

He said nothing and played music with the volume turned way up.

"What's your car situation?" He broke the silence.

"Car situation?"

"Did you talk to your grandparents?"

"Yeah." I turned my attention to the brake lights in front of us as we pulled to a stop at the light.

"And?"

"And they're not going to give me the money for the Porsche, which is stupid because it's *my* freaking money."

"So you get the Forester?"

I shrugged with a single shoulder and sighed. "I suppose so."

"Great. Get the money in your account and we'll go get it tomorrow if it's still there. Or you can go with Rory or Brendon. I really don't care."

He really didn't care. Just what I wanted to hear. Rose was right. Fisher would crush my heart. As we waited for the light to change, my heart took off. Running away.

Away from the naked fisherman.

I wasn't sure what propelled me to make my next move. I don't remember my brain making some grand decision. It was instinct. Impulse. Survival.

Snagging my backpack from the back and unlatching my seat belt, I jumped out of the truck.

"Reese!"

Weaving through three lanes of stopped traffic, I sprinted through the steep dip of the ditch, my boots splashing in a small pool of standing water.

Down a less busy street.

Across a park.

Through someone's backyard.

Down another residential street.

Stopping at a bus stop.

Bending over, I rested my hands on my knees and fought to catch my breath for a few seconds before collapsing onto the bench behind me.

My phone vibrated in the side pocket of my bag. I ignored it.

How did I get there? Less than twenty-four hours earlier, I was on Fisher's bed. We were laughing.

Touching.

Kissing.

Existing only for each other.

He made me feel hopeful.

My phone kept vibrating, so I pulled it out of the pocket to shut it off.

It was Fisher.

And there were a string of texts from him too.

Where are you?

Answer your phone.

I'm sorry.

Please pick up your phone.

Don't make me call Rory.

Or the police.

I was eighteen. He wasn't going to call the police. And I didn't believe he would call Rory either. Not yet.

When the bus stopped, I got on. And I spent the next three hours taking various bus routes around Denver.

Earbuds in.

Music playing.

My mind sorting through everything.

I just needed time.

After my dad died, family rushed to console me. Feed me. Fix me. So I ran away for twelve hours because I needed time. I took the bus that day too. A bus ride didn't solve every problem, but it was cathartic. The passing miles. The passengers coming and going. Time to imagine that my life wasn't any worse than anybody else's life.

After grabbing a sandwich, I found the bus stop closest to the office and walked the rest of the way.

"Hey!" Hailey jumped out of her chair. "Where have you been? Fisher said you bolted this morning. He told me not to tell anyone, but I've been so worried." She hugged me as I stood limp in her arms.

"Sorry. I didn't mean to make anyone worry."

Except Fisher.

I wanted to make him worry. I wanted him to feel a little bit of my pain. My frustration.

"Where have you been?" She released me.

I set my backpack by Fisher's desk. "I just needed time to think about stuff."

"Reese ..." She handed me a glass of water. I had a fair amount of sweat pooling along my forehead and running down my back from walking in the heat with my backpack.

"Can we not talk about it?" I gave her my best pleading glance.

With worry lining her face, she nibbled the inside of her cheek and nodded slowly. "Okay. But if you do want to talk, you can talk to me about absolutely anything. Okay?"

Plopping into Fisher's chair, I nodded.

Hailey gave me a few easy things to do before grabbing her purse. "Your ride is here. I'm taking off early. Remember, I'm always here."

I was impressed that it took a full hour for Fisher to arrive.

"Thanks," I murmured as Fisher opened the door and Hailey squeezed past him, shooting him a cringing expression.

"You're fired."

My gaze lifted to Fisher. I wasn't surprised, yet ... I was.

"The tile shop where I get most of my tile, they're looking to hire someone to answer the phone. I got you an interview. It's just a formality. They will offer you the job. I'm going to tell Rory I found you a new job because I didn't want you on the job sites where you could get hurt. And Hailey doesn't really need your help most days."

I swallowed the lump of emotion in my throat. "Is this about yesterday? Or this morning?" I managed to say in a shaky voice.

"Yes," he replied flatly, just as flat as the expression on his face.

"Rose promised not to tell Rory," I said.

"She lied. Rose will absolutely tell Rory unless we end it."

I had all these what-ifs lining the tip of my tongue.

What if *we* told Rory first?

What if we were more careful?

What if the world ended?

What happened to living in the moment? Living your best life? Loving the one you're with? That was all I did. Rory left me, and I fell in love with Fisher because he was the one I was with. It was really Rory's fault.

"Rory's taking the morning off tomorrow to help you get a car. The interview with the tile shop is the following morning. You'll be able to drive there on your own."

"Are you mad at me?" I whispered.

He returned a tiny wince before pinching the bridge of his nose and blowing out a breath. "No. I'm mad at myself."

The only thing more painful than rejection was regret. Fisher brought his A game. One brutal punch after the next.

A stupid, selfish, errant tear made its way to my cheek, and I looked away quickly to wipe it.

"Fuck ..." he mumbled. "This is what I wanted to avoid. Rory is my friend. Rose is my friend. I didn't want to be the villain. The guy who broke Rory's daughter's heart."

I stood and grabbed my backpack, refusing to look at him as I shouldered past him to the door. "You're such an arrogant asshole."

Yeah, I said it. No regrets.

"And you're the most beautiful and infuriating woman I have ever met."

I stopped at the door like it was a wall that appeared out of nowhere. All the friends of that rebel tear showed up to ruin my carefully constructed facade, busting open the flood gates.

"And in a different time ... a different place in our lives, I'd tell Rory and the rest of the world to go fuck themselves. I'd prove them all wrong. *We'd* prove the naysayers wrong. But ... I don't think they're wrong. Not now."

Sniffling and ignoring the unstoppable tears, I turned. "I'm beautiful ..." I nodded slowly. "A pretty face. Long legs. Perky *tits*. And I sucked your cock. No college education. No fantastic job. Nothing ... but I'm beautiful. Young. Innocent. And maybe the perfect amount of naive. It makes sense now." I laughed through my tears. A crazy laugh. The edge of my sanity laugh. "Stupid, stupid me. I thought we were this magical thing that couldn't be described. We didn't make sense because magic, fate, and serendipity don't have to make sense. I actually *liked* that we didn't make sense, yet my universe seemed perfect when it was just us. I guess the eight-letter word for that is illusion. You played me. You liked the chase. The game. And what better chase than the virgin wearing a cross around her neck?"

Fisher shook his head slowly. "You don't know what you're talking about."

"Because I'm eighteen?"

"Because you're scared."

"Of what?"

"Failure. Eighteen-letter word. Starts with a K."

I wasn't following him. So I said nothing. I did nothing but blink my tear-ladened eyelashes.

"Kakorrhaphiophobia. An abnormal fear of failure. That's why you're here and not chasing a dream. Not in college. Not making any plans in your life. Your dad died. Your mom went to prison. And you've been left with a Bible that prepares you for death and makes you feel ashamed of anything you do in this life to truly *live*."

He opened the door, and I waited for more, but he didn't give me more. We climbed into his truck and headed home, or so I assumed. We didn't make it home. We pulled into his parents' driveway instead.

"Let's go." He hopped out.

I didn't.

Fisher came to my side and opened my door. I assumed my recent firing allowed him to open my door.

"They're out of town. Let's go."

I eased out of the truck and followed him into the house. He opened a door to a storage and utility room, scanning a wall of boxes and plastic containers. When he found what he was looking for, he pulled a box from the shelf and brought it out to the family room.

"Sit." He nodded to the sofa.

I eased my butt down to it, watching him kneel on the floor and open the box. I couldn't see what was inside. He paused, staring at its contents.

"I told you I played sports. And I loved construction. But my real talent came in the form of spelling bees." He pulled out a stack of plaques, certificates, and trophies. "I took first place at a national competition." His face held a bit of harnessed pride as he set everything at my feet. "I liked words. Dissecting them. Studying their origin. A full year of Latin. My mom used to say I'd never find a woman who really appreciated my word-loving soul. And she was so disappointed in me when I let that love of words die, when I found my new favorite words like..." he smirked "...well, most of them were and still are four-letter words. Sometimes simplicity is best. So gone were the days of winklepicker shoes and ulotrichous women. I gravitated toward fuck, fucker, and fucking. It helped me fit in."

His gaze seemed to be focused on the past or maybe whatever was still in the box. "Who would have ever imagined that a girl ... a young woman ten years younger than me would breeze into my life. Beautiful? Yes. Quirky? Absolutely. Innocent? Painfully so. But also a cruciverbalist." Shaking his head, gazing in the box, and irony curling his lips, he pulled out tablets and notebooks, tossing them at my feet with the spelling bee awards.

I bent down and picked one up. Inside, it was filled with hand drawn crossword puzzles.

"Cruciferous ..." I whispered, easing my head side to side. He pretended to not know what a cruciverbalist was. Fisher did play me, just not in the way I thought.

"An eighteen-year-old cruciverbalist. Really, what were the chances?"

"Why didn't you tell me?" I glanced up at him.

He ran a hand through his hair and exhaled. "I don't know. I think I was in shock. And maybe a little awe was involved. A suffocating dose of confusion. A little anger at the timing, at your age. At the fact that you're Rory's daughter."

I thumbed through more pages of his notebook.

"Do you love me, Fisher?" My gaze remained on the notebook, my voice steady, almost passive as if I was asking him about the weather or his day.

"Reese, it doesn't matter."

My head inched side to side. "You mean it doesn't change anything. And maybe you're right. But ..." I lifted my gaze. "It *matters*."

He climbed to his feet and drifted to the windows overlooking the backyard. Hands in the front pockets of his jeans. "I think I loved you before I met you. But we don't always get what we want. I let go of my crossword puzzles and word obsession because it didn't fit into my life any longer. The thing is ... I don't know where you fit into my life. And I know, I *know* you don't like your age to matter, but it does. I won't be the reason you don't take chances in life. Don't make marriage and sex your life's goals. If Rory found out, she'd want to know why. Why I would get involved with an eighteen-year-old girl? And I don't think cruciverbalist would work. Maybe if our ten-year-age gap was more like twenty-five and thirty-five, I could make a case for word geeks and kismet."

He turned to face me, every ounce of his vulnerability on full display. No walls. No lies. Just the hard truth. "Loving you is my favorite thing to do. It's automatic and effortless. And you're right, that matters. But ..."

"It changes nothing," I whispered, setting the notebook on the sofa and pressing my hands to my legs as I stood. Gazing up at the ceiling, I took a deep breath, closed my eyes and blew it out in one big whoosh. "Naked fisherman, you are incorrigible. Moody. Bold. Unpredictable. Brash ... and a million other things that are bad for me. Yet it felt like you were the first person in my life who just ... fit. The version of myself I dreaded ... the version I blamed on your bad behavior, I came to love it. It started to feel like my true skin. It felt good to smile without something in my brain telling me I should smile. You gave my days this vibrant color, and I don't know what I will see when you're not..." I drew in a shaky breath as emotions stung my eyes "...when you're not mine."

His arms slid around my waist, his chest to my back, his face bowed to my shoulder. And I shook as emotion took my body like an earthquake. Unsettling emotions needed to be released. Grief suffocated my lungs. Reality tore at my heart.

Fisher turned me in his arms and pressed my cheek to his chest. He soothed me with soft kisses to the top of my head and gentle strokes from his other hand down my back.

I was so tired of the unfairness in my life. The unanswered prayers. The testing of my faith.

My dad died, and it made no sense. And I didn't want anyone, not even God himself, trying to convince me otherwise.

Rory's decisions made no sense to me either. It was like one day she was my mom, my world, and the next day she was this stranger being sentenced to five years.

Did I have an unnatural fear of failure? Yes.

Success felt like a myth. Happiness ... an unreachable destination.

And love ... well, it was something blurry and always changing forms in my life. I chased love.

Love for my father.

Love for God.

Love for Rory.

But it always felt just out of reach. Until Fisher. With him, I touched love. I held it in my hands, like reaching the end of a rainbow or lassoing the moon.

CHAPTER TWENTY-EIGHT

I GOT the Forester and the tile shop job. And I missed Fisher. Sometimes I saw him mowing the lawn or working in the garage when I got back from my evening walks or jogs. Sometimes I saw him at the tile shop picking up something.

We mastered courteous.

We perfected our sibling relationship around Rory.

But mostly, I spent my time praying for the crater in my heart to heal and ... missing him.

It would have been easier had I stayed angry at him, had I not known everything, had I not felt his love.

"I'm going to Texas this weekend," I announced to Rory, Rose, and Fisher as we ate pizza and cake on a Wednesday night to celebrate Rory's birthday.

"Oh?" Rory eyed me suspiciously from her favorite rocking chair on the porch.

"It was a last-minute decision. It's Grandma's and Grandpa's fiftieth wedding anniversary, and their church is having a party for them. They invited me. Paid for my airfare. And they'll pick me up at the airport Friday evening when I land. Just a quick getaway. I'll be home Sunday night because I have to work Monday."

"Well, tell them happy anniversary from me." Rory wrinkled her nose. "Not that they'll care. I'm not exactly the favorite daughter-in-law anymore."

"Do you need a ride to the airport?" Fisher asked. It was a rare moment of us sharing direct conversation instead of keeping our focus on Rory or Rose like usual.

"No. I'm leaving my vehicle at the airport since I'll be getting in late Sunday. I didn't want anyone to worry about picking me up." After talking to my plate because I still couldn't look him in the eye, I did the impossible—I lifted my gaze to his for a split second.

"Okay." The hint of a smile touched his lips. It was the Fisher smile I had come to love.

"How's your new job going?" Rose asked.

"It's fine. A little monotonous, but the people I work with are nice."

Rose's gaze slid to Fisher. He glanced away from all of us.

"I'm not implying my last job was bad or the people weren't nice." I should have kept my mouth shut.

Fisher grunted a laugh, gazing out in the distance.

"It's a safer job," Rory added.

Fisher fired me because he didn't want to be around me after breaking up with me. It might not have been an actual breakup. We weren't together in the traditional sense. Still, the breakup, real or not, was thick and suffocating in the air between us.

"It is ..." I nodded slowly.

"Have you talked to Brendon lately?" Nice subject change from Rory. Not that I wanted to talk about Brendon in front of Fisher.

"I see him at church. And I saw him last Wednesday night at Bible study."

"No dates?"

I shook my head. "He's been busy studying, and I've been ..." With a half-smile, I lifted a shoulder. "Not thinking much about dating."

Rose continued to eye Fisher and me. If she couldn't see the distance between us, the emotional distance between us, then she was blind.

"Well, remember what I said. It's a good thing to cultivate the friendship first."

No whirlwind love affairs.

Nothing forbidden.

No passion.

Was that the life I wanted?

I stole a quick glance at Fisher and his slumped shoulders, quiet demeanor, and faraway gaze. It didn't matter what I wanted.

I was eighteen with stuff to do like ... figure out *what* to do.

"How about you, Fisher?" Rory swiped a glob of frosting from her piece of cake and sucked it off her finger. "Rose said things fizzled out with Tiffany.

Any other prospects? Or are you still content with one-night stands and a solid grip on your bachelorhood?"

Was he having one-night stands? After investing so much time in Virgin Therese, he deserved to have a normal sexual encounter that involved ... sex.

"I'm going to get some more ice cream." I grabbed my plate and headed into the house.

"Get it together," I whispered to myself as I set my plate on the counter and rested my hands on the edge, my head hanging low.

"I thought I could use some more ice cream too."

My head lifted as Rose shut the door behind her.

Clearing my throat, I smiled. "Yeah. Of course." Turning, I opened the freezer.

"I think we both know you don't want more ice cream. And neither do I."

I closed the freezer door and leaned against it. "If you're concerned that Fisher and I—"

"You've stopped ... whatever you were doing." She climbed onto a barstool. "I can see that. He's been quite the bore lately. I've been making up excuses for him because Rory sees it too. You've actually done a better job of hiding it. Good for you."

Good for me?

I laughed. "Well, it doesn't feel good."

"I know." She gave me a sad smile.

"Do you? Do you know what it's like to have feelings for someone and them have feelings for you, but you can't be together because the timing in life sucks?

It just ..." I rolled my lips between my teeth and shook my head. "Sucks."

"I fell in love once. And the timing was all wrong. But love doesn't care. Your heart doesn't understand. And the scariest part is you want to believe that someday it will work, but you don't *know*. You just don't know. Will patience be rewarded? Will God answer your prayers with the answers you want? You tell yourself that if it's meant to be ... it will be." She pushed a long breath out of her nose and offered a weak smile. "And sometimes the answer is yes. But sometimes the answer is no. So the most you can do is find love and life in every day. The one thing I can promise you is that life rarely goes in the direction we think it will. And that's not always a bad thing. Some-times it's the most amazing surprise."

My gaze affixed to Fisher on the porch. *He* was the most amazing surprise.

"I want to have this conversation with my mom. There have been so many moments over the past five years that I've thought, 'I need my mom.' And now she's here, but I can't talk to her. And I hate it because he didn't take advantage of me. It wasn't like that. And I know what you said about him being a man whore, but that wasn't who he was with me."

Rose gave me a look like she didn't entirely believe me. Or maybe she believed that *I* believed what I said, but it was just my foolish heart, my naive eighteen-year-old brain blinded by my first real crush.

"Well, I'm glad that's not who he was with you.

354

That at least shows he had a little respect for Rory, but it's not enough for her to overlook the obvious. He's twenty-eight and you're eighteen. He should have known better. He should have had self-control."

I shook my head. "It wasn't all him. Despite what everyone seems to think, I do have the ability to make grown-up decisions. Maybe I'm the one who pursued him."

Rose lifted two sharp-peaked eyebrows. "Did you?"

With frustration filling my head and rekindling my anger, I shook my head. "I ... I don't know. It just ... happened."

"I know it's not the same, but I'm here if you want to talk more."

"It's ... fine. I'm good." I was the opposite of good. Still, I couldn't believe how quickly things flipped. One minute he was tearing at my clothes and biting my nipples, and the next ... we were in his parents' basement as he revealed to me why we were *perfect* for each other.

One minute my mom was braiding my hair—the next she was being hauled off in handcuffs.

One minute my dad was eating pasta with me at our favorite restaurant—the next he was dead.

I really didn't trust *life*.

CHAPTER TWENTY-NINE

"Do you have everything packed?" Rory seemed concerned about my big two-night trip to Texas. "If they ask how things are going here, what are you going to say?"

I rolled my carry-on suitcase out of the bedroom. "Are you chewing your nails?"

Rory jerked her hand away from her mouth. "No."

"Why do you seem so panicked?"

She sighed, blowing her hair out of her face. "It's just that I know they think I'm a complete failure, and I don't want them thinking I'm a bad influence because I've tried to do things right. Ya know? I mean, I let you have a little sangria, but I've tried to make sure you have everything you need. And Fisher has been so great at helping watch out for you too. I just want them to know that."

"Why?" I narrowed my eyes. It made no sense. They couldn't take me away from her.

Pressing her fingers over her closed eyes, she grumbled. "Ugh ... it's just that they used to like me. I went out of my way to impress them. And I don't care what they think of me, but I know they have influence over you, probably way more than I do. And I don't want them to persuade you to move back to Texas because..." she pushed out her lower lip "...I'm selfish. I want you with me for as long as you're willing to stay. It's not that I think I can make up for the years I was gone, but I want the chance to be your mom again. Really be your mom."

I held out my arms and hugged her. "I'm going to tell them that it's been great. You bake and cook. You're appropriately overprotective. You don't go to church with me, but they don't need to know that."

"I love you, Reese. I love you more than anything or anyone in this world. I always have and I always will."

I released her and grabbed my bag in one hand and my suitcase in my other hand. "I love you too." It was the first time I had said that to her in over five years. It felt right. It felt true.

"Oh ... let me run up and get Fisher. He'll carry your suitcase to the car so you don't have to lug it up by yourself."

"I've got it."

"He'll get it. I don't want you tripping or anything." She ran up the stairs.

"I've got it. Really." I started to open the door to carry it up to my car.

"Fisher can you give Reese a hand with her suitcase?"

Gah! Why?

I barely got it out the door before Rory returned with Fisher.

Fisher in his exercise shorts and no shirt. Tennis shoes untied like he'd just slipped them on his bare feet. If he wasn't going to marry me and put ten babies in my womb, then the shirtless thing was nothing more than a big F-you to me.

"I said I can do it. She's coddling me. Again." I rolled my eyes to lighten the mood and give my eyes something to do besides gawk at his unnaturally flawless body.

"Well, I'm here now. I'll carry it." He took the suitcase from me and headed up the side of the house.

"Bye, sweetie. Text me as soon as you land." Rory gave me one last hug.

"I will. See you Sunday." I closed the door and jogged to catch up to Fisher. "Sorry. Really, I had it."

Fisher loaded it into the back of my Forester. "It's no big deal." He closed the back.

"Well, thanks."

"Enjoy your trip."

I nodded, feeling the heat of his body. I always felt him without ever touching him. My body seemed to naturally gravitate toward him like it knew where it belonged before my brain figured it out.

We couldn't work together. We couldn't ride in the

same vehicle. We could barely be in the same room without a clawing need ripping me apart from the inside. That must have been what withdrawal felt like.

"Reese?"

I turned after opening my door.

"I'm sorry."

It was a terrible apology. I didn't want his words. Fisher showed me. That was what he did. He showed me when he was sorry. It meant more. No ... it meant everything. But that ... that sad uttering of apology from his lips felt empty, like he was drained but he'd managed to gather a few drops of apology as if it would quench my thirst. My unquenchable thirst for him.

"I should have known better. It was selfish of me." He added yet another layer of pain to my already throbbing wounds.

Regret.

It was always the regret that hurt the most.

"Well, I'm not sorry. Not for any of it. You know it's..." I shook my head "...ironic. Adults, *real* adults, like to lecture young adults like me. They like to paint this picture of hopes and dreams, endless possibilities, and constantly remind us that we can *do* anything, *be* anything. But that's a lie. Because all I wanted was to live a day at a time and figure things out one moment at a time. That's all I wanted to *do*. And all I wanted to *be* was yours." After a quick shrug, I rolled my eyes toward the sky to ward off the tears. "I don't want your apologies or your help because they don't get me you."

He said nothing. Not a word. Not a single muscle in his body moved. Defeat personified.

"I'm going to fall in love. And some guy will be lucky to have me. He'll love me for me. And he won't care where I've been or where I'm going. He'll just feel so *fucking* lucky to be the one who kisses me goodnight and wakes up in the morning with me in his arms. He won't be burdened by my virginity or aggravated that I don't wear socks with my sneakers. He will be a better man for having found me, and I will be a better woman for having found him. I know they say love is patient, but it's not. Love is the brightest star in the sky. It doesn't have an off switch or a timer. It doesn't wear a watch or look at a calendar. It's why we're here. It's the only true reason for our existence."

Fisher was good at taking punches. He didn't duck or even wince. He swallowed every word and let it settle somewhere deep inside of his mind, his heart, maybe his soul. And if he felt unsteady or even a pang of discomfort, I never knew.

"I have to go."

He smiled ever so slightly. "Have a safe trip."

I returned a single nod and climbed into my car. Then, I made it a full three blocks before I cried all the tears.

It was him. He was the someday guy.

The kiss goodnight. It was him.

Waking in the morning in *his* arms.

It felt like I would forever carry a Fisher-shaped

mold around with me, trying to shove other men into a place they would never fit.

The wrong key.

The wrong piece to a puzzle.

I was destined to settle and that sucked.

CHAPTER THIRTY

THE WORST PART about late flights? When they were canceled for mechanical issues, it meant a night in the airport or, in my case, a trip home only to wake up five hours later and drive back to the airport for an early flight.

I didn't even bother pulling my suitcase out of the back of my Forester. Not for five hours. Rose's car was parked in the driveway, and as I made my way around the side of the house, the glow of the globe lights illuminated the walkway for me. They were probably having a party since I was supposed to be out of town for the weekend. I prepared myself for some new girl Rose found to fix up with Fisher.

It didn't matter. I knew I would give them a quick flight update and go straight to bed.

No obsessing over the real adults having fun without me.

No stressing over a new girl (a new *woman*) for Fisher.

To my surprise and relief, there wasn't a party on the screened-in porch, just a couple of empty plates and wine glasses. I toed off my shoes just inside of the door and set my bag on my bed. I knew Rory wasn't asleep because she wouldn't have left the lights on.

I knocked several quick times on her bedroom door before opening it. "My flight got canceled so—"

She wasn't in her bedroom, but the lights were on.

They were upstairs with Fisher. I wasn't sure I wanted or needed to go upstairs. I'd had enough Fisher time for the night. As I started to shut her bedroom door, I heard a noise. It was coming from her bathroom, so I made my way through her bedroom to her bathroom. The door was cracked open, so I eased it open, hearing the water running in the shower.

It took me too long to make sense of what I was seeing in that moment—too much time letting the vision make a permeant stain on my memory. I knew I would never be able to forget. It would play in my mind on an endless loop for ... maybe the rest of my life.

It just *didn't* make sense.

Rory was in the shower, her back against the far wall, her eyes closed, mouth open. One hand pressed to the wall to steady herself. Her other hand was tangled in *Rose's* hair. *Rose* was on her knees with one of Rory's legs hooked over her shoulder. *Rose* was ...

well, she was fingering *my mom* while simultaneously giving her oral sex.

I blinked again and again. I couldn't stop blinking. I couldn't move. Despite the crushing feeling of complete devastation, my world turning upside down ...

I. Couldn't. Turn. Away.

Had it been literally anyone else, I would have turned and ran, feeling horrified for the predictable reason like, it's embarrassing to accidentally walk in on two people having sex.

Then it happened. Those eyes ... the ones that shot me a final glance before leaving the courtroom ... they opened and landed on me.

Contrite and apologetic.

Like cells dividing at a rapid pace, forming something from nothing, ten thousand pieces of a puzzle putting themselves together ... I saw it.

All of it.

It wasn't a coincidence that Rose was in Colorado. They'd been friends for years.

Friends.

That was why my dad was so quick to divorce Rory after she went to prison. So many things I never fully understood. They all started to come together.

"Reese!" Rory called just as I tore my gaze away from the nightmare in the shower and ran out of the house. As soon as I reached the driveway, Fisher pulled in on his motorcycle.

"Did you know?" I yelled.

He drove past me, parking his motorcycle in the garage.

I charged after him. "Did you know?" My hands balled at my sides.

Fisher pulled off his helmet. "What are you doing here?" He climbed off his bike and carried his helmet to the cabinet.

"Did. You. KNOW?"

"Jesus, Reese." He turned, unzipping his jacket. "What the hell is going on?"

"Did you know that my mom is a *lesbian?* Gay. Homosexual. Are you understanding me now?" I shook my head over and over again, running my hands through my hair.

It wasn't real. It wasn't true.

I didn't deserve that, not after *everything* I'd been through. What was God doing? He wasn't supposed to give me more than I could handle. That was way more than I could handle.

Fisher slowed his movements, easing his arms out of his jacket and returning it to the cabinet next to his helmet. Fisher wasn't tense like me. He wasn't stunned, frozen in place.

No bugged-out eyes.

No jaw dropping to the ground.

Not a single sign that I was presenting him with new information.

"Did I know your mom and Rose are together? Yes."

My anger kept my tears at bay, but just barely.

"How could you?"

"How could I what?" He rested his hands on his hips, staring me down like *I* had done something wrong.

"Not tell me!"

"Rory's personal life is not mine to share."

"Rory's *personal life*? Are you kidding me? She's my mom!"

"Your point?"

"I walked in on them. In the shower. My mom and her *girlfriend*. The friend who just happened to be in Colorado after having been a 'client' of hers in Nebraska. She cheated on my dad. That's why he divorced her."

"Is that why you're losing your mind? Because you think your mom cheated on your dad? Or are you upset because Rory is a 'lesbian, homosexual, gay?' Because I'm not sure why you're freaking the fuck out about this."

"You should have told me."

"And what would you have done? How would you have reacted? Like this? I hate to be the one to state the obvious, but your dad died, and that's terrible. Your mom went to prison ... also terrible. But that's in the past. If you want to be a grown ass adult, then start acting like one."

"I'm so tired of the age card." I shoved his chest. "Just because you don't understand my feelings doesn't make it my fault—a product of my age. *Nobody* likes being lied to."

"Nobody lied."

"Omission of the truth is deceptive ... a lie."

"So have we been lying to Rory about us?"

"There is *no* us."

Fisher nodded slowly. His control angered me even more. I needed to be angry. I needed to yell at someone.

"We might choose who we're with, but we don't choose who we love."

"Are you making excuses for her?"

He shook his head, scratching the nape of his neck. "What if I'm making *excuses* for us? Would that be okay with you? Would it be okay because we're not gay?"

My jaw clenched as I swallowed hard. "That's not it."

"You continue to tell yourself that."

I kept shaking my head. It wasn't about Rory's sexuality. It wasn't. Was it?

"Then why are you one blink away from falling apart? Because you're ashamed of her sins?" He held up air quotes. "Or because you need it to be wrong? If you let it be okay, you'll have to question everything that those people put into your head. You'll have to look within to find *your* truth. And then what will you be? Lost? Isn't that the point? Bring the lost to God and they will be found?"

"She cheated on my dad." I blinked, falling apart like he knew I would do.

"She fell in love."

I shook my head. "She was supposed to love him."

"Well, life never goes like it's supposed to. So what are you going to do about it?"

"Reese," Rory said my name.

I kept my back to her, my head bowed so I didn't have to look at her or Fisher. "I'm moving back to Texas. There is nothing for me here."

"Reese, let me explain."

"Explain?" I scoffed, walking toward the corner of the garage where I didn't have to face anyone. I wasn't sure I could ever look at her again. "No explanation needed. Everything I just saw, and will never be able to erase from my mind, was self-explanatory. The reason Dad divorced you. The reason he didn't want me to see you. It's so very clear now."

"You only know half of it. His half, not mine."

Resting my hands on my hips, I stared up at the ceiling, the shelving above the garage door. "I don't want your half. I don't want anything from you ever again. The lesson was mine to learn, and I learned it. Dad was right. You're incredibly selfish, and you don't care about anyone but yourself."

"Reese."

I heard the emotion in her shaky voice, but I wasn't going to look at her no matter how emotional she got, no matter how hurt she felt.

"Don't talk to your mom like that."

That demanded my attention. Fisher's way-out-of-line comment.

I whipped around to face him. "You ... *you* out of

all people don't get to tell me how to talk to her. If she knew the things you've said to me ..." I shook my head, eyes narrowed, daring him to say one more word. "If she only knew ..."

Fisher didn't back down. It wasn't his personality.

"What is she talking about?" Rory asked while Fisher and I stared down.

I was on the verge of blowing up everyone's world, including my own. Rory would be mad at Fisher and Rose. Rose would be mad at me. Fisher would be angry with ... well, I wasn't sure. But since I was livid with *all* of them. I didn't care.

"I'm out. You two figure your shit out. I'm done." Fisher escaped into the house. Still ... I couldn't look at Rory because all I'd see was the face she made when Rose was doing those things to her in the shower.

"How long have you known that you're gay?"

"I think my whole life."

I grunted, shaking my head. "Yet you married Dad and had me. Why?"

"Because it's a sin. Against God's will. That's what I thought at the time. That's what you're thinking. That's what you've been brainwashed into thinking."

"Let me rephrase." I forced myself to look at her with her wet hair, baggy sweats, and fitted tee. "When did you stop caring? Stop caring that it's a sin? Stopped caring about Dad? Stopped caring about our family?"

"Those are unfair questions."

"Oh?" I canted my head. "What are fair questions?"

"Ask me when I decided to honor who I am? Ask me when I decided I could love myself *and* love you?"

After a few silent seconds, I rubbed my lips together and shrugged a shoulder. "Well? What are your answers to those questions?"

She hugged her arms to herself and stared at her bare feet. "I met Rose when you were ten. She literally walked in off the street to see if I had time to trim her bangs. I was booked solid that day. I didn't have time to pee. But I couldn't say no because I knew ... with one look I knew ... she was the piece of me that I'd hidden and suppressed my whole life.

"So I cut her bangs. And she came back the following week for a full cut. Then she scheduled a highlight. Then she just showed up one day with a plate of cookies. That led to lunch. Then meeting at the same coffee shop every morning for coffee. A movie here. A concert there. We became friends. She was married and so was I. And I remember the day I was going to say something to her, confront the elephant in the room. I'd worked it out in my head a million times. Maybe I didn't know what it would mean for my family or her marriage, but I knew even if it didn't change any of that, it would change me on a cellular level. I knew it would be the most honest moment of my life."

I didn't care. I told myself I didn't care. She lied to Dad. She lied to me. It felt unforgivable, yet I found myself asking her, "What happened?"

Rory glanced up at me. "Well, she had something

to say to me that day too. And from the pain in her expression, I thought it was the something I wanted to tell her. The 'I love you, but I don't think we can be together, but I just need to tell you.' I knew ... I just knew that's what I saw in her eyes. But it wasn't, not that day. No. She needed to tell me she had stage three colon cancer, and her husband was leaving her because he didn't have the strength to watch her die. She needed someone to take her to treatments and doctor appointments."

I don't care. I don't care.

"And you did?"

She nodded. "I did. Then I drove her here, to Colorado, right after they legalized marijuana. It helped her a lot." Rory's lips turned into a sad smile as she averted her gaze. "It helped me a lot. It made dealing with my reality a little less stressful, dealing with the possibility of losing Rose a little less painful. Then one day Rose decided to grow her own, in the very illegal state of Nebraska, but she didn't have a great place to do it. So I suggested we use the back room of my salon. No one besides me ever went back there. For years all that had been back there were some old chairs, cracked sinks, and expired products. A few tables and grow lamps and we were growing our own marijuana. No more tiring trips to Colorado. No more paying for something we grew on our own for pennies."

She chuckled, running a hand through her wet hair. "It was stupid. Most things people do in the name of love *are* stupid. I never thought about getting caught.

I was too busy worrying about Rose. Besides ... who would ever think to look in the back of my salon? I was a mom with a child and husband. We went to church every weekend, never cheated on our taxes. I hadn't ever received as much as a parking ticket in my life."

"Dad said it was a break-in."

Rory nodded. "Yes, in the middle of the night, someone broke into my salon. The security alarms went off and whoever broke in didn't stick around. But the cops came and that's how my world shattered. I lost your dad. My freedom. Five years with you. And according to her doctors, it was unlikely Rose would make it to see me get out of prison. But she did. She made a full recovery."

"And Dad? How did he find out about the two of you?"

"We talked before the trial. He didn't understand why I would grow marijuana for a friend, a friend I'd met through my salon. Why would I risk so much? And he kept digging and digging until I cracked. I told him I did it because I was in love with Rose."

"You loved her more than you loved me."

Rory shook her head over and over. "No. I have never nor will I ever love anyone the way I love you."

"Yet, you chose to do something that took you away from me."

Her head continued to shake as she squeezed her eyes shut. "I ... I wasn't for one minute thinking I would get caught. I wasn't thinking that someone would break into my shop and therefore bring the police right to me."

"Well it happened. So do you regret it?"

Rory hesitated. That was my answer.

"I'll sleep at the airport." I stomped past her.

"Wait! No! Just ..." She grabbed my arm, her hand sliding down to my wrist as she inched her body to hunch in front of me, head hanging low. "Yes ..." Her voice broke.

I didn't want to cry for her. She didn't deserve my tears. Rory destroyed our family. She destroyed *us*.

"Yes ..." She sobbed. "I regret the st-stupidity and r-recklessness. I regret risking s-so much when *you* were ... *are* my w-world. I'm so *very* sorry."

Her honesty and apology meant something, but I wasn't sure what. I needed time to think. After believing one thing for five years, I wasn't able to erase my thoughts and feelings to embrace her version of the story. Not yet.

"I'll be back Sunday, but I don't know if I'll stay here. I just ... don't know." I pulled away as she continued to sob.

I ARRIVED in Houston by noon on Saturday. My grandparents took me to lunch. I put on a brave face and gushed about how much fun I'd been having in Colorado. An interesting mix of truths and lies.

On the way back to their house after we left the restaurant, I got a text from Fisher.

If you're not dead, text Rory and tell her you made it safely to Houston. Don't be a total asshole about it.

I read the text three times to verify what I was seeing on my screen. Fisher was calling me an asshole, or at least a partial one since he insinuated not texting Rory would make me a "total asshole."

Like the impure and sinful thoughts that often made their way into my head, but were never allowed to leave my head, I typed my knee-jerk response knowing I would never actually send it. Sending it would be equivalent to saying it, and I would never say this to anyone, not even Fisher.

Reese: Go fuck yourself!

I smiled at the screen, allowing myself to enjoy my bravery for just a few seconds before deleting it and responding with a WWJD attitude.

"Stay in your lane!" Grandpa honked the horn as he quickly swerved, moving my thumb just enough to send the text.

It sent.

"Oh my gosh," I whispered.

"You okay, honey?" Grandma looked over her shoulder at me.

On a thick swallow, I nodded slowly, but I wasn't okay. I was horrified.

My phone vibrated with a new text from Fisher.

I'll let her know you're not dead.

I was in a quandary. Reply? Tell him it was a mistake? Autocorrect? Would my autocorrect default to go fuck yourself?

I didn't text him back.

Instead, I focused on my grandparents, got ready for the party, fielded a million questions at the party about my summer in Colorado, and made it to bed just after ten.

The next morning, we attended church service and fellowship dinner. More questions. More fake smiles and half-truths.

On the way to the airport that afternoon, I picked my grandma's brain.

"I work with someone who is gay. She's so nice and so is her girlfriend. Do you think that's wrong?"

"Of course it's wrong, Therese. The Bible says unnatural desire is an abomination punishable by eternal fire. You know this."

I nodded once while twisting my lips.

"You should pray for her."

"Yeah," I whispered. "Do you think it's worse than any other sexual immorality?"

"It's not my job to judge that, but I know your

friend will not be welcomed in Heaven if she doesn't stop her actions and accept Christ as her savior."

"Well ..." I bit my thumbnail. "Saying that sounds like you are in fact judging her."

"No. I'm simply stating what the Bible says. I tell you, I don't envy your generation. This LGB etcetera etcetera stuff has gotten way out of hand. I don't understand why everyone feels the need to stand out."

"I'm uh ... I'm not sure it's about standing out. What if it's just about fitting in? What if they just want to be themselves without being seen as different or inferior or less worthy? I'm just ... thinking aloud."

"I'm worried your friend is brainwashing you. Honestly, I worried that your time in Colorado would be difficult on you. I really hope you're not skipping church. I hope you're spending time in God's word every day."

Looking out the window, I murmured, "Yeah, I am."

After landing in Denver, I took my time getting my car and making my way home. To my disappointment, Fisher and Rory were on his front porch, drinking beer and it was nearly dark.

Rory gave me a reserved smile as I wheeled my carry-on suitcase up the driveway. "Hey, how was your trip?"

"It was just overnight, barely a trip, but it was fine."

"Did they have a nice anniversary party?"

I nodded.

Things were so awkward. After leaving Rory in

tears, with the uncertainty as to whether or not I'd ever forgive her, and sending Fisher a F-you text, I wasn't sure what to say.

"I'm going to go unpack and do a load of laundry."

"Need help?" Rory asked.

"I'm good."

"Have you had dinner?"

I shook my head. "I'm not hungry."

"Rose and I are going for pizza. We'd love for you to come too."

My head continued to shake. "I'm not hungry. Enjoy your pizza," I said, my voice void of all emotion as I turned and started to head toward the basement. After a few steps, I turned back toward Rory. "I don't know how God feels about you and Rose." I shrugged. "I just know that I've felt lost for the past five years. The lie didn't protect me. And my reaction the other night wasn't really to Rose ... or you and Rose. I know this because I've had time to sort through my feelings. It wasn't Dad. It wasn't even your arrest that destroyed our family; the fact that you tried to live the wrong life ... that's what destroyed us. And it might take me awhile to come to terms with everything, but I can imagine it must have been painful to find the right person at the worst possible time." I kept my attention laser focused on Rory. Had I given Fisher the quickest of glances, I would have lost it.

Rory returned a smile. It was a little sad and a little relieved. "Thank you." Tears shined in her eyes.

AFTER I UNPACKED and tossed in a load of laundry, I grabbed one of Rory's beers from the fridge and took a seat on the porch, music flowing from my phone and my gaze on the sun setting behind the mountains.

"I fucked myself."

I didn't want to grin as Fisher stood at the door to the porch, but I couldn't help it. I took a swig of the beer to hide my grin.

"I'm pretty good." He stepped onto the porch and sat in the rocker where Rory usually sat.

"I don't doubt that." I rubbed my lips together. "But what do I know? I'm just an asshole."

Fisher eyed the beer in my hand, but he didn't say anything about it. "Rory grilled me on what I said to you while she was gone. Thanks for that."

I nodded. "You're welcome." After a long pause of silence, I caved. "What did you tell her?"

"I told her I used a lot of swear words around you."

"And she believed you?"

He lifted a shoulder. "I don't know. I guess so."

I took another big swig of beer, praying for a little buzz to soothe my nerves.

"What are you going to do, Reese? Move back to Texas because your mom is going to Hell?"

"I don't know, Fisher. Would that make me a *total asshole*?"

"Probably."

I rolled my eyes and refocused on the view. "Well, you would know what it's like to be a total asshole."

"Why? Because I wouldn't fuck you?"

"Well, from what I hear, I'm the only single female in a twenty-mile radius you haven't put your dick into. That makes me a unicorn. Maybe that makes me the *one* woman you can't have."

He stood and took two steps in my direction, snagging the bottle of beer from my hand and drinking the rest of it in one shot. "If I wanted you, I could have you, and we both know it."

"No." I shook my head. "You can't have me. Not now. Not ever. I don't want you anymore."

"You do." He handed the empty bottle back to me.

"I don't!" I stood, chin up, shoulders back, teeth clenched.

With a smug expression, he eyed me like he used to do, but I didn't fall for it. "It's almost too easy."

"What's too—"

He kissed me. Hard. Harder than he had ever kissed me. And I fought him, but I lost because I *did* want him to kiss me. It's *all* I wanted. But it didn't mean I was going to give myself to him. No matter how much I wanted his kiss, it didn't change what had happened between us.

My hand dropping the empty bottle to the floor so my fingers could dive into his hair didn't change anything either.

His hands grabbed my ass and lifted me off my

feet. Fisher kissed me and carried me up the stairs like a drunk man on a mission.

Through the door.

Down the hallway.

Onto his bed.

His demanding mouth made it impossible to protest, not that I had one ready to go, not yet. We'd been there before, done that. It wasn't sex. I was still in control.

He discarded my shirt. I still had control.

When he ripped down the cups to my bra and did things to my breasts that made me moan and claw at his back, I *still* had control. I could play his game.

Fisher sat up, kneeling between my spread legs, eyes hooded, lips parted as he unbuttoned my jeans and peeled them from my legs.

I ... I had control.

He kissed his way down one leg, pressing his lips to the inside of my thigh as his finger slipped beneath the crotch of my panties, circling my clit once before sliding lower. Keeping his mouth on my leg, that finger pushed inside of me.

I sucked in a breath. It was a finger, larger than a tampon but not his dick.

In. Out. In. Out.

Agonizingly slow, my vision began to blur. Fisher removed his finger and slid off my panties. After tossing them aside, he unbuttoned his jeans and pulled down the zipper.

"I'm ..." I breathed embarrassingly heavy. "I'm not

having sex with you." Despite my slightly compromised position and lack of blood going to my brain, I felt proud of my will power. The days of being Fisher's toy ... his favorite game ... were over. I was the master, the powerful queen who would take down the king.

Checkmate.

"No?" He leaned forward and slid his hands behind me, unhooking my bra. As he slid it off my arms, he smirked. "We'll see."

"Ah!" I jerked when he bit my nipple, when that finger slid inside of me again, when he added a second finger partway, making me feel so filled. Was he going to take my virginity with his fingers?

His mouth latched onto mine. My hips and legs braced, not moving an inch because Fisher's fingers edged me out of my comfort zone.

What if he pushed them inside of me the whole way? Would it hurt? Would I bleed?

And then ... they were gone. He stood at the end of the bed and removed his jeans, challenging me. I saw it in his eyes.

"I won't do it. You don't deserve it. You had your chance." My bravery tank nearly hit empty.

"We'll see." He crawled onto the bed and his tongue went to work. Swiping between my legs. Flicking my nipples. Making a trail up my neck, and finally landing in my mouth, making slow strokes as his pelvis settled between my legs. That dangerous thin layer of cotton the only thing separating his dick from my entrance.

Thrust.

Thrust.

Thrust.

I reminded myself that we had done this before. We'd been in that position. And we didn't have sex.

Thrust.

Thrust.

Thrust.

My hips lifted from the bed to meet him. That was when he pulled back. That was when he rolled onto his back, taking me with him so I sat on top of him, my legs straddling him right *there*.

With one look, he dared me to quit. *And* he dared me to keep going.

"No sex," I nearly choked on the words.

Fisher jackknifed to sitting, his face a breath away from mine. "We'll see." He kissed me, tangling one hand in my hair while his other hand guided my hand beneath the waistband of his briefs.

So warm.

So hard.

I stroked him as he teased his tongue against mine.

I stroked him as he fingered me again, but just that agonizing partway.

Slow. Too slow.

The more I stroked him, the more I wanted *more*. Not just more. I wanted all of him.

He broke our kiss and stretched his torso to the side, opening the drawer to his nightstand and pulling out a condom.

That was when things got real.

Using his teeth, he tore it open, tossed the wrapper to the side, and pushed down the front of his briefs to roll it on.

He grabbed my face and kissed me a little softer than just seconds earlier. Dragging his lips across my face, dotting it with kisses, he whispered in my ear, "Your husband can thank me."

Those words stopped my heart. The warm blood in my veins ran cold, sending an icy jolt along my spine.

Fisher lifted my hips and positioned me over him, pushing into me an inch, maybe not even.

Tears filled my eyes as I stilled, not letting him move my hips any farther. And I saw it in his eyes.

The pain.

The love.

The conflict.

More than anything, I saw all the reasons I fell for Fisher Mann. He knew we weren't at the right place to make *us* work, but he was willing to give me the one thing I thought I wanted. He wanted to give me all he had to give, even though he knew it wouldn't be enough.

My hands pressed to his face as tears covered my cheeks, the saltiness pooling at my lips. "Thank you, Fisher."

I eased off his lap.

He said nothing. There wasn't anything to say.

After I dressed, I lifted my teary gaze to him. "I'm volunteering to go on a mission trip to Thailand for six months. And then ..." I lifted one shoulder, drawing in a shaky breath that elicited more tears. "I don't know, but I'll figure it out. I'll figure *me* out." Turning, I took several steps and turned, giving him a sad smile. "There's more to life than crossword puzzles, right?"

His jaw stiffened as he swallowed hard and nodded, his eyes a little red. "I hope so."

To be continued ...

ALSO BY JEWEL E. ANN

Standalone Novels

Idle Bloom

Undeniably You

Naked Love

Only Trick

Perfectly Adequate

Look The Part

When Life Happened

A Place Without You

Jersey Six

Scarlet Stone

Not What I Expected

For Lucy

The Fisherman Series

The Naked Fisherman

The Lost Fisherman

Receive a FREE book and stay informed of new releases, sales, and exclusive stories:

Mailing List

https://www.jeweleann.com/free-booksubscribe

ABOUT THE AUTHOR

Jewel is a free-spirited romance junkie with a quirky sense of humor.

With 10 years of flossing lectures under her belt, she took early retirement from her dental hygiene career to stay home with her three awesome boys and manage the family business.

After her best friend of nearly 30 years suggested a few books from the Contemporary Romance genre, Jewel was hooked. Devouring two and three books a week but still craving more, she decided to practice sustainable reading, AKA writing.

When she's not donning her cape and saving the planet one tree at a time, she enjoys yoga with friends, good food with family, rock climbing with her kids, watching How I Met Your Mother reruns, and of course...heart-wrenching, tear-jerking, panty-scorching novels.

www.jeweleann.com

Printed in Great Britain
by Amazon

87185957R00231